The Podcast Matrix Murders

A Matrix Mystery
Book 1

D. J. Laing

Manhanset House
Shelter Island Hts., New York 11965-0342

bricktower@aol.com • absolutelyamazingebooks.com

Library of Congress Cataloging-in-Publication Data
Laing, D. J.
The Podcast Matrix Murders
p. cm.

1. FICTION / Thrillers / Suspense. 2. FICTION / Mystery & Detective /
Hard-Boiled. 3. FICTION / Thrillers / Crime. Fiction, I. Title.
ISBN: 978-1-955036-92-4, Trade Paper

September 2025

The Podcast Matrix Murders

A Matrix Mystery

Book 1

D. J. Laing

WHODUNIT MYSTERY WRITING COMPETITION

AWARD WINNER

An Imprint of ABSOLUTELY AMAZING eBOOKS

Habent Sua Fata Libelli

Books by D. J. Laing
(D.J. Laing is the pen name for the Wilmington, DE couple who
have produced numerous nonfiction titles in the past. This book is
their first collaboration in the mystery genre. They have been
producing and hosting a variety of podcasts since 2005.)

JoAnn M. Laing
*RECALCULATING, 97+ Experts On Driving Small Business
Growth*; Winner of Independent Press Award

Small Business Guide to HSAs

*The Janus Principle,
Focusing Your Company on Selling to Small Business*

Solutions to Today's HR Challenges

Consumer's Guide to Health Savings Accounts

Donald Mazzella

Ruler of the Waves (trilogy)

An American Sampler (trilogy)

Frankie, If You Get Hurt, I'll Kill You

Table of Contents

"Matrix is an environment in which something develops; a surrounding medium or structure. Free choices become the matrix of human life."

—Anonymous

The Crime, Wednesday, 1:15pm

Anger fueled by the thousand disappointments in his life added strength to the killer's downward motion splitting the victim's back skull at the point of impact. The blow's low bone-shattering sound echoed loudly in the silent motel room. Just one involuntary gasp escaped the victim's lips; the murderer didn't care whether of anguish or surprise.

Crumbling to his knees, already suffering brain collapse, the victim did not feel the other four skull-shattering blows cracking his braincase repeatedly. Falling forward, he lay on the floor. Brains and blood spread around his head and into the rug from his opened skull. Within seconds, when his heart stopped, the oozing ceased. His body gave one involuntary jerk, and lay still.

Stepping back to avoid the gore, the murderer sucked in his breath heavily, gasping for air, feeling the first surge of relief from the myriad tensions eased by this one act.

Not wanting the victim's body fluids on his shoes, he stepped around the body and went into the bathroom. Taking one washrag from its place on the shelf, he wrapped the murder weapon. Returning to the room, the murderer saw the briefcase on the bed. A phone was on top, and another phone had fallen from the body to the floor. He picked up both phones and the briefcase.

Touching the body gingerly, the murderer looked for the recorder the victim always carried in his handkerchief pocket, but it was gone. Straightening up, he checked the two drawers in the room, both were empty. After a quick scan of the room, he ended his search. It was enough to assume it was not in the room.

Having touched nothing but being aware everyone left DNA residue, his eyes searched the room for any noticeable trace of his presence. Accepting that there might be something the crime lab people might find, he prepared to leave, unsure how to identify or erase them. Carefully walking around the body, he strode to the door enjoying the thought of what he had just done to the victim.

Peeking out, he saw the unattended maid's cart down the hall; it was apparent she was inside another room. Taking advantage of the empty corridor, he quietly closed the door behind him, forgetting to leave the "Do Not Disturb" sign on the latch. In just a few steps and seconds, he was out the back stairway door. Hugging the outside wall to avoid being recorded by either or both surveillance cameras, he made himself invisible to them as he exited the parking lot. Confident he had not been seen, he made his way to the adjoining lot behind an IHOP restaurant.

As he made his way to his car parked one block away, the killer decided that ridding the world of one oppressor who had disappointed him wasn't enough. There were others. Mentally reviewing the long germinating list of his most deserving oppressors, the persistent pain in his brain eased. What he just did would alert law enforcement officers, but until he did an encore with another oppressor, they had no clue pointing to him.

While this first killing was spontaneous, its accomplishment sparked thoughts of other revenges. But to accomplish the plan forming in his brain would need careful planning. The anger generated by the latest betrayal in a long line of shattered relationships resulted in this savage. spontaneous act. When faced with this latest betrayal, instead of swallowing his disappointment, he struck back. The results were so satisfying, he wanted more than this one taste.

Today, a lifetime of meekly accepting these hurts ended in that motel room. Now it was his turn to display his anger and resentment. But before he acted, he needed a plan whose elements would come to him when the rush stopped.

Looking down, he noted the patterns of the cement sidewalks, crossing his vision every 30 inches. Their repetition reminded him of his adversaries. He knew patterns identified serial murderers. Once the police discerned the reason for the killings, they caught the murderers. He would not let them see why he killed until all the people died.

Thinking further ahead, he realized it was just a question of time until he was caught. That this would be the inevitable outcome did not stop him. Cradling in his mind the vengeance he was about to bring to these people eased his fears or regrets. In this instance, he confirmed his mission.

Crime Scene, Wednesday 3:10pm

Sensing the flesh was dead, the fly was not worried the body would move. Longer than it usually did, the fly remained occupied with sucking up distress from the skin. Busy digesting the skin's secretions, it ignored the men in the room. They didn't overlook the fly.

Engorged, the fly was slow to rise as detective Sawyer Henderson swatted downward with his incident pad. Dislodged by the blow's force, the body's hand and the arm fell with a thud to the floor along with the now-dead fly. Like the man's brains, the fly's blood stained the rug in the twin-bedded room. Unlike the fly, the body had the two detectives' undivided attention.

The arm movement, so easy, alerted both men that rigor had not occurred, meaning the man wasn't dead for too long. They both mentally noted that the early discovery of his body would forestall alarms about his absence. That no one seemed concerned yet meant his movement before reaching the room might be more easily traced.

Someone knew where he was yesterday and the day before, which could help narrow down possible suspects. The 48 hours before and after the killing were the most critical times in any murder case. If an investigation was to be solved, the pertinent clues came from events during that period. They wondered who would report him missing, if at all.

Surely someone must be wondering by now. The man was too well-known and visible to be away from his associates for too long. The detectives made a mental note to remind whoever caught the case.

Of course, they knew who that would be but waited for the official word. Without exchanging words, both bet the lead investigator was on his way already. Knowing his habit, they didn't touch anything in the room. The first officer to respond to the emergency call had

4

remained in the room. He was at the door now, smart enough to retreat when he saw the body. The maid who walked in on the scene waited in a vacant room down the hall with another officer. Only the two detectives had crossed the threshold since the body was discovered.

The victim on the floor was enough of a visitor to the police department that they both recognized the body even in death. Formal identification would wait till later. Neither detective liked him happily in life; others in the department had dealt with him. They hoped, in the end, that this would remain true as well.

Since so many people had police scanners, they had used their cell phones to call in his identity after identifying who lay on the floor. God forbid they alerted anyone to his identity before it could be officially released. When they mentioned his name, the Chief said to sit tight and let no one in the room. Looking at each other, they set to waiting.

Given whom the victim was, his death would bring much media attention. Whoever handled the case would be second-guessed, whatever the outcome. Police careers were often broken by too much media exposure, particularly unsolved cases. If this murder was to be solved, the man coming would be the one to find the clue to break it open.

They also knew that if murder cases were not solved in the first 48 hours, only long slogs involving detailed attention to minor facts were needed to bring murderers to justice. But with the media attention this case would bring, the journalists and commentators would be demanding quick action. The pressure of media attention critical of the often slowness of investigations was a growing feature of 21st-century police work.

Both men would be happy to assist the lead detective. They did not need to face as the lead detective the gauntlet of questions and innuendo from legitimate media and, lately, the many would-be bloggers, podcasters, and such.

Heading a murder investigation was not good if it couldn't be solved quickly. Getting media attention early in any detective's career wasn't the best route to advancement. Neither man had been in the detective bureau for more than three years. With that short tenure, there was reason enough that neither wanted the job of going out there every day facing the gauntlet of questions about efforts to find his murderer.

There was no doubt the man was murdered. Suicide could be ruled out by the injuries he suffered. His brains stained and covered a large area of the room's rug. The man did not hit his head four or more times. The room's undisturbed order indicated that he knew and trusted the murderer. Second, the victim was surprised by his assailant's attack. It seemed logical from the position of the wounds the murderer struck from behind. With his back to his assailant, he had no chance to defend himself. There were no struggle signs in the room. The room was too undisturbed but for the mess on the carpet.

Mentally, Sawyer thought the innkeepers would need to replace the entire rug, paint the walls, and change the beds. On the other hand, when word got out who the victim was, he wondered if some ghoulish patrons might want to sleep in the same room just for the thrill. They'd be welcome to it, but he couldn't.

From the impressions of the twin beds, the detectives could see two people sitting across each other, each on their beds. The covers were still on the beds, and indentations showed patterns of side bags. Either they were purses or briefcases, one placed beside each participant. The victim was left-handed, and his suitcase was to his left. The visitor had their bag to their right. It was logical to assume they passed something between them. But the victim's briefcase was gone.

Sex was not the reason for meeting in a Red Roof room on the outskirts of town in the middle of the day and could be ruled out from the undisturbed nature of the beds. Only one of two other reasons for meeting like this seemed plausible: blackmail or drugs. Either explanation would involve cash, but both would mean something illegal, so the chances the other person would come forward were slim to none. Whatever it was, they wanted to leave it to others to figure out.

They also noted that the tape recorder they knew the victim always carried was not in the room. This observation made the younger detective tell one of the uniformed police officers outside in the hallway to go and scout the outside of the motel and nearby trash receptacles for the missing items. He did not expect the officer to find them, but it was a task any investigation required. The sooner it started the better.

Waiting around, both saw from the force of the blows that whoever killed the victim wanted him dead. Squatting down but not disturbing the body, they squinted at the head, which lay parallel to the nearest bed. The detectives counted at least five blows to the head by examining the skull breaks. The man was probably dead or dying by the second strike. The last blows were just added in fury or hate. This was murder for very personal reasons.

Given these facts and who the man was, at least three people were involved. They were: the victim, the other person in the transaction, and the murderer. An added factor: the events occurred in the middle of the afternoon,

"Let's hope the cameras were working," Sawyer, the younger, said to his partner.

"I have a hunch they aren't," Carmichael Winston replied. He was the more experienced one in this team.

"The chain requires them. For safety and legal protection," Sawyer said.

"This is a no-tell motel during the day," Carmichael laughingly replied.

"You know from using it?" his partner asked. Aware of Carmichael's devotion to his family and still fearful of his mother's wrath should he stray, Sawyer didn't expect an answer.

"When I was on patrol, I had a few calls during the day."

"Thought this place didn't cause any trouble but didn't the day clerk go to jail?"

"Yeah, he was renting rooms during the day to couples who paid in cash, and instead of recording the charges, at the end of the day, no record and no requirement to report the revenue, so he pocketed the money."

"I thought everyone used a credit card nowadays?"

"Too many guys were getting caught by wives seeing motel charges on their credit cards."

"Yeah, the regulars started paying in cash, and he started dipping in and not reporting all the income."

"The front desk clerk was smart; if anyone checked, no one would admit they were here during the day."

"No, he made money; they kept secrets from their wives, and the only loser was the owner. Everyone was happy until some wife shot her husband and his secretary here when she trailed the spouse here when they wanted to have a nooner."

"Yeah, now that I recall, the newspapers labeled the murders as "the Thursday-afternoon Turkey shoot or something like that." One detective took up the story.

"In her anger, the wife missed the husband with the first shot but killed the secretary underneath him." The other detective finished the tale while both laughed.

"She got him with her third shot. Both dead by the time she fired the sixth bullet." Both still laughed.

"She got off with manslaughter. Due out next year," his partner chortled as he finished the line.

"Well, we know she didn't do this one," they said in unison.

Intuitively, neither policeman thought the first visitor was guilty. Call the idea police officers' intuition, karma, or experience; both men sensed the second person was gone when the murderer entered the room. Given the nature of the meeting, they didn't think the first visitor would come forward voluntarily.

It didn't matter to them how they knew; they expected finding the other person indicated in the bed depression would not necessarily mean finding the murderer. Looking at the body, the room, and knowing what he did and how he did it, all they wanted right now was for someone else to have the dubious honor of ending this mystery.

Whoever got the case would need to find people who probably didn't want to be found. The victim dealt with the unsavory side of life. The people he worked with often claimed to be as pure as the driven snow but were as black as a hearse. In cases like this, when the police started examining people's lives, they uncovered things and details many people wanted to be left hidden. First, investigators discovered the venal happenings, such as hating the co-worker, loving the in-law, or wanting little or nothing to do with them.

As investigations dug deeper, most witnesses offered more significant and extensive lies with something to hide. Delaying the search was that innocent participants would often tell these falsehoods for reasons unrelated to the case. It was up to the police to identify which lie pertained to the case and which did not. When patrolmen became investigators, they quickly learned they could not accept any minor detail without verifying from another source to confirm these facts.

Another hampering trend often showing up in small towns was how citizens used their perceived or actual political clout to steer investigations away from themselves or their families. Witnesses claimed the protection of political names or titles even if they were innocent. This sometimes worked but mostly threw more smoke around themselves or others. In some cases, these efforts resulted in crimes not being solved or permitting someone to escape justice.

The media didn't help. All the time the case was open, the press would be around sniffing at the heels of law enforcement. The media wouldn't be too careful with the truth just like this particular victim. Nor would they wait for the police to update anything discovered during the investigation. The pressures of 24-hour news cycles led to many publicizing rumors as facts.

Nowadays, the media tells people what they want to hear, not what is true. It was bad enough when newspapers competed with television and radio, and today, bloggers and podcasters are competing for viewers and readers.

Because the victim was one of their more controversial podcasters, this was a case media people would chew on over the air for months, if not years. As facts emerged, they would be twisted into narratives that fit the theories of the media person delivering their version of the events. Finding 12 jurors who had yet to hear about the topic or form an approach would be much more challenging when the case was solved.

Even if the murderer were caught, confessed, or found guilty, someone would propose an alternative theory. Others would pick it up, amplify the approach into fact, and there would always be people who would believe them. While the police needed to stick close to the points, others would make money twisting those facts to fit their take on events. But for right now, the police would be left with the dreary, mundane job of assembling the details one by one.

The two men pondered all this, waiting for the crime crew, coroner, and, most importantly, the man who would take this case off their hands.

Thinking Ahead, Wednesday, 3:30pm

Detectives seldom get to use their sirens. This meant the two lead detectives, Carter Williams and Raleigh Butler, expected to solve this murder were moving with the slowness of afternoon congestion. In the emerging South Carolina town of Skye Landing, traffic out of town was slow at this time of the day. In bigger cities, the volume would be considered moderate and moving. Once prosperous as a textile and lumbering mecca, by the 1970s, the town lost both industries to foreign competition. After decades of slumbering, the town's now bustling economy centered on data servers, call centers, and as a bedroom community to Charlotte. With the new life came traffic and most inhabitants welcomed the change. The traffic jams told them the town was booming once again. For some of its residents at this time, traffic was slow, painful, and unwanted regardless of the reason.

Like every change, some things inside the town became worse. In Skye Landing's case, it included traffic sprawl. When shift change hours began to cause mild traffic jams, some older folks almost gleefully said it was heavy. The newcomers thought it was little to pay for the benefits bestowed on the South Carolina hill country town.

As a result of being a rapidly expanding tech hub, the jams were discussed at every council meeting. No solutions were adopted because nobody wanted to do anything that stopped the rate new companies poured into the town. Most citizens shared an unspoken smugness that such a problem existed in Skye Landing.

High ceilings, oversized windows, and long, unbroken floors made the old yarn spinning, clothing manufacturing, and dying plants ideal settings for new tech operations. Their morphism to housing tech centers made Skye Landing a prosperous and growing town once again. With few exit points from their location along the river that divided the city, shift changes created long delays at certain traffic lights. Using police officers to speed the traffic only directed anger at the patrolmen assigned to the task and slight improvement.

For Carter, the newly minted detective, the traffic-snarled slowing his boss and himself getting from police headquarters in the middle of town to the motel murder scene on its outskirts took up time that could have been shortened by siren use. There was no doubt in his mind that Carter Williams felt the time sitting in traffic would be better spent at the crime scene. Unfortunately, his immediate superior didn't agree. He said nothing, knowing from experience in the limited time they had been together making any comment would be useless and bring on a withering glance Carter did not enjoy seeing.

So, he sat quietly in the traffic in his car and looked at the scenery, dashboard, and watch., Any place than at his front seat companion. That man didn't care if Carter was unhappy sitting in his car on the spring day and waiting for traffic to clear. People said spring was the best time to be in Skye Landing, and they pointed out the pleasure people got from seeing the blossoming foliage. Today, the trees were just sprouting leaves, and some bright petals appeared here and there. He ignored them.

Carter wanted to use the siren to clear the way for them to the motel. But since his first day in the bureau, the man beside him forbade its use. Angry at the delay, Carter continued saying nothing. If an opening in oncoming traffic appeared, he occasionally deftly steered around some cars ahead of him. Despite his best efforts, they were still making slow progress at the crime scene. The slowness did not seem to bother the man to his right.

Included in the many things he found irritating and surprising about being a detective originated with the man beside him. Using his siren was the part of the job Carter missed most since joining the detective bureau. But the first time they rode together, the man beside him said no siren.

Things were different when he was in uniform and on lone patrol. Then, he was pretty liberal in using the loud wail to move drivers out of his way as he raced to the local sandwich shop. More than once, wailing his way to some non-emergency location, he was caught by a superior officer and reprimanded. He didn't care; within six months of joining the Skye Landing police force, he had made three spectacular arrests based on his intuition concerning suspicious loiterers. With his third collar, he thought his career was made. He did not count on the police chief not liking how he did it.

Despite its southern location, the weather was still chilly even for February, and the cold kept many people off the streets, just like Carter preferred them to be. He caught a wanted murderer from Washington DC hiding on mid-day patrol in the downtown area, thinking no one would notice him in the South Carolina town with many new inhabitants.

Luck was riding with Carter that day when his interest was piqued because the man turned away from the patrol car as it passed. Noting the man's actions, he became suspicious. Most citizens ignore passing police cars, only looking for them when in distress. Criminals avoided looking at police vehicles, whether marked or unmarked, because they knew good cops developed an instinct about nefarious doings or people. Most criminals instinctively turned away when they saw law enforcement personnel passing by. Given the general benign environment in Skye Landing, most law-abiding citizens did not turn away. Carter had no interest in the man. It was the middle of the day, and Carter was loafing in his car, counting the minutes till his lunch break. What caught Carter's attention was that the pedestrian had no apparent reason for turning away.

His suspicions aroused, Carter circled the block. The returning police car prompted the man to run in the opposite direction. First in his vehicle and then afoot, Carter chased after the man shouting for him to stop at the top of his lungs. The minute the culprit saw the car return around the corner, he started running. Using his shoulder-mounted microphone, Carter called for backup. Following the man down the town's narrow streets, the runner crashed into a side alley. Without thinking, exiting the car, Carter followed. Midway down the side alley, the culprit realized there was no exit. Drawing his hidden gun, he turned and fired at the policeman.

Instead of going to a shooting stance, Carter dove to the ground, held his gun between his outstretched hands just above the cement, and fired three times. All three bullets struck the man in his right arm and left leg. Surprised as anyone at his marksmanship, Carter stood over the man when help arrived.

Luckily for Carter, some citizens captured him on his phone, standing over the killer. The image went viral, praise rang in from around the country, and Carter knew he was now earmarked for the detective bureau.

Following the mandatory investigation five days later and displaying modesty he didn't feel, Carter strode into headquarters the following week. He expected kudos, and he had been told promotion was in the air from others inside and outside the department. This was true; reluctantly, giving in to public pressure to reward the officer, the Police Chief approved his promotion which Carter thought was right. But not before he got an earful from the Police Chief for all the procedures he violated, including firing while civilians were in the area.

"If you think you're a hero in this department, Carter, think again." Amanda Harris shouted at him behind her closed door.

"But I got a murderer off the streets."

"For which we are all properly grateful, and the Washington DC police will send you a nice certificate. But don't you dare hang that in this building."

"But I."

"Shut your fuckin' mouth and listen to me. You're a cowboy, and there is no place in my department for a cowboy. Now that you're a national police hero, I can't fire you. But if I had my way, I would. And you know why?"

"No, I don't know why."

"Because your way of doing things will get a fellow officer killed one day. That's why."

"That's not true."

"Here's a policeman nine months into the job telling the police chief with 22 years as a patrolman, investigator, and supervisor what's true or not in police work."

"The arrest was a good one. You just wish you'd made it."

"Bull Shit, get out of my office and take your hubris. Take the rest of the week off to bask in your self-glory and report to Greenville for three weeks of detective training. I got you into the next course. Then when you come back report to the detective bureau. For some reason, Raleigh thinks you'll make a great detective. I think he's wrong, but time will tell. I'm pairing you with Raleigh Butler; maybe you'll learn how to be a detective from him. I do know you'll learn how to be a policeman."

"You can't stick me with that plodder."

"I can, and I have. If anyone can get something out of you, he will."

"But his methods are as old as dinosaurs and just as extinct; everyone knows that."

"I don't know that, and do you know his clearance rates?"

"No, it must be pretty low. It seems he just sits in his office and shuffles papers, looks at some pretty stupid things, and just thinks."

"You believe that's all he does? Do you think that? You know what, I've changed my mind. There are no days off for you now. Until you go to Greenville, you will sit in the detectives' bullpen and read all of Raleigh's cases for the past ten years. It's a good way to start learning how to be a detective."

Shocked by the turn of events, Carter was still reading the cases when he went off to Greenville. What irked him was that Raleigh solved four of the cases studied in his classes. He thought the word baffled was more appropriate because, after reading all the cases, he couldn't tell how the detective had identified the evidence to put him on the killer's trail and then convict the perpetrator. Reluctantly, Carter admitted he would learn a lot more working with the older man than he thought. What he saw and heard in the course still didn't change his mind; the man was a dinosaur.

Still cocky from his arrest, his introductory course over, Carter walked into the detective bureau but all Raleigh did was just nod while telling him that they had some work to do. Carter's new life started the moment they reached the police parking garage. Motioning for him to drive even though he was the junior team member, Raleigh showed immediately things would be different for Carter. After giving him the address they were going to, the only conversation was Raleigh saying he had a strict rule against using the siren. He told the new detective the wail hurt his ears.

Victim's Background, Wednesday, 4:00pm

Weeks into his new role, with painful lessons instilled through multiple incidents, Carter had learned to keep silent going to any crime scene as his chief thought about what they were about to see. Now, with their potentially explosive murder case in the offing, he was sitting quietly as a silent Raleigh reviewed his three-step approach to any crime scene. The first rule was to decide how big the crime scene was relative to the victim. The boundary, in this case, was easy to establish, the motel room. Second, observe as much detail as possible and get as many photos as the police budget allows. Finally, examine the victim and work outward from there.

Raleigh hated it when the victim was removed from the scene to a hospital or morgue before his arrival. Over the years, the tech people knew that it was best to disturb as little as possible until Raleigh arrived. When triage had been attempted before the victim expired, they noted every discarded or bloodied item they used, turning over the list as soon as possible. They now felt confident to move the victim only when he had his look. Even when the remains were only bones or parts of skeletons, Raleigh wanted everything in situ until he was satisfied nothing more could be learned.

In Greenville, they still talked about his identification of a candy wrapper he observed tossed aside during a body dump. Its identification led to the conviction of the murderer. The wrapper didn't appear to belong at the body dump site, and Raleigh spotted the anomaly. This fact led him to ask every suspect what candy they liked. When one suspect fessed up to selecting this particular brand, Raleigh honed in on him. The rest was just building a case, which he did. Sometimes luck is a factor in homicides. He didn't have the heart to tell his fellow officers that he noticed it only because his great-niece had eaten one the day before.

As they crawled through traffic, he thought about his dealing with the victim. Like everyone associated with the Jenny Couri case, he was angry at the victim for bringing up this particular 12-year-old case. Many media outlets bring up unsolved cases, and sometimes the new publicity results in someone remembering something or spurred confessions from guilty consciousness. Those programs he welcomed even appeared in two.

But Jenny Couri was gone, dead of natural causes, according to official documents. What the official documents said hadn't stopped Henry Cain. Now, trusting the two detectives' sureness of the body's identity, Raleigh realized Cain, the podcaster, was now the subject of a murder investigation. He laughed to himself. But Raleigh was afraid this murder was somehow connected to the Couri case.

Cain had put himself out there by claiming there was a killer still at large and was questioning the motives of everyone involved with the case, starting with Raleigh. What's more, no matter how outrageous the claim or the outcome, some part of the mud would continue to stick to everyone involved. After Cain leveled his charges, no matter what other facts emerged, there would always be some doubters and snickers.

These thoughts made Raleigh angry. He knew the truth about that girl's death and the falseness of the new innuendos. With that as background, Raleigh was angry. He was furious Henry Cain was the victim whose murder he would need to solve. Raleigh would like to say good riddance to lousy trash at one level.

But the murder came too late to avoid the damage. Raleigh knew no amount of Band-Aids would cover all the wounds Cain had opened. To date, nothing good had come from Cain's poking around. Bad enough that the police, coroner, and elected officials were caught in his net, Henry had painted others with a worse brush. Now, with his death, Cain left them all tainted. No matter how tenuous the thread is, the media will link the girl's death to Cain's killing.

On his last show, Cain had promised to reveal the names of three men, one of whom he asserted was the murderer of the teenager. Cain could say many things without needing to prosecute them and being careful how he told his accusation.

He'd done it in other cities. Why not Skye Landing? Why one of these men killed her was easy for Cain to claim. Waving a file in his hand, he said these men all had sexual relations with the teenager. He based his claim on evidence he claimed the police withheld in the original investigation. During the video portion of his last broadcast to the average audience member, his delivery holding a small box up for the camera left no doubt that an innocent teenager was killed to cover someone's sexual misconduct.

Knowing how the media would spin his murder, Raleigh's team would waste precious time confirming their alibis when Cain died.

Nor would others be spared additional scrutiny. In the broadcast, Cain named Raleigh specifically, with the aid of the current coroner, who had ruled the death as happening by natural mischance. To the public, Cain's display of the evidence box in his last broadcast proved a police and coroner cover-up. Henry asserted the material came from the department's evidence box holding all pertinent Couri case materials and was supposedly buried in the vaults below the police station.

Stung by what Cain claimed, the entire box on the Jenny Couri case was gone when Raleigh and Amanda went to look. Now, all 86 members of the force, staff, and service personnel were under suspicion. Given the wide net of possible culprits and involving local law enforcement, Amanda asked the state to assign one of their detective lieutenants to handle the investigation. Unfortunately, barely beginning his task, he suffered a massive heart attack. His replacement was due to be named shortly.

On one level, Raleigh was glad to be shucked of the victim. He was sure many others would be equally happy to hear he was gone, which made them all potential suspects. Cain's past muckraking certainly earned him enemies. Identifying them wouldn't be easy. Knowing a motive could help him find the right direction but seeing the crime scene was the first order of business.

The funny part of today's events was that Henry Cain came home to die. Raleigh was sure the man didn't want to die in the town he was born and reared in but came back to demonstrate how successful he had become. That success was based on finding corruption which led to a highly popular podcast.

Skye Landing citizens duly noted his success from what had come to him in his background checking after Cain made his charges, but most people in town ignored him and his show. Cain knew that would change. He wondered if someone from his past had become jealous of his success. That was one motive to pursue. Or someone feared Cain would uncover some information best left unhighlighted.

Jealousy was often the motive for murder; more likely, it was money or passion, the motives most often found as the cause of violence. If the detectives on the scene were correct, which he expected, it appeared one citizen did something dreadful to the podcast host.

When Cain first made his accusations, Amanda asked Raleigh to find out as much as possible about the man. In building his profile of Cain, Raleigh discovered from some of the older teachers that Cain made the perfect media host. Cain was cocky in high school, always on the edge of being disrespectful, but not enough to elicit punishment. Upon graduation and attending college, he moved to Los Angeles 13 years ago. None of the teachers thought the town lost much in his leaving. Nor gained anything in his return. Raleigh wondered if they would feel the same when Cain's death was announced.

Why he returned would also need to be determined, Raleigh knew. There appeared to be no reason for the man to move back to Skye Landing. His mother died, and his father was in Greenville with his sister. Yet, Raleigh felt there was. Raleigh knew there was always a reason people returned to their roots. He made a mental note to dig at that angle.

Also, from his investigation after Cain's first allegations, Raleigh uncovered nobody in town who had heard from him for seven years.

He did not return for his mother's funeral, and his father and sister only knew about his fame from others. Indeed, Raleigh was to learn later in the investigation; he visited with them only once after returning.

Going farther afield, Raleigh looked at Cain's years away from his hometown. He had asked police friends in Los Angeles to fill him in on what they knew about Cain. The reports were still coming but apparently Cain left Hollywood under some cloud. One contact gave Raleigh the impression they were glad he had left town. After Hollywood, Henry started his podcast railing against politicians.

When that approach did not gain traction or audiences, he pursued a tip from one of his few listeners. He discovered the sheriff of a tiny Illinois town was renting women prisoners to men for carnal purposes. Cain got the man indicted and convicted using information from inside the department and another listener. Other leads poured in, and soon he was hopscotching the nation taking down one law enforcement or political official after another.

What made Cain successful was his ability to choose the correct targets. Cain knew which tips could lead him to identify the most exploitive, wide-reaching, and audience-attracting crimes. Parlaying his drumbeat of coverage into attracting a national audience who believed he would solve any case or dislodge any politician who crossed his path, ratings and downloads exploded. Worse from Raleigh's position, based on early successes, his audience had come to believe whatever he said was the truth.

As a podcaster, Henry need only say someone was a crook to make it accurate in his audience's heads. Cain used the old saw: "When did you stop beating your wife?" Either answer gave integrity to the question. Unlike the police, Cain didn't need to prove it in court. He often established 'an innuendo idea that some crime was committed and left it to others to legally prove. People seldom notice how few of his "scoops" ended in guilty courtroom verdicts.

When his first accusation broke, Raleigh discovered Henry's return to Skye Landing delighted some people. Based on his record of finding criminal civic leaders in other towns, people in this area expected him to expose corruption in Skye Landing. Both podcasters and citizens hoped Cain would prove the town's rapid growth had been a breeding ground for corruption.

Much to his chagrin, Cain was surprised to find he couldn't identify any big-time graft or corruption in since arriving. In fact, despite his best efforts, he could report on nothing beyond some building inspectors taking payoffs for minor infractions. While tips from other towns and cities kept his program's downloads high, Skye Landing remained off-limits to his fulminations.

No one knew what prompted him to look into the Couri girl's death. Some whisper concerning the case sent him on the trail of an official cover-up. He had that story in his teeth, thanks to the purloined evidence box. If his accusations were believed, he hit his kind of pay dirt in Skye Landing. His death would spur public interest and mean it would be given far wider circulation. Raleigh knew no way of stopping the whirlwind about to descend on his town.

During his broadcast this past Sunday, Cain also demanded Raleigh sit down with him and explain his actions on Jenny Couri. Well, Raleigh knew if he sat down with Henry, no good would come of the interview for him. Aware he would look silly sitting in a chair and not producing more answers than his department already stated, he told Cain he wasn't coming through the township PR team on Monday.

Like he expects everyone else, Raleigh wondered if the two cases were related. Warning himself against premature theories, he hoped not. Jenny Couri was gone, and what happened to her was finished. What he didn't need now was the media becoming frenzied over a case that should have been long forgotten.

Raleigh glanced over at the driver. Raleigh wouldn't admit it just yet, but Carter could become a good detective if he overcame his ego, selfishness, and lack of empathy. In Carter's book, everything was black-and-white. He had yet to learn; law enforcement often came in hues both soft and hard. Sighing to himself, he put those issues aside. It wasn't time yet to deal with them. It was time to teach him the nuances of detective work.

There was also a nagging feeling Raleigh had Carter also possessed some dark streak. In some policemen, this trait played out in their home life or problems like drinking or gambling. He had seen it destroy colleagues. The only way to resolve them is to confront them.

Some did, and a majority did not. Most of the latter ended up in prison, suicide, or derelict. Raleigh looked closely at Carter to see if it was something Amanda needed to worry about. He reminded himself to get Carter's personnel file which he had neglected to do before coming on board.

Raleigh knew Carter was brilliant, he was thorough, and he was also lucky. In police work, sometimes luck had more to do with success. Finding the one clue, getting tipped from a jailhouse informer, or making the one connection that breaks apart the investigation often happens because of blind luck.

Raleigh knew this because each happened to him during his career. Figuring the younger cop to be one of those lucky types, Raleigh suspected Carter would also get his share. Raleigh thought Carter would go far if he didn't piss Amanda off before finding his feet.

"*The body will still be there when we get there, Carter,*" Raleigh said, trying to relax the anxious man beside him.

"*It's the 48-hour rule I'm thinking of,*" the driver said.

"*This case isn't going to solve itself in 48 hours, Carter.*"

"*You think not?*"

"*No, whoever did this knew the victim. Knew the meeting was being held. Took advantage of the situation. Unless we get fortunate, he or she just might get away from any punishment.*"

"*You really think that?*"

"*No, every crime is solvable if you go about the investigation in the right way.*"

"*Meaning, in this case, we jump to no early conclusions. Go down every road, and check every clue or tip. That means solving this case will take time and effort.*"

"*In a nutshell, you just named our poison,*" Raleigh said encouragingly.

"*What else do you think?*" Carter heard the approval in Raleigh's voice.

"Every media outlet in the country is going to be following what we do, so be careful, cross every T and dot every I. And above all, keep your mouth shut,"

"So you think?"

"Don't want to think 'til after I see the room, the victim, and anything else the crime scene tells us."

"You don't think Sawyer and Winston found everything already."

"Been my experience, eight eyes are better than four."

"Wish this traffic would go away."

"We'll get there when we get there."

Biting his tongue, he swung around two lanes of traffic into the oncoming roadway and rushed ahead. Raleigh said nothing, swerving back in line nervously; Carter did want to use the siren.

The Victim, Wednesday, 4:30pm

Driving around to the hotel's side, the two arriving detectives pulled into the back lot, next to three other police units. They saw two officers beating the bushes against the back fence. Waving at them, both signaled back there was nothing so far. Raleigh appreciated the two detectives' initiatives. He noted that two officers would need to be sent to the other side of the fence and comb that yard. Raleigh expected them not to find anything, but according to the manual, it was a necessary procedure to be followed.

After three weeks as his partner, Carter had learned to wait for Raleigh to enter the crime scene area first. His initial foray into death with Raleigh, a crack overdose, earned Carter a kick in his backside from Raleigh for entering ahead of the older man. No word was spoken the first time, but Carter got the message.

The first two detectives stepped back from the motel room door upon seeing Raleigh enter the hallway. Raleigh stopped in the door frame and took in the scene. First, taking a deep breath, he inhaled the room's odor. In the room, a scent lingered, combining the smell left by the dead body, some cologne or perfume Raleigh couldn't identify, and disinfectant.

"Who discovered the body?" Raleigh asked over his shoulder.

"The maid. There was no "do not disturb" sign on the door, so she went into the room to do a final check. She usually waits until the end of her shift to do a ready room check."

"She touch anything?"

"She doesn't remember touching anything. It's funny; she's the same woman working here when that wife shot the husband and secretary."

"Remind not to come here on the days she's working," the other detective laughed.

25

"Thought you didn't go in for hanky-panky?"
"Might be a time when I'll be tempted."
"Either of you sit on the beds or chairs?" Raleigh asked.
"No, we know better till you get here."
"Notice anything about the chairs?" Raleigh asked.
"Something, but we couldn't figure what?"
"Chair's out from the desk as if someone was going to write something." Raleigh opined.
"What would you write in a motel room," Carter blurted out.
"A check," Raleigh said as the county coroner arrived.

For 15 years, Jules Hagerman was the County Coroner for Skye Landing's County. Jules feared this was shaping up as his last year. Now that its pay and benefits were attractive, he was fighting real competition this time in the next election. Raleigh hoped Hagerman would hold on, but County Coroners face the voters every two years in South Carolina. Seven terms seemed about the limit for tenure hereabouts. Two men were gearing up to run against him in the next election. Jules would have had no trouble beating either man if it weren't for the victim lying on the floor.

For the past month, Henry Cain, today's victim, had been questioning and harassing Hagerman about Jenny Couri. Earlier broadcasts hinted at some sinister allegations against the coroner would be revealed. Finally, last Sunday, he blasted Jules for incompetency in the Jenny Couri case. The tirades and disgorged facts would not have been so bad if Jules didn't know Cain was right. When the Couri case came around, he had been a novice at being a coroner. Not overly sure about how she died, he had been bullied by local power leaders into skipping any lab tests, editing his autopsy reports, and ruling it death by mischance. Worse, he permitted the cremation of the body without taking any samples from her stomach or other fluids.

The allegations could mean the end of his career as County Coroner. Since the Couri affair, Jules studied many disciplines to make his office a model for the state. Jules took science courses on the newest, best procedures and trained himself and his staff so thoroughly as to create one of the better county offices. Unfortunately, that meant nothing to Cain, and Jules knew he could be through come November.

Waiting for Raleigh to finish his observations, Jules thought of the number of cases he and the older man had worked together. The total now passed a hundred, he knew; most were ordinary. Some were difficult. All were interesting. They had both thought the Couri case was buried, but Cain had come along and bitten them on their asses.

Some people were saying it was time to hang up his instrument case. Jules didn't believe that, but he tried to accustom himself to the coming reality.

Raleigh stood aside for Jules and told him he was through looking at the crime scene so the body could be moved. Jules grunted acknowledgment and proceeded with his preliminary exam. Looking up at the four detectives, he surmised they all could render an accurate verdict in this case. However, it was up to him to say the words.

"Victim appears to still be pre-rigor; been mashed at least five times; no signs of struggle. Don't know if he had anything to drink." He said, looking around the room. *"No liquor is evident and none in the form of odor emanating from the body."*

"TOD Jules?" A voice asked.

"Probably before 2pm today. Body's still warm. Temp seems to be in the eighties. I can give you a precise time when I probe back in lab."

"That helps, Jules," Raleigh said quietly.

He turned to the other detectives and asked if they had a check-in time. Both answered negatively, and he motioned for Carter to go to the front desk for that information and any tapes they might have at the front desk. Jules finished his examination and hollered for two workers to bring a stretcher. The body was gone in minutes, leaving the room strangely empty.

Before someone who always attracted attention, even in death, he was the center of interest. With the body gone, it was an ordinary motel room that held important clues if the detectives only knew where to look. Before the body left, everyone still viewed it as his room, and now they referred to it as the murder scene.

Carter returned with two video discs plus word that Henry checked in about noon and paid by credit card, and that surprised three of the four men but not Raleigh.

"Sonofabitch wanted us to know what he was doing, if we kept tabs on his credit cards."

"Do you think we were?" Carter asked.

"He was hoping but we weren't going to get caught in that trap."

"If we had been keeping tabs, he would have found out and trumpeted on his broadcast," Raleigh said to no one in particular.

Carter filed that fact away with the others he was rapidly accumulating.

"No booze, no sex, nothing," Raleigh said almost to himself. Turning to Carter, he asked: *"Did you ask how long he wanted the room?"*

"No, I didn't but he asked for this room in particular."

"Right next to the door leading to the back parking area."

"So no one would see whoever was coming to meet him," Raleigh finished his sentence. *"Go find out if this was booked as an Afternoon Special or what."*

Carter almost crashed into the woman standing outside the room, flying out the door. She was past 30 with bright red hair and held her laptop in front of her as a shield. Managing to avoid most of the blow, Carter ignored her in his haste to determine what he knew should have been asked earlier.

The Press, Wednesday, 5:15pm

As he raced to the main lobby, Carter's brain registered the red hair and the whiff of perfume moving down the hall. Like all the other policemen and women he knew, he followed Amanda's mandate not to disclose information, and someone must have violated that dictate if she was here. Glad it wasn't him; he was in enough trouble with the chief. Since bawling him out and assigning him to Raleigh, she had not said another word to him.

The two detectives turned to the woman and were about to shoo her away when they realized it was Caleigh Butler Jenkins. Each of them had been featured in one or more stories written by Caleigh before she became editor of the Skye Landing Eagle. They smiled at her and stood aside, not wanting to get between her and Raleigh.

"What are you doing here," Raleigh asked quietly.

"Trying to confirm it is Henry Cain they just carted out of here."

"Now what gave you that idea," Raleigh said menacingly.

"A little bird."

"Birds should tweet and not talk."

"Many people tweet nowadays."

"Then they should keep their mouths shut."

"Can't happen in this day and age."

"Figured as much."

"Well, is it?"

"Until we get someone to notify us officially, he's still a John Doe in our books."

"Well can you tell me what killed him?"

"Waiting for the birds to tell me."

"Oh, come on, Raleigh, Henry's big news hereabouts, and if he's gone, the paper will need to spread it across our front page."

"*Better to write about the Garden Club.*"

"*Readers don't want that. Ever hear of 'If it bleeds, it leads?'*"

"*What are you doing here? You're the Eagle's editor, for heaven's sake.*"

"*With the young reporters the home office sends me, I couldn't trust them not to blow my scoop.*"

"*Well, you're not getting confirmation from me.*"

"*So, you mean to say that the body they just took out of here maybe is Henry Cain.*"

"*Or maybe it's not.*"

"*I think I'm going with the fact it's presumed to be Henry Cain.*"

"*Do what you like.*"

"*Don't I always?*"

"*Since you were a little girl.*"

"*And you held me on your lap.*"

"*Only way I could keep tabs on you.*"

"*Remember, we have lunch Saturday.*"

"*If I'm not working this case.*"

"*Even if you were, Sue Ellen expects you.*"

"*Can't disappoint Sue Ellen now, can we?*"

"*You haven't in 16 years, so why start now.*"

Raleigh permitted himself a small chuckle. Since she came to live with him and his wife, Ellen, his niece had wrapped him around her finger to get whatever she wanted. Caleigh taught his grand-niece to do the same as her daughter grew up. Raleigh admitted that their needs were the only things he permitted to come between him and his job in his few reflective moments. He would be at that luncheon no matter where the case stood on Saturday. He wished he had learned to do the same for his wife while she lived.

Within minutes of Caleigh's departure, Carter returned with the sign-in information from Henry's registration. What interested Raleigh was Henry's intention of staying the night at the motel. His home was less than a mile away, and his office was closer.

Raleigh pondered that a moment before telling the other detectives to supervise the tech crew when they arrived. He also told them to take everything portable from the room, including the glasses, ice bucket, and one open soap bar in the bathroom. Noting the seat was down, his eyes swept the bathroom, checking off that two towels were in disarray, and he told the men to take them.

He called Amanda on her private line using his phone, confirmed it was Cain, and asked her to set up a 7pm press conference through their PR person. He picked the time deliberately to miss the 6pm news broadcast and give Caleigh a chance to scoop them via her Internet feed "Bad cess to them," he thought.

Office Visit, Wednesday, 6:30pm

Good investigative procedure mandates detailing one officer to monitor who enters or leaves the crime scene perimeter and logs collected evidence. It is an important, thankless task, often assigned to the most junior patrolmen or patrolwomen. Raleigh detailed Sawyer for this task, assuring him that this case was too important to give the task to a patrolman.

Taking Carter with him, Raleigh drove to the outdoor shopping strip where Cain's office occupied the second-floor corner suite. Deliberately parking their car far away from the building to avoid being stuck when the usual horde of media people came, they walked across the lot to the elevator leading to the second-floor offices. No one seemed to be about, so they assumed word of Cain's death had not yet spread. If it were known he was dead, the media and fans would be outside.

The hallway was quiet, making it seem like no one worked in the building. Raleigh let Carter try the door to Cain's office, which was locked. The detective then knocked firmly after hearing some scurrying around inside. Not wanting to draw attention to themselves, they waited quietly.

After a few minutes, they heard the click of the lock opening; the door slid slightly ajar. Carter pushed the door in at a signal from Raleigh, knocking the occupant down. She proved to be a short, fat woman in her early to late fifties who was having difficulty rising to meet the visitor at the door.

This didn't prevent her from emitting howls of protest from the ground. In a fury, finally reaching her feet, she rushed the detective. Carter easily held her off as Raleigh's booming voice shouted that they were the police. Still struggling, Carter wrestled the woman around and put her in handcuffs behind her back.

Two other people peered out from cubicles at the spectacle. The fat woman commenced spewing curses at the men, and she seemed to hate all policemen without exception. Sawyer sat her down on a chair in the reception area while Raleigh walked nearer to the other occupants. A wispy, emaciated blonde in a pale blue sweater and black pants shrank away from the detective.

"And your name?" Raleigh asked gently, not wanting to spook the woman more.

"Henriette Percy."

"What do you do?"

"Answer phones. Edit interviews. Make sure guests are comfortable." Arrange Mr. Cain's trips. Act as a script girl for the radio broadcasts.*

"What does a script girl do."

"If a program is live, keep the timing, so we hit the commercial times correctly. Warn when the guest is running overtime. Anything that needs to be done I do." And then:

"We didn't know who you were, and we haven't heard from Mr. Cain all day."

"Does he often disappear without calling in?"

"No, that is why it's so strange. He left yesterday in mid-afternoon and said he would be gone until this morning. This morning he called and said he would be gone for the whole day."

"Unusual?"

"Yes, he never wants to be away from the office, visitors, or phones for more than a day."

"You tried contacting him?"

"On both his phones."

"And?"

"And nothing; he hasn't picked up since 6pm yesterday."

"Ever think about reporting to the police he was missing?"

"Oh no. Mr. Cain thinks it will be the police who will make him disappear."

"You believe him?"

"Of course, look at how they ignored that poor teenager. This town is rife with corruption."

Carter started to speak, but Raleigh's look silenced him. Letting the comments pass, Raleigh focused on getting the support team's help.

"Is that why you didn't answer our knock?" he asked the woman, who resumed her seat in front of a bank of phones and recording instruments.

"No, we have had some strange visitors recently. We were careful because Mr. Cain is not here," she answered.

"How do you reach Mr. Cain when he is out of the office?"

"We dial his private phone. He usually answers that one. The other he might ignore because he believes the police know about that one and tap it. The other is one he buys for cash, and they don't know about."

"So Mr. Cain has two phones?"

"Yes, one for the general public and the other for his most intimate friends. Those who can't get around to see him or don't want to be seen with him."

"And these phones are always with him?"

"Yes, he was never without them," they almost chorused together.

Raleigh pondered that and fit it in because no phone was found with the body, and his briefcase and recorder were also missing. The detective was glad that Sawyer ordered a sweep of the motel car park but was sure that none of those items would show up.

With feigned indifference, Raleigh asked casually if Cain had contacted them in any way since last night. All three looked at each other, debating whether to say something. Finally, the blond woman spoke up, barely whispering:

"Nothing this morning but this afternoon at 2pm, he reassured us everything was okay."

"Voice or text?"

"Oh, text. He did that sometimes in case anyone was listening. He preferred text to any other way if he was on some new trail."

"You sure it was him?

"Yes, very sure, it was from his private phone. Except?"

"Except what? Raleigh continued to act casual.

"He didn't add his usual postscript."

"Which was?"

"Keep Hanging."

"Are you from around here?" He asked the blonde employee.

"No, I joined Mr. Cain when he first started. Been with him now six years."

"Where are you from?" Raleigh said more harshly to the older woman.

"I'm from Peoria, Illinois."

Raleigh turned away from the woman and strode to the other cubicle. Its occupant was the male version of Henrietta. He took a defiant stance and blocked Raleigh from moving too far into his cubicle. Taking this as a challenge, Raleigh used his stomach to drive the man back.

Once inside the cubicle, he saw a wide array of computer equipment and communication gear. It was apparent the occupant had taken care to shut it all down. The only instrument still on was a scanner tuned to the Skye Landing police frequency. Raleigh listened for a moment and then turned it off.

"Your name?" he asked harshly.

"Geoffrey Wallace," he answered firmly but trailed off at the look on Raleigh's face.

"What's your job?"

"Research."

"What's the meaning of research?" Raleigh said in a not-so-friendly voice.

"I verify facts and identities and assure the truth of anything Mr. Cain says on the air is true."

"You don't do a very good job," Sawyer said, keeping the struggling man away from the others in the office.

"So you examine all the papers, documents, and film Henry uses in his broadcasts?"

"Almost all, sometimes Mr. Cain gets material so sensitive only he handles it."

"Like the contents of the police evidence box."

"On the advice of our attorneys, we disclaim any involvement with that material."

"Whose, your attorney?"

"Beau Jenkins."

"Might've known Beau would be involved someplace."

"He's a brilliant attorney."

"He's a turd, and you can tell him I said so the next time you see him."

"I would not dignify it with any transmittal."

"Okay, where's Henry's office?"

"At the end of this corridor. But it's locked, and none of us have a key. And you can't go into in without a search warrant."

"We don't need a search warrant; this is a murder investigation."

All three employees reacted to the word murder.

"Who died?" the fat woman shouted from her chair.

"We want to know," the other woman shouted in agreement.

"We demand to know!" the man squealed.

"Why do you want to know? Why should I tell you?" Raleigh egged them on, preparing to use the moment to his advantage.

"Then why are you here?" the fat woman got up from her chair and rushed at Raleigh.

"Because your boss said one of three men was a murderer. And now there's been a murder."

"We had nothing to do with it," Geoffrey almost shouted.

"With what?"

"With whatever murder you're investigating."

"How do you prove it?"

"When did this murder occur?"

"This afternoon."

"Ah, ha. We've been together in this office all day."

"Convenient. Why's that?"

"Because we're preparing for Sunday's broadcast and wanted to be here whenever Mr. Cain returned," Geoffrey said to the group.

"So what was so important you couldn't leave."

"Mr. Cain said he would be bringing proof that one of the three men was a murderer."

"He say what the proof was?"

"All he said was this town wouldn't be the same after his show."

"And you believed him?"

"Of course, it was something he always said when he had final proof of some miscreant."

Savoring the words as he spoke them, the little man acted as an individual would if talking to someone who did not know their meaning.

"And he always came through?"

"Oh, yes. He even ordered his favorite champagne for all of us."

"So, given all this, you're not worried Henry hasn't shown up."

"Of course, we're worried, especially after that man came in earlier today looking for Mr. Cain," the fat woman babbled as she sat back in the seat as if suddenly realizing something.

"Do you know who the man was?" Raleigh asked.

"No, but he had a wild look in his eyes. Demanded to see Mr. Cain."

"How did you get him to leave?"

"I picked up the phone and said I was dialing the police."

"So, we're good for getting rid of unwanted guests."

"Oh, no, I would never call the police".

"You're all thugs," Geoffrey said, seemingly oblivious that he was confronting two police officers.

"That seemed to sober the man," the fat lady said smugly. *"After throwing a chair against Mr. Cain's door, he left. That's when we started locking the door."*

"What time did this happen?"

"About 3pm. Mr. Cain wasn't here, and he didn't seem to want to deal with us." This came from the fat woman in the chair while she slipped further back in the chair. Her face drooped, and she seemed to shrink more into herself, reviewing the situation.

Pleased with himself, Raleigh went over the last few minutes in his mind. The three employees could be eliminated as suspects unless they were conspiring together. The next step was to secure the office and computers before they had a chance to wipe them or hide evidence from the Couri case.

While Raleigh was thinking, the fat lady made the final leap and screamed out in anguish.

"*Mr. Cain is dead, isn't he?*" She shouted at Sawyer, who was closest to her.

"*I'm afraid so,*" Raleigh said softly.

"*No, it's not true,*" Henrietta spoke quietly.

"*You must be mistaken!*" Geoffrey yelled.

"*You killed him,*" the fat woman shouted, lunging at Sawyer.

"*No, we didn't have the pleasure,*" Sawyer said maliciously, savoring the moment.

"*Where did he die?*" The other woman asked.

"*At a motel just inside the city limits.*" Raleigh replied.

"*What was he doing at a motel?*" the fat woman asked herself.

"*Getting the evidence,*" Geoffrey said gleefully.

"*More likely have an illicit affair,*" Sawyer replied.

"*He wasn't married. He could go out with anyone,*" Geoffrey said almost to himself.

"*Surprised he didn't go out with you,*" Sawyer said, twisting the knife more into the man.

"*He was my boss; I wouldn't complicate things.*"

"*So you knew he played for the other team?*" Sawyer asked.

"*We all did,*" the blonde woman spoke up quickly.

"*So you all thought he was out on a love date?*" Raleigh asked.

"*No, no, he distinctly told us last night he was getting the evidence he needed to make Sunday a ratings blockbuster,*" Geoffrey said, clearly disappointed his boss had not succeeded.

"*Well, he's gone, and we need to sequester this office,*" Raleigh brought the conversation back to his original goal.

"*But what about Sunday's broadcast?*" Geoffrey wailed.

"*Not our concern.*"

"*Where's his briefcase, tape recorder, and two telephones? Do you have them? I bet you do,*" Geoffrey pushed back at Raleigh.

"*If we had them, they would be police property until we solve this case. But we don't.*" Raleigh said with finality.

All three employees started weeping. The two detectives looked on. In his career, Raleigh had broken death news to many families, and Carter had also done his share of notifications. Eying each other, they thought the staff was exhibiting excessive feelings. The way the three employees carried on, an onlooker might consider them family. Raleigh let them go on for a few minutes and then told them to leave.

"You can't make us," Geoffrey said, retreating into his cubicle.

"I can, and I am," Raleigh said. *"We are securing these premises until we can be sure there are no clues to his murderer."*

"You just want to find the evidence in the Couri case and bury it again. Well, I won't let you!"

"And you'll stop us how?"

"With Beau Jenkins' help."

"Well, you go on outside and call good ole' Beau, and you tell him if he comes within one mile of this office, I'll kick his ass from here to Greenville."

"You wouldn't dare."

"You ask Beau if I haven't done that already. Now empty your pockets so I'm sure you're not taking anything out of this office but your asses."

After giving Carter their contact information and home addresses, the three employees reluctantly complied with Raleigh's request and left much subdued. When they examined Henry's door, the two men discovered it was steel with a triple lock. Raleigh called headquarters and asked for two patrolmen to guard the office and Amanda to find someone to get them past the door.

"Might've known old Beau would be mixed up in this thing somehow," Raleigh almost whispered.

"Knew you've had dealings with him before."

"Too many for my liking."

"People say he's running for mayor."

"People say a lot of things. In this case, it's true. Bad cess for this town."

"You know Beau well?"

"Too well. Man's the most selfish person I know."

"Heard you kicked his ass."

"Not hard enough. Should've done more."

Examining the keys Geoffrey had left behind, he found one labeled Henry's House. Waiting for the patrolmen, he tried booting up the computers but quickly saw passwords guarded them. Before considering calling Geoffrey for the passwords, Sawyer rummaged through the cubicle and found the passwords taped to the bottom of one drawer.

When the tech crew arrived, he reluctantly started to leave, looking longingly at the computers on the way out. Both Raleigh and he were confident their contents would give them some clues. Raleigh and Carter left for Henry's house when officers arrived to stand guard. Their final instruction to the two men was to bar entry to anyone, especially the employees.

Victim's Home, Wednesday 7:15pm

On the drive over to Henry's house, Carter queried Raleigh on the case so far.

"Well, we know why he was at the Red Roof at noon. We don't know where he was from two yesterday until checking into the motel," Raleigh answered.

"At home?" Sawyer shot back.

"Don't think so. I have a hunch those three had a way of knowing if he was home."

"Maybe he was catting about."

"Perhaps, but I think knowing where he was last night is going to be important to finding his killer," Raleigh mused almost to himself.

"But not why he was spending the night at the motel," Carter completed his sentence.

"Nor why somebody wrote a check in that room and to whom," Raleigh continued.

"Could check with the bank in the morning to see if any new checks show up in his account."

"We could check his regular accounts, but no, I think that check was made out to or deposited in an account we will have great difficulty finding."

"Think so?"

"Henry Cain was a man of many parts, most of which he didn't want people to know."

"In what way?"

"Take that fat woman. There's a story with her. She reacted to his death way out of being just an employee."

"I thought all three identified themselves with Henry Cain."

"I think the other two identify with what he did. Her life was projected around him and him alone."

"What about the man who showed up yesterday afternoon after Henry was dead?"

"Either he's innocent or playing it very smart. I'll wait on him."

"What about the three men he planned to name and the one he says murdered the girl."

"We need to talk to all three tomorrow. But I will tell you one thing, none of those three men killed that girl."

"So she did die by accident."

"No, she was murdered."

Upon hearing Raleigh's calm declaration, Carter nearly ran their car into the side roadway.

"You mean Cain was right?"

"Yes, she was murdered. But we know who did it. We know why. And that person has been punished beyond our laws. No, we didn't cover up a murder, nor do a sloppy investigation. We protected innocent people from great anguish. That's the side of the law you need to learn."

"That's why you're not talking or defending the department?"

"Because people will be hurt, and they don't need to be hurt."

"And you're not going to tell any of us more?"

"When the time's right, I will. Either Sawyer, Carmichael, or you'll figure it out yourself. Sawyer and Carmichael already understand law enforcement is about balancing grey areas. That's something not for me to tell you but for you to learn."

"Shit, I knew that going in."

"Knowing it and doing it are two different things."

"So, killing Cain wasn't to prevent him naming someone for killing that girl?"

"No, he was so far wrong on that case he would have lost half his audience. Amanda would have waited for him to name the so-called murderer and then showed the world why that person couldn't have been the killer. But that wouldn't have quieted speculation or straightened him out. Those men are doomed to the bad publicity from Cain's show. Now that he's dead, it will be even more difficult for them. Amanda

can't help them. Things got complicated when the case box went missing—turned a bad light on our department. Hell, the whole department. We need to find out who stole the box. Whether it has anything to do with Cain's murder is yet to be determined. No matter how you look at it, Cain's death really opened a can of worms."

"So fear of exposure didn't motivate this killing?"

"I didn't say that. I think Cain might have overturned another rock without realizing it. Someone else feared exposure. That's why I think the motive for this murder is not the Couri girl but something or someone else."

"What or who else?"

"If I knew the answer to that question, Sawyer, we'd have our murderer. This is one of those crimes where we will need to find the motive to identify the killer."

Arriving at Henry Cain's house, they saw Geoffrey and the fat woman going up the steps to the front door. From their body language, the man had a key to open the door, and the woman carried a largely empty shopping bag. They turned towards the approaching car and then tried to flee back to their auto.

Swooping up the driveway and around the parked car, the two detectives jumped out and pushed the interlopers against their vehicle.

"What are you doing here?" Carter shouted.

"We wanted to get some items that belong to Hilda here," Geoffrey said sullenly.

"There're papers that belong to me and some clothes," the woman shouted plaintively.

"Why are you in Skye Landing?" Carter pressed her.

"No, Mr. Cain helped me get out of jail, and I came here because I feared for my life."

"From whom?

"The sheriff in my hometown."

"What's in the papers?"

"Documents concerning how women in his jail were rented out as prostitutes prove I'm not crazy."

"And you stole the records?"

"*No, after I was released, I got into his office and managed to xerox them and get them to the state police. Mr. Cain turned them into PDFs for my safety.*"

"*Why are they in Henry's house?*" Raleigh asked.

"*For safekeeping.*"

"*Safekeeping from whom*" Carter said viciously.

"*My children and the sheriff.*"

"*Your children?*"

"*Yes, Henry exposed their attempt to have me put away. I thought I was safe, but they've come after me. Henry was keeping all my papers and documents.*"

"*What's your real name?* Carter pushed her.

"*Hilda Rensozo,*" she said.

"*The Peoria heiress who blew the whistle on the sheriff.*"

"*Yes, for him to escape prison, he claimed I was insane. My children couldn't wait for my money, so they went along.*"

"*How did you get involved with the Sheriff?*"

"*I was in jail on a motor vehicle charge and saw what was happening. I tipped off Henry, and he brought down the sheriff. Now he and my children have common cause to get me certified as insane.*"

"*Why are they so important to this sheriff?*"

"*They were used at the sheriff's trial, but somehow, the copies have gone missing, and I have the only ones left. He's asking for a new trial because the evidence disappeared. Everything was going smoothly for them until they discovered I had copies. They didn't know I had copies until last week, and we're sure he's headed here to destroy them.*"

"*We'll check your story; we're going into the house, and you two are going elsewhere. I'll have an officer standing guard so no one will get in.*"

"*But I know the ex-sheriff is coming. He called and threatened Mr. Cain last week, after he learned I was with him here. He threatened Cain to get the papers back and said he was coming to get us both.*"

"*What did Henry do?*"

"*Laughed. Said he had more on him, and if he didn't leave me alone, he would give more damning evidence about something worse than prostitution to the people in Peoria. They're still trying to get him on* more charges. *After being found guilty, the judge only gave him three months in jail, but he lost his job. They're afraid he'll run again and get elected if he gets a pardon or the case is thrown out."*

"What's this guy's name, and where is he in town."

"Arturo Gonzalez, but we don't know when he's coming. He usually drives a Blue Cadillac and has two companions who were two former deputies thrown off the force."

"Okay, I'll put out a search and arrest circular for him but in the meantime, go home!"

"This is my home!" the woman shouted again.

"Sorry, you can't get back in until we searched his house. Is there any place you can stay?"

"I guess Henrietta will let me stay with her."

"Go there. We'll let you come by and get your clothes when we finish. The papers will remain with us until this case ends. As to ownership, we'll cross that bridge later."

To reassure them, Carter radioed in a description of the three men and their car. The two employees seemed somewhat mollified. After watching the two people leave, Raleigh and Carter entered the house.

Still having a new construction smell, Carter called headquarters, asking for someone to run down the construction details. They saw a staircase led from the front foyer to what they assumed were bedrooms. Hallways to the back flanked each side of the stairs that divided the house. To their right was an archway leading to the large living room that was more suited for people waiting to see the master of the house. A closed door on the left opened to Henry's office. There were two bathrooms under the staircase. The kitchen ran behind the stairway.

Both men felt the house closed in on itself and was not designed for entertaining but for accommodating the owner's business style. Like Cain's life, the house was a series of compartments arranged, so rooms remained separate enclaves with no two designed to permit easy flow between them. Further along, the hallway was a dining area opening onto the back patio. These two areas were not linked for easy circulation, and both looked unused.

The men didn't go further, concentrating instead on unlocking the office. To their surprise, it wasn't made of steel and opened without a key. But all the heavy cabinets and desks were locked tight with tamper-proof crossbars in front. The desk held only a calendar. The only one notation for today was: motel. On previous Monday's date was only one word: PAYDAY in big block letters.

When the guard duty officer arrived, Raleigh repeated his order that no one was admitted till they had a chance to inventory the office contents. He mentioned the aggressive sheriff in passing, giving the officer permission to be extra strong in preventing entry. Knowing the patrolman from other occasions when crime scene protection was necessary, he knew not to worry.

Leaving the officer inside, Raleigh and Carter stood on the mansion steps, realizing they were hungry. They drove back to Skye Landing's main thoroughfare and picked the Waffle House. As they waited for their food, Carter pressed Raleigh for more details on the Couri affair

"In good time," the older man said.

"Now's a good time."

"No, I want you to concentrate on this case and solve it before I do."

"If you can't figure it out, how can I?"

"Using your God-given brains," Raleigh said with half a smile.

"We have so little to go on."

"Think so"

"Yes, the three main suspects aren't suspects. We don't know who Cain met. Forensic probably is a dead end. We got zip."

"Well, you're wrong. We know something's up in this town. We know Cain was in on it. We know someone who met with him before the murderer is out there and can tell us a lot if we can find them."

"Where do we start?"

"Not with the Couri girl? I don't think she's the reason for Cain's death, but I think her death sent someone on the trail of a good story that they could peddle to Cain. They needed that police file to convince Cain to do the story. Why they wanted the story told is as important as well."

"I'd like to look at that file."

"Come to my house; I have a duplicate file you can look at tonight. Give you a head start for the morning."

"Keeping duplicate files is against the law," Carter said in half-disbelief.

"Or you using your police siren in non-emergency situations. There is no harm just as long as no one sees you; if they don't, you have no worries."

After Hours, Wednesday 9pm

Carter pondered that until their food arrived, sitting back in his booth seat. They didn't talk further until arriving at Raleigh's house. There, Carter got another surprise. The woman from the motel was just getting out of her car and entering the house.

"*My niece,*" Raleigh said laconically and followed her into the building.

The house had what real estate people called a "used look." Talking to other agents they would say the house looked as though the occupants fixed things when they broke but left the rest to deteriorate on their own. Following Raleigh into the front corridor, he saw the woman's heels disappearing up the hall steps. As she reached the top of the steps, a shrill voice yelled "Mother" in a not-friendly tone. Raleigh ignored the upstairs commotion and ushered Carter into a back office packed with boxes around one large desk. Folders and papers sat in the desk's center. Raleigh went to the desk, took out two thick binders, and handed them to Carter.

"*Start here, the files on the crime itself and the first interviews. That will bring you up to speed to understand the rest,*" Raleigh said as he packed his gun into the wall safe, open and empty when they arrived but now shut with his gun inside.

"*Where do I sit?*"

"*At my desk, I'm going to take a shower,*" Raleigh pointed to his big chair as he exited the office and went up the stairs.

Putting his jacket on two file boxes occupying one of the other two chairs in the room, Carter sat in the comfortable desk chair and attempted to read the reports, review the forms, and squint at the pictures. Within minutes he was distracted by the shouted voices coming from overhead. The younger voice was shouting about trust, parental control, and some party, the substance of which Carter could not catch what the other person was saying.

He presumed it was the woman who walked ahead of them. For ten minutes, the exchange continued. It ended with someone slamming a door with such violence the windows shook. Quiet reigned, and Carter was able to concentrate on the case files.

A whiff of perfume he smelled in the motel corridor awakened Carter to the fact that someone was standing in the doorway. To Carter, she was framed by the light behind her creating a halo effect. The red hair atop the green silk blouse added color to the apparition, and the result was breathtaking. Sitting at the oversized desk, Carter realized his prick had betrayed him.

"Don't you hate the smell in this room?" The vision said.

"Didn't notice," was all Carter could say.

"It's all these files and what's in those boxes," the vision said in lowered tones.

"I was so engrossed in the files; I didn't smell anything."

"The Couri case?" she said with a question mark at the end.

Caleigh was the Editor of the Eagle, and knowing Amanda's rules about talking to the press, Carter said nothing,

"Don't worry; Raleigh will tell me the details when they can be released. That case is closed.

"Not according to Henry Cain."

"Well, he's dead, and hopefully that poor girl will rest peacefully again."

"Do you know where she's buried?"

"Yes, her ashes are in an urn behind Pastor Bob's church altar or what serves as their altar."

"There are about a dozen people from Skye Landing there. People who have no family to remember them by. Pastor Bob says, saying prayers for them to keep their memories alive."

"Good thought."

"I don't know. Maybe that was one girl the town should forget."

"Why?"

"*Because she left nothing behind but heartache. Look, we have another murder.*"

Just then, the shower turned off in an upstairs bathroom. Carter realized he had not heard it before then.

"*That's Raleigh taking his shower. No matter what time or for how long he is home, he has a shower first,*" said Caleigh dryly.

"*Funny didn't know what he was doing.*"

"*Well, you will. Sometimes, she would run in there with him when his wife was alive. It was funny hearing them giggle like two young kids.*"

"*I can't imagine him giggling.*"

"*I grew up in this house and can tell that was their routine.*"

"*You grew up in this house?*"

"*Since I was four. My mother came in one day. Dropped me off and roared off in a red convertible and hasn't been heard from since.*"

"*I can't believe she just left you. Raleigh's wife was her sister, right? Didn't they try to find your mother?*"

"*Only when they were adopting me. They had no luck, so they just took guardianship.*"

"*What about your father?*"

"*My mother would never tell anyone who it was.*"

"*Must be tough on you?*"

"*It was and is. I'm lucky to have had Raleigh and Ellen.*"

"*Has she been gone long?*"

"*Be eight years July 4th. Raleigh woke up, and she was dead beside him.*"

"*That must have been tough.*"

"*For him, a disaster. He wasn't the same for months. He took the mattress and bed and burned them in the yard. To this day, he sleeps on a sofa in his room.*"

As Caleigh finished this thought, the phone rang on the desk and somewhere upstairs. She motioned for Carter not to answer it. They waited in silence until Raleigh yelled down.

"Sonofabitchen sheriff tried to rush Cain's home with his two goons. The guy I left there flattened all three and they're at the jail. We'll talk with them in the morning. Good night," he yelled back as he climbed back up the stairs.

"So, if you're going to stay and read those reports you'll need coffee. Let's go to the kitchen."

"If it's not too much bother."

"It's either coffee or bourbon, but I got a long day tomorrow and a 16-year-old daughter."

"She mad at you?"

"Perpetually. Right now, it's because I won't let her go to a party in Charlotte."

"I see."

"No, you don't see. I was the original party girl. I know what happens at these parties."

Wild ideas crossed Carter's mind as she spoke these words. Along with Caleigh's Kelly-green silk blouse, she had changed into tight denim pants, and gold sandals.

Nothing went together, but the effect on her and the bright red hair left Carter bedazzled. He could only think, *"What was the color of the hair under her pants?"* as they walked into the kitchen.

Turning on the kitchen lights revealed an ultra-modern arrangement that included a six-burner stove, a deep cold refrigerator, and enough pots and pans for the most demanding cook. Caleigh explained.

"Eleanor Hightower was Ellen's best friend. When my daughter was four, I got promoted to night editor. For three weeks, chaos reigned in this house with me trying to be both mother and editor. One morning Eleanor showed up with two suitcases and took the spare bedroom. She was a widow, but she and Raleigh worked out a salary arrangement that fit them both. I once offered to pay part of her salary, and Raleigh just walked away. She is a marvelous cook and terrible housekeeper, but wonderful with my daughter and me. In recent years, she's taken to giving cooking lessons and redid the kitchen five years ago. We thought she paid for it herself, but local stores donated most in return for her steering business to them. It seems to

work for them, and Raleigh doesn't mind. Hell, she even put in a back door so husbands who wanted to learn how to cook could sneak in without going through the front door. This is a nosy town."

"Why are they learning to cook?"

"To surprise their wives."

"That they can cook?"

"No, so they can survive on their own after the divorce they are anticipating."

"Really?"

"Two ways you can tell a couple are on the verge of divorce. She's losing weight, and he's learning to live independently. Ellen can predict divorces better than anyone in town."

"Are there that many?"

"Enough that she has almost as many men as women in some classes. But for gossip, she keeps several classes for women only. They're also good for more lessons. Men want to learn how to make breakfast and a dish to help them seduce all the women they think will flock to them once their single again."

"At least someone's making money."

"Money wasn't her first concern when she started those classes."

"What was?"

"Having something to do while she waited."

"For what?"

"I think she's just waiting for Raleigh to ask her to marry him."

"You think so?"

"I know so. She doesn't say anything but occasionally gets a wishful look towards him."

"He doesn't reciprocate?"

"Too busy being a detective. Same with Ellen, no time."

"What do you think he wants now?"

"Ellen."

"Seems that's passed."

"I think he realizes what he lost by not spending more time with her."

"No children?"

"Now, that will need to wait for another time."

"Long story?"

"Long Tragedy."

"We all have them."

"Not like those two."

"Tragedies in your life?"

"None I couldn't handle, thanks to Raleigh and Ellen."

"You were lucky."

"Don't I know it."

"Where's Raleigh's luck?"

"His job."

"Shouldn't there be more?"

"For him, there's nothing more. Nor does he want anything more."

"It will need to end sometime."

"He knows it but is putting it off as long as possible."

"What do you want in a marriage?"

"Now, look, Lover Boy, I'm not one of your young things. I bet I'm a decade older than you and two decades wiser. So don't try wooing me with your slick questions. Grow up first and learn from Raleigh."

"From the sounds of it, he didn't do such a great job on the personal front."

"See, that's why you're so young. Ellen worshiped him, and he, her. Raleigh just didn't know he needed to come home more. Now he does, but it's too late. Maybe the next time, he'll know better."

"Don't see him finding love at his age."

"You know you look for companionship in a marriage at some point."

"I wouldn't know."

"I'd bet that about you. You're still footloose and fancy-free."

"And you're not?" He said hopefully.

"Not with a 16-year-old daughter."

"Who's her father?"

"Don't laugh, Beau Jenkins."

Despite himself, Carter did laugh, and she gave him a rueful face.

"Ain't he the guy Raleigh said he would kick around the block again?"

"The one and same. Raleigh found out I was pregnant just after Beau walked out on me for Corine Goodman. People tell me Raleigh tossed him down the stairs from his office and then pushed and kicked him up and down Reed Road."

"No one stopped him."

"No one stops Raleigh when he's mad. Once, when he found out this local father was abusing his two daughters, Raleigh went over and dragged the man from his house to the jail right down Main Street so everyone would know what he'd done. Yes, Raleigh is mean when he's mad."

"Wouldn't know it to work with him."

"You'll see and maybe need to get between him and the object of his anger."

"Seems to me as if I don't know the man."

"I suspect you don't. Few do."

"They sure know him in Greenville."

"I know; whenever I go there or Charlotte, all they want to talk about is him."

"He must be past retirement age."

"Yes, but what else will he do?"

Changing the subject to keep his erection from showing again, Carter asked about Beau.

"Beau went for the money with Corrine. Her father is one of the richest men in town. Hell, I think in the state. Unfortunately, they can't have children. So, they wanted my daughter to come live with them. But after Raleigh gave him that beating, he didn't want any part of her. So he gave up parental rights before she was born. Beau settled $25,000 on her in return for freeing himself from all obligations. He thought he got the better of the deal until they found out she wasn't fertile. They offered me all sorts of money to give her up. They sent private detectives to prove I was an unfit mother when I refused. I'm telling you this because you'd find it out anyway. They brought me to court and laid everything out, all they could find to dirty me up. For six months, it was ugly. Only reason it was settled was because Judge Caleb owed Raleigh a big favor. I don't know what it was, but he ruled against Beau and told him to go home. Lucky, just about then, they adopted Jill Sukenik's two kids. She was Corine's sister. I'm surprised how well Corine's done by those kids. Both are smart, well-behaved, and love Corine. What Beau thinks, I don't know. I wouldn't be surprised he's still catting around. The only time I see him is in a lawyer's office or court. We're discussing now whether he should give money for my daughter's college. Beau seems to think he's free and clear. But Sue Ellen can sue him when she reaches 18. I'm trying to avoid notoriety. So does he, if he wants to run for Mayor. Corine's offered to pay for her college, but I want it to come from Beau's pocket."

"This Corine seems okay for a rich kid."

"You know, I've come to the same conclusion. Been talking to her on-and-off and what she's done with those kids. It's tough losing both parents when you're toddlers."

"What happened?"

"Their father was a Rabbi. His father-in-law wanted both daughters near him, so he built the synagogue for Hyman Sukenik and got the congregation to call him as Rabbi."

"I don't think they "call him," Carter interrupted as he felt his erection dwindling.

"Well, whatever. He and Sarah, Goldman's other daughter, settled into the town. About 12 years ago, Hy was at the scene of an auto accident involving down electrical wires. Somehow, he stepped on a live wire."

"Wow, how did that happen? Usually, those power people are really careful at those scenes. Been on a couple of cases and couldn't get close to those lines."

"No one seems to know. The power company was really afraid of a lawsuit, but Sarah wouldn't move ahead despite her father's wishes."

"How old were the children?"

"The boy, I think his name is Josh, was two. Sarah was pregnant with the girl. She has a funny name for a Jew, Joyous. But naturally, everyone calls her Joy."

"What happened to Sarah?"

"She had been diagnosed with cervical cancer the week before her husband's death. They refused many treatments so that the baby could survive. She went to full term and died two weeks after was born."

"How do you know all this?"

"Wrote the story, but it was killed thanks to the grandfather. No details ever appeared. They call Corinne Mama, but she told them the truth. Beau let it slip during one of our arguments in my lawyer's office."

"That's more detail than I ever wanted to know."

"We did wander from our main topic. Jenny Couri."

And got my mind off your crotch, Carter thought. Then he realized that despite all the profound revelations Caleigh shared, he still found his eyes wandering to her crotch. Seeing his focus, she smiled.

"You know many guys have wondered what you're wondering now, Carter," she laughed. *"Very few have found out. Maybe you will, but you've got some growing up to do."*

Taken aback by her bluntness, Carter managed to blurt out a feeble protest.

"You've come to town. Established a reputation but don't see what's around you in any clear light."

"Clear light?"

"Yes, clear light. Do you know every new police officer works with Raleigh for a month during their first year?"

"I didn't. "

"Because you went off to be a hero."

"What's wrong with that?"

"There's more to police work than being a hero."

"Doesn't hurt."

"No, but it could hurt you."

"Says you?"

"Your what 24, 25?"

"26."

"Where will you be ten years from now?"

"Police chief."

"Not here."

"Why not here?"

"Because two of the people you will need on your side right now aren't too sure about you."

"Who?"

"Amanda and Raleigh."

"They won't be here ten years from now."
"But they can help or hinder you before then."

Stung by her comments, Carter stopped talking. Sensing she had said enough for one night, Caleigh steered the conversation to the files. She gave him his coffee and took hers to the parlor while he read the first binder in the kitchen.

Getting sleepy, he wondered if he could take the second binder to his apartment. He went looking for Caleigh and found her asleep on the sofa. Cradling the second file, he locked the door from the inside as he left past midnight.

Media Frenzy, Thursday 9am

Despite the rain falling in torrents, three television crews and assorted print and podcast producers were camped out in front of the Skye Landing police station the following day, waiting to be admitted to the space for the press conference. Their bosses were not satisfied with the meager details in the previous night's press conference and scooped by Caleigh's better access, the appetite for news drove them to exaggerate what little facts were known. Angry at Amanda, they were prepared to be harsh in their questioning, and she sensed their anger when she walked into the room.

Wet, angry, and surly, they waited to hear Amanda Harris. Amanda scheduled her press conference for 9am to avoid the early morning news cycle. Hoping to help Jules keep his job, she invited him to give the autopsy report. Raleigh prepped her on what he knew, suspected, and doubted. They agreed to be forthcoming on many aspects of the case but knew that each station and podcaster would provide their own interpretation no matter what was said.

Opening the meeting by formally identifying it was Henry Cain who was murdered, Jules confirmed head trauma as the cause of death. Neither mentioned they thought the murder involved extreme passion. Nor did they give details on the number of blows, the missing briefcase, and absent phones. Also left unsaid was the search for the other possible visitor before the murder.

By narrowing the time of death, Jules hoped to help the investigation. He told the assembled there was a two-hour window for time-of-death ending at about 1:30pm. Before the press conference, he informed Raleigh death was before 1:30pm, meaning he was seen at 12:30, so there was just one hour to be accounted for. When Amanda opened the conference to questions, the fun began.

"What about the three men, one of whom Henry Cain claimed killed the Couri girl?" the ABC network affiliate reporter asked.

"As we said 12 years ago, told Mr. Cain repeatedly and reconfirmed again today, there was no murder of Jenny Couri. She died because of some illness that we could not identify. She was not beaten, strangled, assaulted, shot, or otherwise harmed," Amanda replied wearily.

"What about the evidence he claimed to have from your case file box?" Asked NBC's representative.

"We have not yet recovered the box despite our search of Mr. Cain's office and home. We are in the process of examining his papers, tapes, and witnesses to identify what he found and planned to disclose, suggesting her death was murder. We know his intentions to name particular individuals, and we are trying to determine if he communicated that fact to anyone. So far, we have not talked to the men. As part of our elimination process, we are confirming their activities yesterday."

"So there could be something to Mr. Cain's claims," she followed up.

"No, there was and is nothing to his claims. But to make doubly sure we are thorough investigators."

"Who are these men?" some reporter from Greenville shouted out.

"Since they are not under suspicion for any crime, we are not releasing their names and repeat, here again, Jenny Couri died a natural death."

"Why wasn't a complete autopsy done?" ABC shouted over the crowd.

"Her death occurred during a time of transition period at the coroner's office, staffing was short, and some steps were missed. However, at the time, both the new and outgoing coroner concurred on a natural cause of death. Please remember, we have only Mr. Cain's unsupported claims of murder in this case."

"But if there was no first murder, what was the evidence Mr. Cain claimed to have from your evidence box?" Fox jumped in.

"We are not precisely sure what evidence Mr. Cain would reveal Sunday. Last week, he showed our chief investigator and me pictures of material that he claimed came from the box. We are still in the process of verifying what he took from the box and planned to display. Since we had ruled no crime was committed, the material was held under civil bond. If, as Mr.

Cain claimed, there was a crime, by law, that material cannot be shared publicly without court approval. But Mr. Cain appeared determined to move ahead."

"Has your department found who gave the evidence box to Henry Cain?" the late-arriving CBS reporter asked.

"That investigation has been hampered by the illness of the officer assigned from Montgomery County."

"You don't seem too anxious to find out who took the box," the reporter followed up before her colleagues could ask another question.

"Believe me; I am very anxious to find out who gave it to him. She or he will have a tough time keeping their job if I have anything to say about it."

With all eyes riveted on Amanda, Geoffrey Wallace yelled from the back of the room.

"I have Mr. Cain's list of suspects. You can have the list," he shouted as he released a sheaf of papers.

All at once, the pack of journalists ran to the back of the room, scrambling to grab a copy. Left alone on the stage, the three officials watch the scrum. Realizing the names would be smeared across the media in minutes, Raleigh left the stage. He went to the police communication room and directed squad cars to each man's home and business.

Amanda went to her office and called the township attorney.

"Thankfully, we're not responsible," Neely Brighton said from his office.

"But these men are now going to be suspected of murder," she almost yelled into the phone.

"Can't be helped. Cain did the accusing, even if it was from the grave. By the way on what was he basing his claim?"

"You know, Neely, as far as we can tell, he thought we buried the case because Jenny wrote three names on the paper she wrapped around the positive pregnancy test result we found in her room after she died."

"Since everyone will soon know, who were the men?"

"Do you really want to know?"

"Afraid I'm going to need to know if this blows back on us."

"Somehow, I think it will." She paused. And then named names.

"Charlie Stewart, the theatre teacher, Knox Alexander, our local landowner, Henrik Gunderson, the banker."

"A perfect trifecta of community male leaders all of whom would not want it known they were fooling around with an under-age girl, based on his other shows, they are Cain's preferred targets."

"But Neely, we know none of them killed Jenny Couri."

"Then who did?"

"That's exactly what I mean; no one killed her; she died of natural causes."

"Sorry Amanda, no one believes that now," he said as he hung up.

Almost defeated, Amanda put down the phone and took the whisky bottle out of her drawer. It was there for emergencies and celebrations, and this drink was more a salute to idiocy than anything else.

Almost like a cooling brush in a warm spring, the Mayor came into Amanda's office closing the door behind him.

"I think we got a problem that won't get buried with press conferences," Provender Gibson said gravely.

"Oh," Amanda replied non-committedly.

"That Charlotte reporter has been puttering around asking people lots of questions ever since Cain started peddling his garbage about the Couri girl." the Mayor said.

"Braced me in my office last night asking me what I think."

"What did you say?"

"I told him I left police matters to the police but if he thought there was something fishy he should talk to you," Provender said.

"He hasn't asked for an interview."

"Says he'll wait until let the investigation proceed. I think he was using me to give you a warning."

"Damn, I thought we had dodged that bullet. No pun intended."

"Maybe you have and maybe you haven't. I think there are ways of heading him off."

"Let's worry about this when we catch that killer.. We've all been under a lot of pressure."

"I agree, but be wary, he might try to hit you during the day."

"Hope not, I've got enough stress."

"But we got another problem, this one involves me more than you."

"Oh no, let me guess - Beau."

"The one and only. He's looking for some edge in the upcoming mayor's race."

"I thought you weren't running."

"Don't want to but doesn't seem there's anyone else around that can beat him but me."

"What's he doing now to beat you over your head?"

"Well to start, tomorrow's edition of the Eagle will have a front page interview featuring Beau questioning decisions you made in this case and others. Says the police force is out of control because I, the mayor, I'm not paying enough attention."

"You're kidding me?"

"No, Beau will use that to jump off into other areas where I'm failing to deliver starting with the new high school. He's got the people on Dane Hill all riled up wanting their own school."

"I'm sorry Provender."

"Don't be, I can handle the other stuff, just be prepared to have the Eagle coming out after you."

"I would think Caleigh would give me a heads up," Amanda mused.

"Don't say anything but they are sending in some hotshot to run the paper over her. He called me today by way of introduction. During the conversation he seemed to be indicating Caleigh may not have a job. Something about being too close to the police. I guess he means Raleigh."

"She got the paper some good scoops."

"Seems the people who own the paper thinks the police and the police chief need to face a stronger advocate for the public."

"So I'd better watch out?"

"It seems to me to be the prudent attitude. Don't give the paper or the city council any reason to cry for shame."

"You know me better than most. I run a clean ship and a clean department."

"Yeah, that's what I told the man before hanging up on him."

"But that still leaves Beau."

"*Yeah, Beau wants to be mayor and he'll stop at nothing to get there. Saying the police are incompetent is one way of rousing the citizens.*"

"*So, Beau's criticizing me about how I handled this case?*"

"*He's hinting you know more about Cain's activities than you've let on.*"

"*Boy is that calling the kettle black.*"

"*I know it but the people that vote don't.*"

"*You know we've held something back you can use, if you want.*"

"*No, Amanda, if I'm going to win it will be because the people like me, not that they don't like the other guy. I love this town and I fear people like Beau are entering township leadership to gain advantages for themselves and the people behind them.*"

"*People like, Beau?*"

"*Especially people like Beau. You know his father-in-law gave me a big check to get into the race. He knows what his son-in-law is like.*"

"*Once those two grandkids go off to college, I don't think Corinne will tolerate Beau's ways.*"

"*I can't wait for that day. Love the way she's raising those kids. Money isn't going to spoil them if she has any say in the matter.*"

"*No, think not.*"

"*When he does interview me, what can I do when it comes to Beau?*"

"*Steer that reporter to his shenanigans with Cain, the Mayor said on his way out. "We can help the citizens know a little bit more about old Beau.*"

No Answers, 9:15am

Minutes later, Raleigh came in, taking the chair opposite Amanda.

"Got the cars there just ahead of the hyenas," he said.

"Seems all three men met Cain last week and told them how he was announcing their names on his show this Sunday."

"Could he have done it?"

"I'm no expert, but Alexander and Gunderson said their lawyers thought he could if he did it carefully. Ironically, if all he said was about the pregnancy test with the list, he could get away with it."

"Getting away with it is a great way of saying it," Amanda said ruefully as she drank her whiskey in one gulp.

"Who would ever take an old evidence box out of our police station?"

"That's just it; who? You know the council will ask me that question on Tuesday."

"Let 'em. You've got nothing to hide!"

"You know Raleigh I've been in this job 13 years; some people are tired of me."

"But they wouldn't dare fire you," he almost shouted.

"There are some people that would, and if your friend Beau Jenkins is elected mayor, his first order of business would be getting rid of me."

"Council does the hiring, firing."

"He would make it worthwhile for some of them."

"Hogwash!"

"No, reality. You need to find our murderer fast and hope he or she had nothing to do with Couri's murder.

"Will try, Chief, but I think this case will drag on for a while."

"Do your usual job Raleigh but if there is any way to shorten things for Christ sakes do it."

"Could use Sawyer and Winston full-time."

"They're yours; tell Barrow I authorize any and all overtime."

When the subject of Ned Barrow came up, both people winced. Nominally the Chief of Detectives, Barrow was also COO of the department. When he became head of the department, Ned and Raleigh worked out an arrangement that worked for them both. Ned would administer the department, schedules, promotions, expenditures, etc. Raleigh would supervise the investigations and keep Ned apprised of all significant developments. When it came time to appear in public, Ned was the face of the department, and Amanda ensured he also appeared at events involving her. To date, the arrangement worked well for all parties.

There were three power positions in an organization like the Skye Landing Police Department. Police Chief, Chief of Detectives, and Patrol Chief. Nine years before, again at Raleigh's suggestion, Amanda brought Daw Perdue from the Washington police to lead the patrol division.

Daw, like Amanda, was black. He was also from the nation's capital, and Barrow was passed over for the job he thought he deserved. Swallowing his anger, Barrow took on all the other departments for Amanda. Since Raleigh more or less ran the detective bureau, Barrow was too smart to interfere, there were few administrative duties, so in reality, the Chief of Detectives had little to do. This gave Barrow time to be seen at many civic events and special occasions, attend training courses, and perform everything but police work.

Admittedly, he was popular and well-liked in the community, but Amanda and Raleigh doubted his loyalty. More importantly, they doubted his ability to maintain Daw's standards the newcomer had established for the patrol division, let alone improve upon them. Amanda had put off announcing the appointment for weeks even though Daw was leaving that week to head up Washington's Patrol Division.

"What are you going to do with Barrow?" Raleigh asked as he rose from his chair.

"Much as I hate to do it, I guess he's the new Chief of Patrol."

"Well, he's waited this long; I guess he deserves it."

"Cow chips. He's not right for the job, but there's no one else. Daw leaves for Washington this week. We need to make the announcement soon. We hate to lose him, but we knew we'd lose him when we hired him."

"But now you have a first-rate patrol division."

"Which Barrow could ruin in a matter of days."

"Just keep him on a short leash."

"There isn't a short enough leash for that man once he gets his hands on that division."

"He did okay with the detective division."

"That's because I had you there. Care to go back to a patrol car?"

"No, I'm too old to pass the pursuit test."

"What do we do with those three clowns in the holding cell. Don't we owe them professional courtesy?"

"Not really. He's a convicted something or other, and the other two are muscles. Let 'em stew until Carter and I get back from talking to those poor dumb bastards. Geoffrey just made meat for the media."

"Will do. How's Carter doing?"

"Better than you expected. When he gets his head out of his ass, he will make a good detective."

"Keep him on a short leash for now."

"Think it's time to let him go off on his own. Thanks for Sawyer and Winston. They can do all the backfill."

"You trained them."

"Yes, are you jealous Daw is going back to Washington?"

"No, I really like it here. Think I'll stay no matter what happens in the future."

"Always glad to have you. Knew that the first time I met you."

One of the fastest-rising stars in the Washington DC police force, Amanda Tubman Harris was born in the city she policed. A lieutenant by age 26, she was on a fast track to captaincy. Two things sidetracked her career, one related to the other: Seth Harris and the birth of her two sons.

Seth Harris starred in football, track, and baseball before making the fatal mistake, career-wise, of not choosing one sport to concentrate on towards the end of high school. Forced to accept a two-sports scholarship to Bethune Williams, his skills sputtered out.

With nothing better on the horizon, he joined the DC police force. Some breaks, the right friendships, and attention to detail got him Captain Bars at age 30.

From the first moment they met, Amanda and Seth became a much-talked-about item at black police retirement parties, finally publicly admitting to being a couple and ultimately married. While Amanda stayed home with their two sons, Seth rose in the department.

When the time came, the boys could be left with their grandmothers, and Amanda wanted to rejoin the force. Seth thought she should stay home, and against his wishes, she returned much to his displeasure. Discovering she possessed a sense for numbers, she soon headed the department's Crime Analysis Section. Using data from all sources, including supermarket product sales figures, Amanda began to anticipate crime surges or identify them. At the same time, the department could do something about containing criminals and better protecting civilians.

Soon Amanda got her captaincy and wider exposure inside and outside the department. On one such speaking engagement, she met Raleigh. With her career rising, Seth felt somehow eclipsed. Soon Seth was stepping out of the marriage, and when the boys were 11 and 12, he left permanently.

At the same time, Skye Landing was looking for a progressive police chief. With Raleigh's support, Amanda became the first black female police chief in South Carolina. She and the two boys and her mother relocated to South Carolina.

Her boys, by now teenagers, couldn't make the adjustment from Washington to rural South Carolina. They were back with their father in the nation's capital within a year. Her oldest succumbed to a drug overdose within three years. Her youngest was discharged as a bad-conduct police recruit. He drifted west, and she had lost touch. Her ex-husband was now deputy chief.

In the past, bigger cities had asked her to apply for their chief's job. After one or two experiences where she was the token black and woman candidate, she had given up leaving Skye Landing. She calculated the two pensions on the back of an envelope, and consulting would keep her quite nicely. She was still young, but ambition could be traded for living well in Skye Landing.

Suspect Elimination, Thursday 9:30am

Acting swiftly after leaving Amanda's office, Raleigh called in Sawyer and Carmichael to start assembling the case file to keep all pertinent information, report, phone log, and photos. They immediately started the process but reminded him the coroner's report was still not forthcoming. In his mind, this raised red flags, and he noted to call Jules as it was not like him to delay such an important document.

Looking out his office window into the squad room, he saw Sawyer and Carmichael busily rounding up the sheets and notebooks that always prove crucial later when preparing for trial. Because he had trained them, he was confident the two men would keep everything together and away from prying eyes.

Losing the Couri file was bad enough, but having someone outside the department reading their case notes would be 10 times worse. For this and a hundred more reasons, Raleigh eschewed using a whiteboard, now standard practice in many departments, because he felt too many outside people saw it during the investigation. Raleigh preferred to keep his investigations tightly focused and as confidential as possible.

That thought brought him to Carter. First question: Where was he? The second question flowed from that: What was he doing? The third question quickly followed: Should I be worried? Raleigh shrugged and reached for the phone to call Jules.

The coroner answered his private line with a cheerful greeting. Pausing to close the door, he lowered his voice and hunched over the desk to impart two nuggets the detective was pleased the coroner omitted from his report.

"*Raleigh thought you should know two things are not in the autopsy. Mr. Cain was not wearing any underwear and he had coitus within 12-hours of his death. But there were no female fluids on his body but I think I got some male fluids.*"

"*Can you type them and give me a name.*"

"*Sent them to the state lab with a rush order but its 50-50 and their bogged down.*"

"*I could make a call.*"

"*You do that. Even if they get something, they need to match it.*"

"*You sound doubtful.*"

"*Got a hunch he won't be in our databases. Don't ask me why but got that feeling.*"

"*Okay Jules you're usually right.*"

"*Not all the time.*"

"*Will you just get the Couri case out of your mind. We did the right thing.*"

"*Till it bit us in the ass.*"

"*I'll put some ointment on this whole thing before long.*"

"*Hope so Raleigh.*"

Before proceeding further, Raleigh thought about briefing Barrow who he knew would be prudent and keep his mouth shut. He went by the man's office and saw it was dark. Walking past, he said the office was often dark these days. Passing by Daw Perdue's office, with a quick glance through the open door, Raleigh saw it was also dark, and most of his awards, certificates, and diplomas were already taken down.

Along with Amanda's recommendation, Raleigh felt good about spotting the man for chief of patrol. He just wished Barrow had learned from Daw. Well, a man couldn't have everything in his job.

During Daw Perdue's time with the department, he had turned the patrol division into a model followed by other cities and earned the city accolades as one of the safest in terms of crime in America. Too bad it cost Perdue his marriage and kids, and maybe going to Washington could salvage it for him. An idle thought struck Raleigh. He couldn't remember the last time Barrow mentioned his wife or son, and he dismissed it. Divorce was part of cops' lives, almost like breathing.

Raleigh turned to see the missing tyro detective as ~~the younger man~~ Carter exploded through the door carrying two precariously held boxes striding to the office. He plopped them down on the nearest desk noisily to attract attention. He got everyone's and opened one box, revealing numerous video discs.

"Went back to the motel and confiscated all their tape discs."

"Thought we did that yesterday?" Sawyer said somewhat jealously.

"I did too, but then I remembered there were pole cameras front, back, and side."

"And you got 'em?" Sawyer barked.

"No, the manager did and gave me his secret recordings of the desk clerks. It seems he doesn't trust them anymore."

"We need to look deeper, but Cain was dropped off down the block from the motel. Someone didn't want to be seen on tape."

"Now that's interesting," Sawyer admitted.

"Get's even more interesting. Look who registered right after Cain," Carter said as he put one disc into the office disc machine.

Before Carter could run the disc, Raleigh stepped in.

"Men, we run nothing in the squad room. Let's use my office so no stray eyes see these discs."

Adjourning to Raleigh's office, he pulled the blinds, leaving it almost total darkness. Plugging in the machine, Carter savored his forthcoming moment of triumph. They rolled the disc, and the image of former detective Sandra Bing filled the screen. She confidently handed the clerk bills to cover the cost of a room. At seeing the picture, Sawyer and Winston laughed.

"Bing went private in Greenville three years ago, she's probably working with Red Roof management to identify whose pocketing money from these afternoon affairs, Guess they're still paranoiac from the last clerk." Winston said.

"Yeah, she'll stay there for two hours then leave nervously and obviously from the front," Sawyer added.

"When the day's tally is done, she and the manager together search if her marked bills show up," Winston twisted the knife.

"We questioned her yesterday but she was in the other wing. Would've been nice if she saw something," Sawyer said with finality.

"But you guys don't see this dark four-door turning right at the corner to avoid the next CCTV camera. He did it deliberately after dropping Cain off, but how did he know the camera was there?" Carter said, trying to regain the initiative.

"CBS affiliate ran three nights of special reports detailing where they were last month," Winston said ruefully.

"Well, let's add a note about the dark sedan and go out and interview the three men Cain was going to expose on Sunday," Raleigh said carefully.

"See, you're already thinking of them as suspects in two murders," Sawyer said.

"No, I just think they're three men caught in a public relation vise for which there is no loosening until we find the real murderer," Raleigh retorted. *"Carter, you go find and interview Charlie Stewart, the theatre teacher. See where he was yesterday and if we can eliminate him as a suspect for his sake. I'll take Gunderson and if I know Knox he'll waltz in here this afternoon, attorney in tow and prove his innocence."*

"You think so?" Carter said half in admiration for Knox or Raleigh; no one could guess.

"Yeah, known the man for 20-odd years, he is always ahead of everyone else. He'll be ahead of me here too. This crime doesn't fit how he does things. Slow, careful, and without him getting his pants dirty. No, he didn't kill Cain, I'll bet but I believe he has some information he wants to impart. He'll be here."

Evidence Accumulates, Thursday 10am

Elated to be left on his own, Carter called the high school only to discover Stewart was on leave from his duties before being let go. A call to his home got only his answering app. Carter called the school back and strong-armed the secretary for Stewart's cell phone. That number found him in the local community theater building. Carter drove there quickly, itching to use his siren but afraid Raleigh might find out.

A waifish man, no more than five feet five inches, Charlie Stewart wore clothes that looked expensive but worn like their owner. Carter's arrival seemed to stop him from aimlessly clearing his office. His pale eyes peered from behind his desk through maroon-rimmed glasses that did nothing to hide his flaccid face.

"Going someplace?" Carter asked.

"Dismissed by the board."

"When'd that happen?"

"Two nights. Mrs. Stone wasted no time getting me out of here when she found the excuse," Charlie said bitterly.

"What excuse?"

"I'm about to give you another reason to look at me for Henry's murder."

"How's that?"

"My lawyer says I should keep quiet but you'll find out soon enough."

"Find out what?"

"12 years ago I made an audition tape with Jenny Couri."

"A tape."

"Yes, it was a scene from the play Equus she thought would show off her talents."

"So 12 years ago she made a tape. Was it porno?"

"No, just the nude scene from the play."

"And she played it naked?"

"Exactly as they did on Broadway."

"Any good?"

"That's the sad part. She was terrific. You know she was the most chameleon-like person I have ever known. She acted in three school plays and each year she got better and better."

"So, she was a good actress."

"She was manipulative! Vicious! Selfish! The day after she graduated, she showed up at my apartment and threatened to say I slept with her while she was a student."

"Really?"

"I went to college with Jane San Suber. At the time, she was a big producer in Hollywood and we kept in touch. Over the years, I'd done script reading, revision, critiques and she valued my opinion. In my first years in town, to build up my artistic credibility, I at times, I mentioned our friendship in class."

"Let me guess, Jenny wanted you to do an audition tape and send it to this producer?"

"I was new to town, didn't have anyone to help me so I made the tape and we used the stage at the high school."

"And what happened?"

"We made the tape and she was terrific. It didn't hurt that she had a fabulous body the camera ate her up. Her performance was so erotic I thought Jane would at least be interested."

"So what happened?"

"Don't you remember, Jane was killed by that crazed actor in her office?"

"No, I don't remember."

"Maybe because you were still so young," Charlie chided Carter.

"So how did Mrs. Stone find the tape?"

"That's the part that really hurts," Charlie sighed.

"I posted the tape three days before Jane died. When she died, I told Jenny to forget about a career in Hollywood. She looked at me and said: "There are other ways for me to get what I want." Chilled me to the bone

the way she looked and talked. A month later she was dead. I forgot about the tape until Cain came waltzing into my apartment one night with a copy in his hand."

"How did he get it?"

"Seems the tape was, for one minute, big on the Hollywood party circuit. He saw it one night and recognized the high school auditorium and knew Jenny because she was a year behind him. He put two-and-two together and figured out who produced the tape."

"You know, even if he was a son-of-a-bitch, Cain was quite a savvy guy," Carter said half admiration."

"And twice as vindictive."

"You still haven't told me how Mrs. Stone found out about the tape."

"Anyway, Cain takes out this piece of paper and says my name along with two others is on it. I say so what. He retorts it was wrapped around a positive pregnancy test."

"And you said?"

"I laughed and said my only involvement with that devil girl was making the tape. He called me a liar. I said go to hell. He says I will and leaves." He paused.

"This was two weeks ago. Last week Mrs. Stone gets the tape in the mail. Being relatively new in town, she curried favor with some of the older, more conservative members of the arts board. I guess she figured canning me would be a good way to get in good with them. I think she was afraid I might find out something about her. She knew other board members were after me for some of the shows I've done here in this theatre. She called the board demanding I be fired but they backed me. Not wanting to be thwarted, she waited. I think she's trying to cover up a sordid past. Two years in town and she is its arbiter of sin. Cain's acolyte makes my name public and I'm out. End of play. Final Act. Despite the recent changes it is still a small Southern town with some pretty rigid morals. You're from Atlanta, don't get sideways with their orthodoxy, they'll expel you without hesitation."

"Still doesn't tell me where you were yesterday between 11am and 1pm."

"Easy, I was at the High School picking up my things."

"*Anybody see you?*"

"*My drama class, English class, writing class. They all said goodbye.*"

"*Lucky for you,*" Carter said as he closed his notebook.

"*How is that lucky for me?*"

"*That's when Henry Cain died.*"

"*About two weeks too late for me,*" Charlie said, staring at one of his posters of his past plays.

Exiting the theatre, Carter mentally crossed Charlie off his suspect list. The time for Charlie to kill Cain was before the victim went to Mrs. Stone. Knowing Raleigh would ask him, Carter went to the High School to confirm Charlie's alibi and returned to headquarters. He filled out the interview forms on the computer and thought of Charlie's ruined life. Realized there was nothing he could do and hit the enter button.

Learning More, Thursday 11am

Looking at the modest house Henrik Gunderson owned, a stranger would not believe he ran Dan Hurst Bank. It nestled at the cul-de-sac farthest from the main thoroughfare bisecting Dane Hill above Skye Landing. Not the richest neighborhood, this section catered to affluent but not wealthy Charlotte commuters and downtown techies who flocked to its clean streets, highly-rated schools, and low crime.

Henrik considered he was lucky to be where he was. Thirteen years ago, Henrik was summoned to the office of the conglomerate's patriarch Lars Andre Hurst. Seated at the large table were his boss, her boss, a man he didn't know, and the family head. Motioned to a chair facing all of them, Lars spoke.

"For the sake of our American visitor we will speak in English. We are thinking of opening a branch in South Carolina in America," Lars began.

Not asked to comment, Henrik waited for the old man to continue. He did but in English.

"You have experience in banking and America," Lars continued more a statement then a question.

"I have run branches here in Denmark and spent two years in New York," Henrik said carefully, replying in English.

"Yes, you were born in America and have dual citizenship. But your wife is Danish."

"True, from Copenhagen," he said again, not knowing where the conversation would lead.

"Would she go to America with you?"

"I have not asked her but I think so. She is happy here but anyone would be interested in running a bank. But why South Carolina? There are better banking states and localities."

"Told you he was smart," his boss said, hiking her skirt slightly higher.

"Is he smart enough for our friends in America?" Lars asked, in Danish using the collegial Danish word for a person who is brainy.

"I know so." She said emphatically in English.

"The people in this room think you may be the man to run our bank," Lars continued.

"I would do a good job of it," he replied, this time in Danish forgetting the injunction to speak English in his excitement.

"Henrik, the Hurst family is investing with Mr. Goldman here and some others in a massive project in, what is the name of the town, ah, here, Skye Landing. We want you to represent the bank in this effort. Your job is to protect the bank. Not the family. We have enough people on that side. The bank will be heavily committed and you are to represent the bank and protect its assets. Do not ever consider my family's interest. Is that clear? No matter what anyone says, you worry about the bank."

Hearing Mr. Hurst's emphasis, Henrik sensed a lot of money, ego, and family dynamics at play. Whatever they were, he knew he was in for a tough time.

"I would like this job very much, Mr. Hurst. I will not fail you."

"I don't think you will. It's settled."

"I will not fail you."

Dan Hurst Bank was registered as an American bank and operating in Skye Landing one year later.

Henrik found he was conflicted with Dane Hill Development Limited; the company developing the project almost from the start. Henrik's responsibilities included managing the construction loans and infrastructure financing while also arranging financing for the transfers of the 4,000 acres being contributed to the venture by the Hurst family.

Maintaining property values, avoiding financing shortages, and finding outside capital fell on his shoulders. Henrik was pleased the elder Hurst sided with the bank when contentious issues arose between the two entities. Three years into the project, the 30-40 homes a month were delivered to new and old Skye Landing residents.

Would-be buyers were encouraged but not required to obtain their mortgages through the bank. Thanks to Henrik's leadership and despite his difficulties with the development company, many were sold with Dan Hurst mortgages.

Within seven years, Dane Hill was so successful other community builders studied it for tips on creating wealth for its owners and desirable places to live for its occupants.

After moving from Denmark, Henrik and his wife, Daniella, slipped into the upper echelon of Skye Landing leaders. Their three children moved there as young teenagers and thrived. Tragedy struck when Daniella was stricken with Multiple Sclerosis in a particularly vicious form. As the disease progressed, she became almost totally housebound.

All this Raleigh mentally reviewed as he rang the doorbell at the Gunderson house. Henrik answered the door and invited the detective to their sunroom. Daniella was in her wheelchair, her head drooping, but dressed for company.

"Good to see you, Henrik," Raleigh said.

"Wish this was a better occasion."

"Me too, but the quicker we get this settled the better for all," Raleigh replied.

"What do you want to know?" Daniella asked angrily.

"Did you talk with Henry Cain?"

"I talked with him in my office two weeks ago," Henrik said.

"He said he had some paper with my name on it with two other men."

"Did he tell you who the other men were?"

"No, but I knew Knox was on the list."

"How?"

"He told me. He said he saw my name when Cain flashed it at him."

"What did Cain want?"

"He said he was going to name me as one of the men who had an affair with this Jenny Couri."

Daniella stirred angrily in her wheelchair and spat out the word *tæve*. *"That tæve (whore) baby sat for us twice. I saw what she was and told Henrik never to employ her again."*

"Why?"

"Ah, Raleigh, a woman knows when someone is sniffing around their man."

"You were worried about losing Henrik?"

"No, not that I would lose him, but that she would cause trouble. She is like cat in heat. There to be smelled but dangerous to play with. I would never permit Henrik to be alone with her."

"Afraid he might stray?"

"No, afraid of the lies she was capable of. If it came to a he-said, she-said situation no matter what happened Henrik would lose. I told him that when she was around, he should always need a witness. Did you know one day she came to his office and shut the door trying to be alone with him? I had warned him and he had his secretary ready to open the door. She did just as she came around the desk. She wanted something, but she never got it from us."

All the time she talked, he held her hand, seemingly afraid to lose her.

"Where were you between 11am yesterday and 2pm yesterday?"

"At the Rotary Club."

"I know but no one seems to remember you between noon and 1pm and you missed lunch. You were there for the speeches but not lunch and it's a short way to the motel from the banquet hall."

"Okay, Raleigh, I will tell you but you need to keep this quiet."

"I will if I can, Henrik."

"I was in my car having a conference call with New York and Copenhagen."

"Why in your car?"

"Some matters came up involving bank laws that needed to be discussed privately, away even from the bank building."

"What could that involve?"

"Knox has offered me his private jet to take Daniella and me to Europe. Accepting the offer would violate my company's rules and federal law."

"Why would you need a private jet?"

"Daniela's health makes a commercial flight dangerous and difficult."

"What does Knox get in return?"

"That was what we were discussing. He wants nothing just giving us a way to travel back home."

"You're leaving?"

"I'm afraid so. Our kids are in Amsterdam; soon she will not be able to travel at all. We are going home."

"I'll miss you. So will this town."

"It will survive and from the way the media is hounding us the town may want us gone."

"Not if I could help it."

"Thank you. But New York and Copenhagen were trying to determine if it was legal for me to use Knox's plane. He does a lot of business with the bank."

"Did they approve?"

"Funny, old man Hurst was on the call and he finally said to go hire a private ambulance jet to be here July Fifth to take us home. He surprised everyone. When I got the figures yesterday and sent them to Copenhagen, I thought they would renege. But he called me personally this morning to say the deal held. We're going home."

"That's wonderful news for you, sad for us."

"Time isn't on our side Raleigh."

"Then I won't take up any more of it."

"We appreciate it. Please don't say anything. We want to leave as we came, silently," Daniella said as she collapsed back into the cushions of her chair.

Daniella slumping back in her chair gave Raleigh the sign to leave. The two men walked to the front door and then to Raleigh's car.

"One thing," Henrik said." It hasn't been recorded yet, but Cain's $200,000 mortgage was paid in full last Tuesday. Cain came in with a certified check for $207,000 to pay off the money he owed us, and he was laughing the whole time. Naturally, the paperwork isn't finished, but the mortgage is gone."

"That is interesting," Raleigh said.

"One more interesting fact you might want to explore, he asked us to put the papers to transfer the property to a Delaware corporation.

"His?"

"*No it would be owned by someone in town.*"

"*He say who? Give you any details?*"

"*Just the name, it was CH Realty Investments.*"

"*Anything else?*"

"*Said Beau would handle all the details. He was leaving town.*"

"*Why did you lend it to him in the first place?*"

"*Beau Jenkins guaranteed the loan as second signer.*"

"*I might've known he'd be in there some way.*"

"*I heard what you did to him.*"

"*He deserved it.*"

"*Probably did, but he might be our next mayor.*"

"*God forbid.*"

"*Only in heaven is one forgiven.*"

"*Well best be off. Sorry to hear you're leaving.*"

"*I want to spend as much time as I can with Daniella and her family is there and perhaps better medical care in Denmark.*"

As he drove back to headquarters, Raleigh thought about all the time he was a detective and not a husband. Ellen Belmont Butler never complained, but many lonely nights must have been, and he regretted those lost moments.

Unwelcomed Visitors, Thursday 12:30pm

Few criminals left the Skye Landing interview room unshaken when Carmichael Winston finished his questioning. Carmichael ended his Skye Landing high school football career weighing 260 pounds. After three years as starting guard at South Carolina University, he weighed 340 pounds and was also six foot, eight inches tall. Unlike many ex-football players, he lost only fat when his playing days were over.

Despite playing three years for good but not spectacular teams and coaches, his pro football prospects were not bright as graduation neared. His mother made him marry pregnant Sabrina Watts in the spring before his senior year. Despite the extra pressure of having a wife and child, both Sabrina and his mother pushed him to finish college, and he was second-team all-SEC. No pro-team invites seemed in the offing as graduation approached.

Looking at all alternative career paths, he thought being a policeman would give him more excitement than some office job. He joined the township police force after dropping 80 pounds to just clear the physical limits.

At his height and weight, he was a menacing presence, but he was a teddy bear to his three children. On the job miscreants learned to steer away from him. His bulk hid from most, but not Raleigh, the keen mind he used during the five years it took Carmichael to earn promotion to the detective bureau.

Now, Carmichael sat opposite Illinois sheriff Arturo Gonzalez who had gone to fat 15 years after first being elected. Twenty-four hours in the holding cell made Arturo angry and desperate. He knew the evidence hidden in Cain's house or office could spell many years in jail.

Glaring at Carmichael, Arturo surmised these South Carolina racists would like nothing better than put this Hispanic hombre who had made good behind bars. Worse, they wouldn't mind sending him to the same prison where some of the people he had railroaded in the past now resided. From the way he was looking at him, Arturo thought this was especially true of this hulk sitting across the table from him. There was no professional courtesy evident in this interview room.

The two men stared at each other, neither talking. Both men knew silence in this room was sometimes used to power confessions. Arturo kept silent out of fear and Carmichael out of habit. They had been playing this game for almost an hour. The stalemate was broken by Raleigh's arrival.

"*Well Mr. Gonzalez you tried to enter a sealed off crime scene this morning at 1am,*" Raleigh started.

"*We were executing a warrant for material pertinent to criminal activities.*"

"*But you're no longer a sheriff.*"

"*I was acting as a private investigator for an attorney.*"

"*Who, I understand, is up for disbarment.*"

"*He's still an attorney till the Illinois bar says differently.*"

"*He's also your co-defendant, I understand.*"

"*The subpoena's still good.*"

"*It's good In Illinois, but not until we acknowledge it here in South Carolina.*"

"*A formality.*"

"*Which you seem to have neglected to get.*"

"*Time was important.*"

"*So are legal requirements.*"

"*The man is dead.*"

"*Murdered! Even more reason to cross all legal T's.*"

"*We need those papers.*"

"*So you keep telling us. What specific papers are you referring to?*"

"*My jailhouse records! My voucher books! My arrest records!*" Arturo began to shout.

"*No need to shout. It is my understanding they also pertain to a Mrs. Hilda Rensozo.*"

"*Yeah, she's the crazy one.*"

"She didn't seem so crazy to me when I interviewed her yesterday."

"She's loco and if I get my hands on those papers, I can prove it."

"Didn't do so well at your trial."

"It was rigged."

"Against you?"

"Of course against me, and if you were half-a-lawman you wouldn't have kept me in that filthy cell for 24-hours."

"Gee, we clean those cells every morning."

"Not this morning."

"Winston, make a note to can our cleaning crew."

"Will do," Carmichael smiled.

"But you assaulted one of my officers," said Raleigh.

"He wouldn't let us in."

"That house is part of a murder investigation. Which reminds me, where were you and your men yesterday between 11am and 1pm?"

"You're asking me for an alibi?" Arturo shouted.

"Right now you're our number one suspect because we cleared all of our other suspects."

"You're kidding me?"

"In this room we never kid, do we Winston?"

"No, seems to me this guy had a pretty good reason to murder Henry Cain," Carmichael said with a straight face.

Sputtering with rage, Arturo looked at the two men and realized the interview was turning out badly for him. He sat back and thought about his situation. His problems in Illinois were relatively minor compared with facing capital charges in South Carolina. Having framed others, he thought these men might be planning to charge him with Cain's murder. Thinking quickly, he took time to breathe. Exhaling slowly, he said in calm tones.

"About that time my men and I were entering South Carolina. We stopped at a restaurant to eat and figure how best to approach Cain."

"And your decision?"

"We sat there for an hour waiting till it got dark. It was dark before we got here."

"Can you prove it?"

"*You have my wallet? The receipt should be in it.*"

"*Why don't you go get his wallet and other possessions Winston?*"

With lumbering grace, Carmichael got up and went to the property room. He came back with the box containing Arturo and his men's effects. Raleigh permitted the man to rummage in the box and find the wallet and receipt.

"*There's the receipt and time stamp.*"

"*Seems the man has an alibi, Winston.*"

"*Seems that way.*"

"*Well, we now know you didn't murder Mr. Cain. Now there's only the matter of assaulting my patrolman. Carmichael, when I entered the room, he shouted something about professional courtesy. I think we should extend that to him and his men.*"

"*I agree,*" said Carmichael quietly.

"*So, your car is in our lot, we will expunge the arrest form and you can be on your way back to Illinois before dark.*"

"*Back to Illinois?*"

"*Yes, if you're in Skye Landing by the time its dark you'll be charged with assaulting an officer, carrying concealed weapons while on bail, and anything else we can find in the statues.*"

"*We need those papers.*"

"*It's your choice. Leave or get jailed.*"

"*What about our guns.*"

"*We will see they're delivered to the court in Illinois, let them decide.*"

With that, Raleigh got up to leave, nodding to Carmichael to see his decisions were carried out. Arturo said nothing but slumped in his chair. Raleigh could think that this suspect was another dead-end and wasted time.

More Questions, Thursday 1:30pm

When Raleigh reached his office after leaving the integration room, Carter met him at the door. He seemed excited, so Raleigh let the young detective talk first.

"We can wash Charlie Stewart out. Got 30 kids to swear he was at the High School while Cain was getting his comeuppance," he began.

"Gunderson is in the clear as well," Raleigh contributed. *"He's got an alibi we need to check, but I think it will hold water,"*

"That leaves us Knox Alexander, and he's waiting in Amanda's office."

"She let him wait there?"

"Thought better than having him sit in the detectives' area."

"She's probably right. Give me a minute to go to the can then bring him to my office. You can sit in if you'd like."

"You bet I do."

While he was relieving himself, Raleigh pondered where the case was going. Interviewing these men was necessary but a waste of time. He knew one of them didn't kill Jenny Couri. This murder had more to do with passion than a 19-year-old girl or money. But now, more time would be wasted looking for Cain's sudden wealth source. Two facts stood out: he had sex with a man sometime yesterday and planned to have more last night in that hotel room. Two men? Same man? Raleigh wondered as he zipped up his fly.

On his way back to his office, Raleigh told Sawyer to go out and bring Cain's man Geoffrey in for further questioning.

A casual observer would describe Knox Alexander as an aquiline man. Slim, trimmed, and perfectly dressed to fit the occasion, he always looked like he had just come from the dry cleaners. His clothes were put together with care, and he showered at least three times each day.

Yet no matter where he was or who he was with, Knox always seemed at ease. Following Carter, whose attire was haphazard, into Raleigh's office, he took the seat directly in front of the older man.

"Glad you came in Knox, saves us a trip."

"I figured you'd want to talk to me. Sooner you did the sooner I can get out of this mess."

"So, you've nothing to hide?"

"Oh, we all have secrets, Raleigh, even you. But I had nothing to do neither with Cain's murder nor of that girl years ago."

"I know you're no part of what happened years ago, but where were you yesterday between 11am and 1pm?"

"Easy, I was at 24,000 feet coming home in my jet from New York."

"Seems easy to prove."

"Yep, here are signed affidavits from pilot, co-pilot, and stewardess. If you want, I can also give you the names of the two men on the flight with me; but they are potential business associates and I'd rather you not bother them."

"Three's enough, but they all work for you."

"No, they're a charter crew. I own the plane but charter the crews and have a fixed base contract. Let them worry about everything."

"Okay that clears you but tell me, did Cain approach you about the Couri girl?"

"Of course he did. He said I was one of three men who had motive then."

"What motive did he say you had?"

"That I knocked her up."

"Did you have sex with her?"

"Of course not, Raleigh, you know I swing the other way."

"Well you said it Knox, I wasn't about to bandy that around."

"Well Cain was about to say I was a lecher. When that hit, sooner or later some reporter would discover the truth. He had it in the script for Sunday, till I persuaded him to axe it."

"How did you do that? Everyone says he was immune to pressure."

"But that man wasn't immune to bribes."

"You mean you bribed him?"

"As the Godfather said: I gave him an offer he couldn't refuse."

"Meaning?"

"I have a substantial interest in Bluebell Media. They're one of the upcoming podcast aggregators. I had them buyout Cain's company provided he drop any mention of my interests."

"So you bought him off for how much?"

"Half-a-million dollars upfront and $350,000 per guaranteed for two years."

"And he accepted."

"He wasn't flat broke but this deal came with setting him up in New York and promotional help. Everybody talks podcast but many people are going broke producing shows with no audience measurement. We would take care of all that."

"Why would you pay $1 million to stop one story?"

"Raleigh, to tell you the truth I'm sick of living a lie. I've a beautiful wife who is as gay as I am. We've had a marriage of convenience for 10 years but last month she told me she's moving to Atlanta to be with someone she loves. We're working out the divorce details now. I'm the chairman of the Republican party hereabouts and its time I get some return for all the money I've given the party."

"Meaning?"

"After all these years as our state senator, Conerly Scott is retiring. I want his seat and he's agreed to endorse me. When you run for office, you'd better get all your skeletons out of the closet. I'm depending on you to solve this case like you always do. When all this fuss blows over, I'm going to come out of my closet. Tell people it's time for the Republican Party to welcome gays. I think I can survive the blowback from announcing I am gay. Either way, the hiding is over. Didn't want Cain spoiling that. Besides, he would have made a lot of money for us."

"Now he's dead and you've got nothing."

"Except $2 million in insurance money. We take out insurance on all of our hosts. We paid the first premium Monday.

"How's that for luck."

"No Raleigh, you were the lucky one. Your Ellen was some woman. If I wasn't gay, I would've tried to marry her myself."

"*How did you know Ellen?*"

"*While you were out solving cases, she was finding causes. Whenever she needed money for one of them, she knew I was a soft touch. She surely did love you putting up with all those lonely nights.*"

"*How would you know?*"

"*Why did she do all those charities? She was lonely. Can I go now?*"

Raleigh didn't answer, just nodded his head. Carter said nothing pondering all that was exposed in the interview.

Reluctant Source, Thursday 2pm

All his life Geoffrey Wallace was on the wrong side of any situation. Living in a small town, his troubles started with his mother's hatred of his father. Both used their son to find ways of humiliating each other. He was five years old before his mother let him have his own bed. Yes, they did things like that in Indiana. Elementary school years were little better and high school a nightmare. Truant most of the time, only his intelligence enabled him to pass with mediocre grades.

At 18, he went to Chicago but found that city even more degrading than his hometown. When his mother died, she left him an insurance policy that enabled him to go to Columbia College. There he found his gift for editing and electronics. He recorded bands and events by his third year and set up home systems. He also found Gerald, who made him feel wonderful and alive. The two cohabitated just off-campus, building, installing, and refining an elaborate recording set up with the monies earned from his various gigs.

One night, Geoffrey came home and found Gerald dead on the floor and the apartment stripped of every machine. The police came, took pictures, dusted, said little, and went away. Geoffrey wasn't allowed back into the flat and wandered the streets. Alone with his grief, he checked into a motel and began badgering the police in the days that follow. They never found the murderers and finally threatened him with jail if Geoffrey didn't leave them alone. From this experience, he developed such hatred for all law enforcement that it became an all-embracing mantra.

Pulling himself together, he finished college and joined various organizations rallying against police activities. One such rally brought him to Peoria and Henry Cain. Once the two met, Cain knew he had the perfect producer for his shows. Geoffrey thought he had joined the most prominent crusader against the police. Within two years, he realized what a charlatan Cain was, but by this time, the money and occasional victory over the police made it worthwhile to stay.

Riding in the back of the police car, Geoffrey thought of the irony. These men were the only ones who could find Cain's murderer. But to do it, they would need his help. The question he had was, "did he want to give it to them?" He was still deciding when Sawyer opened the car door and motioned for him to get out. Geoffrey felt he was being made to look like a criminal because Sawyer walked him by the camped-out media group in front of the station.

The department's procedure was to use the headquarters building's back entry with any person of interest they didn't want the media to know. For spite and to deliberately mislead the media, Sawyer walked Geoffrey through the crowd assembled at the building's front entrance. Sawyer thought it was fitting repayment for the producer revealing the names of those poor guys. He knew Raleigh and Carter wasted the day clearing the three men on the list.

James 'Jaime' Sawyer hated the media. Seldom did they help the police, and often they hindered investigations. He knew this first hand.

Seven years previously, in his first year as a detective, he let slip to a pretty television reporter the department was looking for an individual concerning the murder of an elderly couple. The television reporter ran with the story displaying his picture on her broadcast. Not knowing the information had been aired, when police went looking at his home, shots erupted from the sought man's house. The first fuselage killed his partner, wounded Jaime, and ignited 12 hours of siege around his home. When, finally, the wanted man killed himself, police also found his wife and child dead inside the house. Yes, the nation needed the media, but he didn't.

Greeting Geoffrey with a smile, Raleigh invited him into his office. Again, he motioned Carter to join him. Before stepping back into his office, Raleigh asked Sawyer to see if anyone had found receipts or papers so they could ask for the dead man's phone records. Then he had a thought:

"Geoffrey, can I see your phone," he asked genially.

"My cell phone?"

"I assume you have one from Cain's company?"

"Yes, we all have one. On the same plan. Quite cheap."

"Good, then I just want our technical people to get Cain's information from your phone."

"Like hell you'll get that from me."

"Look, you can give me your phone and I promise my men won't look at your information or we can sit here until I get a subpoena to do it. In which case you will be here a lot longer and need to answer many more questions," Raleigh said more harshly.

Reluctantly, Geoffrey gave up his phone. Laughing to himself, Sawyer went down the hall to the tech section. Handing them the phone, he simply said: "Raleigh wants the records for every phone on that account." He left with a smile on his face. Raleigh had pulled another rabbit out of his hat.

Back in his office, Raleigh questioned Geoffrey to reconfirm the alibis, the story about the Peoria sheriff, Cain's office, and home. Geoffrey spoke freely but gave him nothing new. Thirty minutes into the interview, Geoffrey slipped.

"What did Cain do for fun?" Raleigh asked; apparently, an errant thought plucked out of the air.

"Tormented us," Geoffrey spat out before realizing what he said.

"Tormenting who?"

"We three. Henriette Percy, Hilda, me."

"How."

"If we had a slow day, he would have Henriette come into his office and strip naked down to her panties."

"Why her and why that?" Carter broke in.

"To remind her what she wasn't any more."

"What do you mean?" Carter pushed.

"She's so pale, skinny, and washed out but six years ago she was Miss Illinois."

"That stick was Miss Illinois?" Carter said, trying to convince himself.

"Yes, that's what one year in Arturo Gonzalez jail can do. He got her on a trumped-up drug charge and then used her in his prostitution set-up."

"I can't believe it. Her real name is Dawn Davis; her parents haven't seen her for five years now."

"Why is she with Cain? Because Hilda and Cain got her out of that Hell Hole. You see her now; she doesn't want to go home in the condition she's in."

"She still using?."

"She will be off the drugs for two or three months and then slip. Cain pays for her to dry out but he loved to see her strip naked."

"The bastard."

"You said it not me."

"What about Hilda?"

"She's afraid to go home. Her children stole her money, but she got most of it back. Now they're afraid she'll cut them out of her will."

"Why this attachment to Cain?" Raleigh asked, fascinated by the dynamics of this couple.

"Hilda has no one she can trust. She gave Cain $100,000 for him to protect her."

"And has he, and did he?."

"Who do you think tipped off Sheriff Gonzalez about Hilda's whereabouts?"

"Cain?"

"Yes, Gonzalez was supposed to bring $100,000 with him in exchange for Hilda and the papers."

"You don't say," Raleigh said menacingly, "He didn't have it with him when we arrested him."

"I'm not surprised. Cain sometimes played dangerously."

"Why did you stay with him?"

"He promised to take me when he landed a big entertainment contract."

"You believed him."

"Until Monday when he showed me the contract he signed, but said I needed to audition with the company. He had made no provision for me. I half expected it but I am not worried. Thanks to my years with him, I have in-demand skills."

"And I bet you have duplicates of everything Cain has done since you joined him."

"What does the FBI say: I can neither confirm nor deny."

"Could the murderer be on those tapes?"

Surprised at Raleigh's accuracy about duplicating the tapes, Geoffrey drew long breaths.

"Perhaps."

"But anything involving the Couri girl?"

"Mr. Cain wouldn't let us hear or deal with any of the Couri girl's material."

"So the tapes you have don't include anything on the Couri case?"

"That's right. If you think the man who murdered the Couri girl murdered Mr. Cain you won't find anything to help you on those tapes," Geoffrey said angrily.

"We'll see," Raleigh said, getting angrier by the minute. *"Those tapes have nothing to do with your investigation,"* Geoffrey managed to add more vigor to his voice.

"That's for us to decide. I'm going to send my detectives with you, and you're going to give us every one of those tapes.

"Like hell I will."

"Like hell you will or you'll rot in our jail until this case is over."

"Beau will get me out; he told me this morning not to worry, he had my back."

"Beau has nothing. If you want to hide behind Beau go ahead, but have people told you what I did the last time Beau did something I really disliked?"

"No, no one did." Geoffrey said, shaken by Raleigh's face and voice.

"Well Beau won't, but there are a lot of people in this town who will tell you. So don't get me madder than I am right now and go get those tapes."

"There's nothing on them to help you find his murderer."

"We'll decide."

"Okay, but I need them back."

"We'll see."

All three men remained silent for a few minutes until, in a gentle voice, Raleigh asked: *"Who do you think killed Cain?"*

Taking his time, Geoffrey let out a deep breath. *"I believe Cain had a male lover and that man killed him."*

Not letting any emotion show on his face, Raleigh asked gently: "*Why do you say he killed Cain?.*"

"*Because Cain was not only gay but vindictive. As a teenager he had a lover in this town. One he had in high school and one for whom he came back to rekindle their friendship.*"

"*An old lover who remained behind?*"

"*Yes, but I think Mr. Cain told his lover the day he died he was leaving to go to New York. I think that is what triggered the murder. The lover killed him.*"

"*Why do you say all this? Did you meet the man?*"

"*No, that's why Cain had the second phone. And it wasn't paid for by the company. He paid for it in cash, a pay-as-you-go phone.*"

"*Do you know where he bought it?*"

"*No, But I gather it wasn't with him when you found his body?*"

"*No, it was not.*"

"*Find that phone and you will find your killer. Personally, I don't think you will.*"

Benjamin Goodman, Thursday 3pm

Under President Ronald Reagan, the 1980's were prosperous years for most Americans. During that decade, Benjamin Goodman widened his father's Chicago real estate holdings into other states. Adding construction and support services as time went on, he realized in 1990 that all the pieces were in place to build whole communities of offices, manufacturing hubs, houses, schools, and apartments. His problem was finding enough contiguous land and a reasonable local government to accomplish his goal.

Benjamin's wife supplied the answer when she bought furniture crafted in Skye Landing in the Danish-owned factory established in the 20th Century by Lars Hurst's father. Never a big money maker but dear to the old man's heart, the furniture line and company survived as a sentimental keepsake by his son and heirs. When he started the factory, the original Hurst acquired 3,000 acres of woodland to supply its raw material. Then it was known as Breed's Hill. Over the years, in recognition of its owner, the natives in Skye Landing came to call the mountainous acres Dane Hill.

After personally and covertly examining the land and investigating Skye Landing itself and the surrounding area, Benjamin hired consultants to understand the dynamics of local government. Realizing five men got things done in the town, he targeted one, Knox Alexander's father, to be the regional leader for his project. His big obstacle was convincing Lars Hurst to contribute his land.

Using intermediaries, Benjamin arranged to meet the patriarch in his Copenhagen office. Much to Benjamin's surprise, Hurst was receptive to his concept. The two men agreed quickly, and the deal was struck. The community of Dane Hill was born 13 years prior and was the model for many other such projects. Benjamin moved his family to Dane Hill but lost his wife to her preference for Chicago. Sarah appreciated the chance for her husband to lead a synagogue of his own. Corinne was fleeing an unhappy marriage.

Often, Benjamin reflected both were happier in Dane Hill, preferring that name to Skye Landing. Building schools along with offices, homes, and roads made Benjamin happy. His only sadness was losing his wife to Maj Jong and Sarah to cancer. Today he sat behind his desk wondering how fate so conspired to leave him rich but unhappy. He waited for Raleigh to once again help him avoid despair.

Driving into Benjamin's front driveway, Raleigh reminded himself how rich the man must be. Yet, his house was relatively modest, dwarfed by his daughter Corinne's next door and the home once occupied by his other daughter. It was empty, maintained for the day one of her children might want to live in it. Raleigh rang the bell, immediately answered by Arthur, Benjamin's secretary. Nodding his head, Arthur showed him to Benjamin's office, surprising Raleigh by departing rather than taking his usual seat beside the older man.

To Benjamin's right, Corinne sat huddled, folded into the side chair, and looking as if she hadn't slept or changed clothes. This caught Raleigh's interest as the woman was known for her immaculate appearance, never seen with a hair out of place. He waited while Benjamin shuffled some papers.

"Good of you to come Raleigh."

"You said it was important."

"It is and I wouldn't drag you away from your investigation if this didn't have some bearing on your case."

"Fire away."

"Actually, I think my daughter Corinne has something to tell you."

Sensing he needed to let the woman speak when she was composed enough, Raleigh settled himself in his chair and waited. The minutes dragged on, finally compelling Raleigh to act.

"When you're ready Mrs. Jenkins."

Hesitating and clearly unhappy with what she was about to say, Corinne swiveled around in her chair and faced Raleigh directly.

"I was the other person in the room with Henry Cain yesterday.

98

Surprised by her statement, Raleigh resorted to the policemen's standby and said nothing.

"Henry Cain called me Monday and said I needed to meet with him discreetly to discuss a matter involving my sister and her husband," with each word sounding louder and more assertive.

"And you met with him? Raleigh asked encouragingly.

"He wanted to meet Tuesday but I told him I couldn't until Wednesday. I had school conferences Tuesday and they can't be changed.

He was irritated but agreed. He told me to go to the Red Roof Inn at noon, even gave me a specific room number."

"You went to a motel to meet a man notorious for his not-so-nice activities."

"Well I brought my gun," she said defensively, pulling the small revolver from her purse. *"I have a carry permit."*

"So you went yesterday?" Raleigh encouraged her.

"Yes, he greeted me at the door as if he'd just gotten there. Told me to sit on the bed."

"And what did he claim?"

"That he was adding my dead brother-in-law to the list of possible Jenny Couri killers."

"Based on what evidence?" Raleigh pressed her.

"What happened in Scarsdale."

"What happened in Scarsdale?" Raleigh asked, surprised at this new turn of events.

"Hyman was accused of having sex with two of the younger teenagers in our synagogue," Benjamin piped in to avoid having his daughter say anything.

"Was it true? Raleigh asked.

"We're not sure. The girls recanted. Hy denied it. Sarah said it wasn't true," Benjamin said, a note of resignation in his voice. From the tone, Raleigh knew it was true.

"It was so long ago. I'm surprised he found out," Corinne said, looking away.

"He's got a good researcher," Raleigh said. *"So, after he told you this what happened?"*

"I begged him not to reveal anything because of the children, Josh and Joy."

"And what happened?"

"He laughed and said they should know what their father was really like."

"And you did what?"

"I said is there anything I could do to stop him from revealing all that stuff."

"Did he ask for money?" Raleigh prompted.

"First he said he wouldn't do it if I stripped down to my panties."

"What did you say to that?"

"I took out my gun and said I'd shoot him if he came close to me."

"And then what happened?"

"He said how much money could I raise?" She paused.

"I looked at him and said I'd give him all our house money $22,000 right then and there."

"He took it?"

"He looked at me and he looked at my gun and he figured this was a bad situation so he agreed."

"And you wrote the check at the desk."

"With him sitting in the corner as far away from me as possible."

"What happened next?"

"He took the check and put it in his briefcase."

"So he had the briefcase?"

"Yes, on the bed. It was locked and he had the key on a chain around his neck."

"You're sure about that?"

"Positive, while he fumbled to open it, I kept the gun on him the whole time."

"What happened next?"

"He looked at the clock in the room. It said quarter to twelve so he checked with his watch and asked me to leave."

"He say why?"

"Said he had an old friend coming and they had a lot to talk about."

"And you left." Raleigh said more as a statement than a question.

"I backed him into the room farthest from the door and left."

"See anyone in the hall or back parking lot?"

"No, I'd left my car down the street and walked to it as fast as I could. Went straight to the bank and stopped the check."

"Why did you do that?"

"Because he was a penny-ante shyster and if he was going to smear Hy's name he could try but I didn't think he could or would. Then I found out he was murdered and realized eventually you would find me."

"Because of the check?"

"No, I'd made it out to cash. But some record would appear sometime."

"That's true, but probably too late for our investigation."

"Can I go now?"

"Yes, I'll handle this down at headquarters."

Leaving the two men eying each other, she left somewhat relieved.

"Drink?" Benjamin asked.

"No, still need to do a lot more digging. At least your daughter solved one mystery."

"Can we keep her out of this?"

"Depends what happens in our investigation. Now I can confirm what we thought. There were two visitors to Cain's room. The second one killed him."

"Any idea who murdered the insect?" Benjamin asked.

"Only that he's gay, still in the closet and angry."

"How do you know he's angry?"

"By the damage done to Cain, guy didn't stop until he made sure."

"Corinne handled herself well," Benjamin added.

"I don't know, meeting a man like Cain in a motel room," Raleigh said.

"She is most capable," her father said.

"She handles Beau."

"Why do you think she has the gun? He gets out of line, she'll shoot him."

"Always said someone would someday."

"Careful, he may be our next mayor."

"I don't think you'll let that happen, Benjamin."

"I can't control everything. Look at this mess coming back to haunt us after 12 years."

"A secret is a secret Benjamin. Like to know who woke the dogs?"

"Perhaps we will never know."

"Doubt that."

"Just be careful out there. Ghosts have a way of hurting people."

"Never did believe in Ghosts." Raleigh said as he began to leave.

Benjamin had a thoughtful expression on his face as Raleigh got up to leave.

Before he reached the door, Arthur opened it from the other side; behind him waited Provender Gibson, the last person Raleigh expected to see that day. Besides being mayor, he was among the wealthiest men in the town. That he was here was not unusual, just the timing. Provender almost never interfered with the police or their activities. Raleigh's first thought that the mayor was there to protect Benjamin. Seeming to confirm this thought, the always discrete Arthur retreated after ushering the new visitor into the room. There was an awkward silence for a moment then things got interesting.

Provender Gibson, Thursday, 3:33pm

Since the first Scots-Irish settlers moved into the hill country of South Carolina, there have been Gibbons. Usually, the family stayed just outside the law, managing to survive root and family for more than 300 years.

Micah Gibson was the first to make real wealth legally. First by buying land from the tax office during the depression, so when cotton and linseed became high-priced crops again, he was in a position to earn steady cash with his large holdings.

Then, he looked around for his next investment. Reading the newspapers and seeing war on the horizon in Europe, he bought the local operating lumber mill and defunct cotton mill. When in 1939, fighting in Europe did happen, he went to Charleston, looked up the British agent, and offered blankets and uniform material on credit. Needing both, the agent gave him contract after contract until the Japanese struck Pearl Harbor.

Before America's entry, Micah had been stockpiling wood in anticipation of the war efforts. When Army and Navy purchasing agents came around, he had almost 500,000 board feet ready to deliver. Most of it was lumbered off of what was then called Breed's Hill, after the family that owned it but had unfortunately been in desperate need of cash had given cutting rights to Micah.

By 1943, wartime restrictions limited how much individuals could deposit in each bank. Micah needed to find banks willing to absorb his profits. Generating large cash hordes and no institution willing to absorb more of his assets, he finally bought the local bank.

As the war progressed, Micah continued to earn profits, but at the cost of employee morale. Labor injuries and deaths had caused many workers to resent the man. When his employees resorted to strikes, Micah had a ready answer.

These work stoppages were won by Micah using a simple tactic resented by everyone. If the lumber mill workers went out on strike, he closed the entire operation. This earned the strikers the enmity of the other laborers not striking. Micah would use the profits from the cotton business to tide over the mill until the workers went back. To add pressure on the workers to settle, his bank also did not extend credit to store keepers and others dependent on the striking workers for sales. They in turn became reluctant to extend terms to striking families. It was a vicious cycle that made Micah even richer but more despised. Despite the wartime labor shortages, unlike many of his competitors, Micah was able to break every strike during the war years.

With the war winding down, Micah turned to buying Skye Landing's stores and businesses. He also realized he needed heirs to keep these businesses growing. For heirs to appear, there needed to be a wife. He chose 19-year-old Mae Hopkins, the daughter of his accountant. To eliminate her concern about the 33-year differences in their ages, he offered her $50,000 per child up to four. Mae jumped at the chance but could only produce Provender Gibson before tiring of Micah and his miserly ways. She decamped to Florida and lived well for years until cancer took her at 54.

Raised by a series of housekeepers, nurses, and tutors, Provender proved to be the opposite of Micah. He flunked out of South Carolina in two semesters due to inattention and returned to Skye Landing only to fall in love with Ellen Breed, whose father had during the lean years sold lumbering rights to his acreage to Micah.

There was just one obstacle to their marriage. In 1959 Micah was presented with an unpleasant clause in his agreement with Barrington Breed. Simply put, the clause enabled the landowner to take back his rights for $25,000. Micah had assented to the clause, never believing the liquor-loving man could hold himself together long enough to raise the necessary funds.

When the Danes first came to town, Micah dealt sharply with them. Demanding high amounts for his wood and often spotty delivery schedules, the Hurst family looked about for alternative sources. By happy chance, an idle conversation brought them to Barrington. When he gave them the contract to examine, a Danish lawyer saw the buyback loophole and the Danes advanced the repayment funds, in exchange for the four tree stands they needed for their factory. Losing his source of low-cost lumber, Micah's mill soon became an albatross.

Bitter, Micah forbade Provender from marrying Ellen. When the couple eloped, he cut off Provender. The couple moved to Atlanta, but the marriage did not survive the difficult times. Ellen married a classmate of Provender and stayed in Atlanta.

Provender returned to Skye Landing and moved back in with his father. Never saying another word, he waited for his father to die. That occasion did not occur until 1980, by which time Provender knew the businesses better than his father.

The day after the father's funeral, Provender started selling all his assets and decided to make Skye Landing his business. For the next 39 years, he was a councilman, Board of Education President, and finally, in 1998, Mayor. With Lars Hurst, Knox Alexander's father, and Benjamin Goodman, they created Dane Hill, the industry sector, and just about every other improvement in town. A small man who inherited bony features, he strode into Benjamin's house confident of his position and reception.

"Amanda told me where to find you Raleigh."

"Always a pleasure to see you but I'm busy."

"Know you are and I am about to make you busier."

"Oh, no!"

"Yep, your slimy murder victim visited me the morning he died."

"He got around."

"Yeah, thought he could push me around."

"He should've known better."

"Well, he tried, saying he was going add my name to the list of perverts associated with this Couri girl."

"How he comes by your name?"

"*Probably Beau put him up to it. Beau figuring a little dirt on me would make his campaign easier.*"

"*You're going to run again?*"

"*No, I'm finished as Mayor, too many votes for Beau up on Dane Hill, they want a high school of their own up there.*"

"*What did Cain want?*"

"*What does anyone want from me, money. He said if I gave him $25,000 he wouldn't add my name.*"

"*What did you say?*"

"*Called Henry and told him to toss Cain out the garbage door.*"

"*He could've named you.*"

"*And then I would have sued him for everything he had. I had a vasectomy in 1980 and can't have children and got doctor's notes to prove it.*"

"*What Cain do when he heard this?*"

"*Well, before Henry got close to him, I noticed he had this device hanging from his lapel. Saw one on another fella years ago, it was a recorder. He had been recording us. I had Henry grab it before throwing him out. Because I destroyed the chain of evidence I originally thought of destroying its. But after my talk with Amanda, I realized you might need to have it.*"

"*Mighty generous of you Provender,.*" Raleigh said angry at the time lost.

"*Don't know how to use it and didn't want to gum it up so I'm bringing it to you.*"

Plopping the unit on Benjamin's desk, Provender stepped back, and Raleigh scooped it up. He didn't bother with a handkerchief as all hopes of prints was lost.

"*Just for the record, Provender, where were you yesterday between 11-2?*"

"*Where I am most days now, on my back porch enjoying Delilah's cooking. I'm getting too old to do much more. Thinking of really retiring.*"

"*They've been with you a long time and happy to lie for you.*"

"*Make 'em swear on a bible, you know they can't lie over a bible.*"

"No, I guess not. I'll bring this to the tech boys to make sure we don't screw it up."

"You do that now," Provender said with half a laugh.

"Drink, Provender, before you go?" Benjamin asked.

"Always enjoy your hospitality."

Raleigh left the two men sitting in their chairs, wishing he could join them but knowing there was some urgency in this case. Why he didn't know, but there was a nagging feeling he was missing something important. He almost used the siren to rush back to the police headquarters.

Secret Cache, Thursday 4:30pm

While driving back to headquarters, Raleigh remembered the detectives at Cain's office and home. Confident they knew their jobs, he hadn't worried they wouldn't uncover evidence if there was anything to find. Therefore he wasn't surprised when Sawyer called him from the house, excited and puzzled.

"You're not going to believe this, Raleigh," Sawyer said loudly.

"With the way this case is going, I'd believe anything."

"We were poking around wondering where Cain kept important stuff."

"You find it."

"Not in his desk, files, or drawers."

"Then where?"

"You know in those old movies where they have bookcases that hide passages."

"Yes?"

"Well, Cain's liquor cabinet moves and there's a safe behind it."

"You open it?"

"Had to get the locksmith back but he did and he ruined the lock."

"And inside?"

"Heck-of-a-lotta stuff. More than we can wade through tonight."

"Then box it up and bring everything to the station. Don't put it in the evidence room, we know someone can get in there. Lock it in my office and have someone guard the door tonight."

"Means overtime."

"So what, Amanda will okay the overtime because it is too important to be left unguarded."

"You're the boss."

"Yes, I am. Where's Carter?"

"I think he's back at headquarters."

"Okay knock off for today after you secure that material."

"Will do!"

Realizing how tired he was, Raleigh decided to go home. First, by phone, he invited Carter to dinner and called Eleanor Hightower to say there would be one more for dinner, and she said nothing but added another filet to her baking pan.

Still in his shower when Carter arrived, Eleanor let him in, inviting the detective to join her while she finished making dinner. Declining liquor and drinking diet soda, he sat on a stool in the spacious kitchen, which also served as an instructional area.

"You know Raleigh a long time?" He asked.

"We went to grammar school together. I moved away for almost 20 years while my family followed the textile migration to Asia."

"So, you were in Asia."

"Almost two decades. Funny, went to Asia to meet a man grew up 25 miles from here. We came back, he was a banker but wanted to be a baker. So, he opened an exotic dessert place that was the talk of the state."

"What happened?"

"Cancer. Gone in six months. I sold the business about the time Ellen died and moved in here."

"Can't be fun not having your own family."

"Oh, I think I'm part of this one."

"I hope I've not inconvenienced you coming tonight."

"Raleigh has had every member of the department here one time or the other. You were the only one he hadn't asked. Besides which, he foots the food bills and just about everything else in this house except my cooking lessons."

"Why's that?"

"He is a very old-fashioned guy. Just like his father and I expect his father's father."

"Allows his niece to save for her daughter's education?"

"I shouldn't be telling you this, but his wife left an education fund for her."

"A very generous family."

"When she died, almost the whole town turned out for her funeral. Wasn't a charity or cause she didn't help."

"Someone told me it was because Raleigh neglected her."

"Now, that's what's wrong with people. People never understand other people's marriages. Certainly didn't understand their marriage. When they learned they couldn't have more children, they turned to each other. She understood Raleigh's need to solve crimes. When he came home, they were fiercely into each other. But she knew what drove him. She told me once every minute with him was like an hour."

"They loved each other that much?"

"Started in the eighth grade and never stopped."

"Wish I had that."

"That's cause you're so into yourself. Caleigh picked it up first time she met you."

"What did she say about me?"

"Said you needed to grow more."

"She said that?"

"Yes, she's had bad luck with men starting with Beau Jenkins. I knew the moment I met him he was a skirt chaser and never would settle for one woman."

"That's a term I haven't heard in a long time."

"It's true. Man just can't help himself. It's a wonder Corinne puts up with him. Now that's a woman who surprises me. Best damn mother I know, and she raises her niece and nephew the best I've seen. Guess she'll tolerate Beau until they leave home. I'm betting she kicks him out on his ass when they do."

"Well, I'm sure she's rich enough with Benjamin's money."

"I agree but most goes to trusts and the kids will only get their mother's inheritance."

"You know an awful lot."

"Half the women in town have come into this kitchen. Some want to learn how to cook, others to add to their skills. What do you think we talk about here, meat and fish?"

"Never thought about that. I should take cooking lessons."

"I keep men and women separate in my classes."

"Why's that?"

"Most men are self-conscious about cooking. They also want to learn different things."

"Like?"

"How to boil water. Enough now I hear Sue Ellen coming in. She'll want a snack. Don't know where she puts it. She's sixteen going on thirty with a figure to match. In short, trouble."

Caleigh's daughter burst into the kitchen, flinging her backpack on a stool and sidling next to Carter.

'So, you're my mother's latest conquest," Sue Ellen said, inching close to Carter's face.

"Conquest?"

"Yeah, heard you last night. She let you into Raleigh's office. Only a few people get to see it, let alone read his files. Learn anything?"

"What should I have learned?"

"How to solve crimes. He's the best and getting to work with him is an honor."

"How would you know?"

"I listen at keyholes. People come from all over to talk to him about hard cases."

"I didn't know that."

"A lot you don't know. Including the fact that if you want to sleep with her you need to take her to Charleston. She won't do anything in this town for fear it will corrupt me."

"Seems, you're already corrupted."

"Not yet, but I'm trying."

"Don't upset the man, Ellen!" Eleanor said sternly but with a smile on her face. *"You'll have plenty of time to get corrupted. Just enjoy your teen years."*

Giving Eleanor what she thought was a withering look, she turned back to the hapless third party.

"How can I with a mother who was wild and now won't let me go to parties and things."

"She just won't let you go to Charlotte because of what happened to her there when she was your age," Eleanor said.

"What happened?", Ellen asked, knowing the answer would be silence as it was on numerous other occasions.

When the sound of the door opening and shutting reached the three kitchen occupants, they tried to guess who would be the next family member to arrive. The footsteps indicated movement up the stairs allowing them to know it was Raleigh heading to his shower.

Ellen ate the cupcake proffered by Eleanor and said nothing. Uncomfortable with the silence but not knowing what to say, Carter also remained silent. Eleanor popped the baking pan into the oven and left the room. The younger woman soon followed, leaving Carter awkwardly alone in the bright lights.

Remaining where he was sitting, he heard the silence of this strange house of three women and one man. The sound of showering ended and within minutes Raleigh wandered in dressed in jeans and a polo shirt. Silently, he motioned Carter to his office, closing the door after both entered.

"What did you find today?" Raleigh said without preamble.

"Nothing useful," he replied ruefully.

"Wrong, everything's useful, we just need to figure out where they belong."

"I worked at his office. We got the door open but any important papers are elsewhere."

"We found them behind his bar at home in a safe."

"What did they say?"

"Don't know left it for the morning when we're fresh. Under guard I might add."

"Smart."

"Hope so, we still don't know who filched the Couri file."

"We will. By-the-way, that guy Geoffrey hung around all day outside trying to get in."

"Did you let him in?"

"'Course not. Posted a guard there tonight just in case he tried to get in."

"What about the computers?"

"We got into them. Geoffrey likes gay porn. The woman likes beauty shows and that heiress searches the Internet for news of her family. As for Cain, he almost never used it. Apparently, he relied on Geoffrey."

"What about e-mails?"

"Thousands, we're going through them but I don't think they'll lead us anywhere."

"Need to cover the bases. Wish we could find his phones and briefcase."

"And his recorder."

"We've got that but the trail of custody is going to get tough to defend."

Raleigh was about to explain Provender's involvement when Caleigh knocked on the office door and said dinner was ready. So engrossed in their conversation, neither man had registered that she had arrived. The two men adjourned to the dining room. Raleigh's niece wore the same jeans but a blue blouse. Seeing her standing there, Carter began feeling the same urges from the previous night. He sat down quickly, happy the others followed suit.

Ellen dominated the conversation by discussing school and world affairs, always bringing the conversation back to parties and permissions. Her mother ignored most thrusts in those directions, and the dinner remained cordial. Carter offered to do the dishes and was vigorously warned off. Declining a drink, he followed Raleigh back to his office. After bringing him up to speed, Raleigh indicated he was going to bed.

Walking out of the house, he glimpsed Caleigh in the parlor on her laptop. Knowing he hadn't spilled any departmental secrets, he left without a word. On the sofa, Caleigh smiled.

Death Visits, Thursday, 6:30pm

Peeking out from the slight crack in the portal, Henriette opened the door wider to let him in once she saw who he was. Just behind her, Hilda retreated into the neat but old-looking room.

In prior years the building housed young adults moving to town. The owner had taken pride in the building and was fussy about who rented his apartments. Gambling was his undoing, losing the building in a rigged card game. The new owners didn't care who rented as long as they paid their monthly rent. Soon, the police made regular calls to the building. Tenants tended to get poorer and more larcenous over time. They also had less money for rent but consistently enough for drugs. What was common in all of them was their ability to ignore happenings in other parts of the building.

Because Henrietta had long lost the right to drive, her apartment was the only one she found that was cheap and near Cain's office. Henriette tried to add little touches to brighten her apartment despite her troubles. The adornments didn't hide the cracks in the walls and stains on the rugs.

Mouthing nothings, the two women bustled about as the visitor sat at the only table in the one-bedroom apartment. He noted the clothes hanging in the bathroom. Neatly folded blankets, sheets, and pillowcases to one side revealed that someone was sleeping on the couch. The visitor bet it was the younger woman.

They asked if he would like some tea. He said yes to gain time to survey everything in the front room. He didn't care about the bedroom, and he was sure no one hid there. As he completed his inventory, the kettle whistled quickly as if they were expecting someone beside him to drop in.

Given their present situations, both women needed help, but they were unsure why he had come. In their need, both women looked at him expectantly. Hilda hoped the visitor could facilitate the return of her materials from police custody. Her supply of narcotics dwindling, Henriette wanted to know if there was still a job with whoever took over Cain's company. Her plight was desperate because she feared returning to drugs.

She had built up some cash reserves and was hoping to find a way to go home. The long descent from beauty queen to her present situation sapped her will. She had run out of hope. Truth be known, all she wanted to do was go home.

Hilda poured the Sassafras tea, not bothering to ask the guest what he wanted. Its fragrance filled the room, momentarily hiding the smells of previous occupants. Saying nothing, the visitor let them prattle on. He waited until they sat down opposite him. As he remained silent, they continued to talk. He occasionally nodded, seeming to agree with them. Finally, their patter faded out, and they looked to him expectantly.

Portraying a grave face, he sat quietly and continued looking at them. They returned his gaze for some moments, and then both looked down. When they did, he took the gun from his pocket and first shot Hilda, knowing Henriette would not react quickly. The bullet went into the older women's head just above the nose and remained lodged in her brain. His gun moved rapidly to the other woman, who did not move but showed a surprised look on her face. Before she could say or yell something, his bullet entered her forehead at almost precisely the same spot, exiting out the back of her head. Her brain absorbed most of the bullet's energy, dropping to the floor midway to the far wall.

Noting there was hardly any noise from the shots, the visitor got up and dumped the tea into the sink with a gloved hand. He searched the apartment, took some items from Henriette's scrapbook, and prepared to leave. There was no one in the hall nor were there surveillance cameras as he went along the wall to his car parked one block away. It was not yet 7pm: time enough to establish an alibi if needed.

Behind him, the two women sat in their chairs, the smell of gunpowder the only clue that he had been there.

Cameras Blink, Friday, 8:00am

Thinking he would be first in the bureau, Carter arrived to find others ahead of him, pretending to work but waiting for Raleigh. The older man appeared with Amanda before the thirty-minute mark was hit. Crowding into his office, they all wondered what clues the two boxes would offer them. No one wanted to admit they were stumped as to motive and killer.

Reaching his hand into the nearest box, Raleigh extracted a thick packet of polaroid photos. After seeing the first, he handed them to Amanda. Shuffling through the photos and realizing she had not interviewed any suspects, she gave the images to Carter. On top was an unknown woman naked except for her panties. Looking at each one, he extracted two and handed them to Amanda.

"The younger one is the former Miss Illinois in Cain's office. The older one is the heiress," Sawyer said to the assembled detectives. *"They're naked except for panties. Seems all the pictures are of women stripped to their panties. I would guess they're all extortion or blackmail victims."*
"Sonofabitch liked to humiliate women," Carmichael exclaimed.
"We know of another attempt but she pulled out her gun and stopped him," Raleigh said, half in humor.

"Who was that?" Carter asked.

"Cain's first visitor. Who she is will remain confidential now unless we need to disclose it," Raleigh said with finality.

"If that's the way you want it Raleigh," Amanda said, reinforcing his words. The others in the office understood.

"What else is there in here?" Raleigh said, pulling out a group of manila files. Without a word, he distributed them roughly equal to the others in the room.

Quickly reading his five files, Carter was the first to speak.

"Looks to me like they're files about every important person in town. I've got Gunderson, the board president, head of the savings and loan, and that tech billionaire up in Dane Hill."

"I've got you Amanda, Daw, and the druggist. Mighty interesting info on the druggist. We should send it to Hawley down in Narcotics," Carmichael said.

"I've got the Neely, the township attorney, and Arthur, Benjamin's secretary," Amanda offered.

"I bet when we're finished we will find just about everyone of importance in town or rich enough to blackmail in this box," Raleigh said thoughtfully.

"Means we need to ask every one of them for an alibi for the murder time," Carter said eagerly.

"We're not doing any such thing, Carter," Raleigh said harshly.

"Why not?" Carter demanded.

"Because I know this was a murder fueled by anger. We need to look for someone who suddenly had a great hatred of Cain. The act wasn't premeditated but spontaneous. Let's concentrate for the moment on these boxes."

Working slowly, the group found Cain's most personal items, including a pornographic video of him and some men in what appeared to be a swank Hollywood mansion. Also inside the second box was Jenny Couri's audition tape. Played naked, the scene was erotic, and even Amanda was moved by the body the young girl displayed. The scene's locale, the high school auditorium stage, was evident to all. Also included were 20 seconds of Charles Stewart feeding lines to the woman who displayed her solid acting talent.

Reaching the bottom of the second box, Raleigh extracted one last item.

"Anybody recognize this?" he said laughingly.

"My god, I got mine at home," said Carmichael.

"Me too," said Sawyer.

"Haven't seen one in years," Raleigh continued.

"Not since we discontinued the program 10 years ago."

"What program?" Carter looked around the room.

"That badge is from Patrolman's Watch, that was Ned Barrow's TV program to encourage boys to become policemen. Ran it for 18-years until some busy body complained that he only took in boys for the program. He didn't want to add girls so he scrapped the entire thing. Boy was Barrow mad. Kept getting his patrolmen to give her tickets. Until I put a stop to that nonsense," Amanda said laughingly.

"I can't imagine Cain as a junior patrolman or a policeman," Raleigh said.

"But it must have meant something to him to keep it all these years," Carter said.

"But what?" said Raleigh putting the badge on his desk?

"Voucher the rest and let's move on," Amanda said briskly.

"To where?" Carter said.

"Raleigh will know," Amanda answered.

In most murder investigations, police often find themselves stumped. When that happens, one solution is to go back and re-interview witnesses and re-examine all available evidence. Raleigh put the badge away and ordered Winston to bring in the two women who worked with Cain. He directed Carter to sort through the folders to see if they offered any clues. Carmichael was detailed to bring in Geoffrey. Three patrolmen were ordered to again search around the motel but to widen the area under inspection. He called down to the two tech officers to see if they had deciphered how the recorder worked.

Putting the badge in the center of his desk, he looked at it again. The number had long faded, but he could assume it was Cain's from when he attended Skye Landing grammar school and high school. He called down to Thelma Wright, secretary to the Police Chiefs for almost 28 years, to see if any records were left about the group. Its demise was national news at the time.

He called Ned Barrow's office, but his aide said he had taken another vacation to drive his wife and son to her mother's home in Greenville. As he hung up the phone, something nagged at Raleigh about that, but he couldn't remember what it was.

Coffee and one of Eleanor's donuts didn't help him. He called Caleigh, who said she would look up any stories her paper did on the

Patrolmen Watch. While waiting for reports, he thought about Ellen, his wife, and Raleigh wondered if he did neglect her. He had tossed and turned during the night, thinking of the comments made to him yesterday.

Another Surprise, Friday, 10:25am

Winston called from outside Henriette Percy's apartment to report no response to his knocking. Ordering him to knock harder and get the women to headquarters, he hung up without saying goodbye.

His phone rang five minutes later, and it was Winston again.

"You'd better get down here Raleigh. Both women are dead."

Before Winston could say more, Raleigh was out of his chair, calling Carter to drive him to the scene.

"This time use the siren," was all Raleigh said.

When the two detectives arrived, two squad cars were already parked in front of the two-story apartment building. Raleigh was glad to see the Crime Scene team was waiting outside before entering the building. He climbed the stairs quickly, followed closely by Carter and the other police.

Winston was standing outside the open door. He nodded at Raleigh and waited for orders.

"Why did you push the door in?" Raleigh asked.

"Something didn't feel right. They had no place to go. Office is still barred to them. So they should have been home. Checked and her car was in its assigned spot. So I broke in."

"You did right. Let's go in."

Pausing at the door, Raleigh looked at the shabby apartment and the two women at the table. There were cups filled with tea in front of each, and another empty cup sat opposite them. Both sat upright in their chairs, each with one bullet in the center of their foreheads.

Raleigh marveled at the speed and marksmanship of the shooter. He must have fired twice so fast that the second victim had no time to react.

Both were dead in an instant. There was a bedroom behind them, and his quick glance showed the bed was still made. The couch where the guest, probably Hilda Rensozo, was expected to sleep was undisturbed.

"*I'm guessing they were killed last night,*" Carter piped up.

"*I think you're right, but let's wait for Jules. Anybody call him yet?*" he almost shouted.

"*I did. He said he'll be here in about 20 minutes,*" volunteered Winston

"*Good. Let's sweep for prints and things, but I'm betting we'll find only theirs and maybe Geoffrey's. Does anybody know where he is?*

"*He's at the office still trying to get in.*"

"*Good, have the officers arrest him as a material witness and hustle him to headquarters. I think he's next on the killer's list. He probably saved his life staying near the office.*"

"*Be careful but look for any papers in this apartment but I think the killer beat us to any of importance,*" Raleigh ordered.

His prediction was correct; some empty folders were found. Only an album showing Henriette as state beauty queen remained on the coffee table. There were two letters, apparently from her parents, and her jewelry was still in the apartment. Hidden in the only drawer were the rhinestone tiara from better days, five dresses, six blouses, four sweaters, and underwear. The other victim's clothes included a nightgown, cosmetics, and new underclothes.

"*Have the guys at Cain's house check if that woman's clothes are there,*" Carter said helpfully.

"*She said she lived there.*"

"*We saw her picture in that stack.*"

"*Yes, but she seemed happy to pose.*"

"*At her age, who else but a pervert would ask a woman who looked like that to pose nude?*"

"*You would be surprised in this day and age.*"

"*At my age, nothing surprises me.*"

As they spoke, Jules came through the door, two attendants behind him. Raleigh told the attendants to stay out until the crime scene people finished. Being careful to disturb little at the crime scene, Jules examined the bodies and looked at Raleigh to give him an estimate of when they died.

"About 6pm last night, I would guess. Probably not off by much. Know better when I finish the autopsy."

"They seem to have been having tea with him or her when the killer shot them," Raleigh said.

"What did he or she drink?"

"Whatever it was is down the drain. The cup will be wiped clean of prints."

"They haven't been moved if that's what you're asking."

"So, they knew the killer."

"Appears so. But I don't think they had many beyond Cain and Geoffrey."

"I know one's dead and the idiot was camped out with our police guard at their offices."

"Wonder what is so important he needs to get into those offices so badly?"

"I think he has a cache of materials he hopes to parlay into a job. I'm thinking we let him in and nab him on the way out. Let's go back to headquarters. There's not much more we can do here."

"They must have known something for the killer to risk being seen," said Carter.

"Ask Amanda for more patrolmen and let them ask neighbors and anyone else they find," Raleigh ordered Carter.

"Helluva time for Barrow to drive his wife to Greenville," Carter said almost as an aside.

"Not the first time he's bugged out of a major crime or snafu. He doesn't like to get his skirt wet," Raleigh said almost silently but loud enough for Carter to hear.

Knowing nothing more to be seen at the murder scene, Raleigh and Carter traipsed out of the apartment. They drove silently back to headquarters, neither saying a word, both knowing the case was nowhere.

Stonewall Collapses, Friday, 11am

After being hustled to headquarters once again, Geoffrey wasn't in the mood to be talkative when he was brought to Raleigh's office. Along with the same detective from Cain's office, a black woman with bars on her blouse's shoulders had joined them. No one looked happy, so four unhappy faces stared at each other than at Geoffrey.

"Geoffrey, you know any reason Hilda or Henriette would know who the killer is?" Raleigh asked softly to open the discussions.

"Those two?" Geoffrey asked disdainfully.

"Yes, those two and don't give me any twaddle about not cooperating, this is important," Raleigh asked more forcefully.

"Those two knew almost nothing about this Couri girl or our efforts," Geoffrey allowed himself this one answer.

"Maybe they knew something about Cain's secret life."

"What secret life?" Geoffrey blurted out.

"That he was gay?" Carter jumped in, starting to act the bad cop role.

"Cain wasn't gay, I would have known." Geoffrey almost shouted.

"Seems he was," Amanda spoke for the first time.

"No, Mr. Cain liked girls, had them in his office all the time."

"To humiliate them," Amanda said angrily.

"No, he always said afterwards how much he enjoyed them."

"Seems all he liked to do was humiliate them."

"I wouldn't know about that," Geoffrey said, retreating from something he had thought but never articulated.

"Still begs the question, would those two women know anything about our murderer."

At this point, Geoffrey decided to go silent with an "I wouldn't know comment." The three police officers saw this attitude and decided to huddle outside. Putting him in a chair at the far end of the detective's desks, they stood in the hallway outside of Ned Barrow's dark office.

"We aren't going to get anything out of this guy unless we find some sort of leverage," Carter said.

"He's right about that," Amanda said reluctantly, not liking to agree with Carter.

"Perhaps, I can get it," Raleigh said. *"Let's call Knox and get him down here."*

"Why Knox?" Carter queried.

"Knox's company bought Cain's podcast company and this guy needs work and maybe Knox can wiggle the information out of him," Raleigh reminded them.

"I'll do it," Carter volunteered to try to impress Amanda. She ignored the gesture.

As they broke up and almost on cue, Ned Barrow walked down the hallway towards his office. Raleigh waited for him to reach the door.

"Glad you're back," he said to the man who was nominally his boss.

"Needed to do some things,"

"Need to be briefed on the case?"

"Have a suspect yet?" Ned asked negligently.

"Not yet. We're working on some things,"

"I figure you will find him, and when you do, let me know,"

"Will do."

"Who's that sitting there?" Ned said, nodding towards Geoffrey.

"A witness, but we're still trying to get some leverage on him."

"Know you will, Raleigh. Now let me get to my office. I'm sure there is a lot of paperwork to catch up on in there."

"You bet," Raleigh said but doubting there was. From the beginning of his tenure, his people had learned to avoid bringing anything of importance to his attention. Most preferring to solve any issue before Ned got involved.

The men parted, leaving Geoffrey stewing until Knox arrived two hours later. Briefed by Raleigh, they brought Geoffrey back into

Raleigh's office. Carter joined them, still frustrated by Cain's papers which continued to no providing any clues as to who may have killed him.

"Geoffrey, this is the new owner of Cain's podcast, Knox Alexander," Raleigh began.

"Understand you're not cooperating with the police Geoffrey?" Knox started out almost as a rhetorical question.

"As a member of the press, I have certain rights," Geoffrey said in a huff.

"And as a member of our staff you must know we cooperate totally and completely with the police," Knox said.

"How do I know you now own Cain Podcast?" Geoffrey said.

"Thought you might have doubts here is a copy of our press release that will go out Monday announcing the deal. We signed our agreements this past Monday which was fortuitous for us given Mr. Cain's unfortunate demise."

Reading the document slowly, Geoffrey debated his response.

"How do I know I'm not talking to a fancy policeman with fake papers?"

"Oh, for God's sake, I'm not used to people questioning me. But do you know the name of the head of Blue Smoke Productions?"

"Yes, Mr. Cain had me call him several times these past few months."

Knox reached into his pocket and used his phone to speed dial a number. A voice answered before the third ring.

"Jim, this is Knox. I am about to decide about one of the employees of Cain Podcasts. He doesn't believe I can. Can you inform him who and what I am for Blue Smoke?"

With that, he handed the phone to Geoffrey and, after confirming who was at the other end of the phone, asked to describe his owner. Satisfied, Geoffrey handed the phone back to Knox, who queried the voice as to who was being sent to manage the Cain podcasts. Satisfied, he hung up.

"Now, Geoffrey, are you going to cooperate, or are you fired? Knox said nastily.

"Don't you believe in freedom of the press, Mr. Alexander?"

"Not when it comes to murder, I don't." He replied even more nastily.

"Will I have a job with Cain Podcasts?"

"For as long as it exists," Knox replied more sympathetically.

"Well, I don't know if it means anything but 10 days ago the two women came back from a shopping excursion all excited. All they would say was they had seen Mr. Cain with someone strange for him to be with. They wouldn't say who, but once or twice they said that person was the last person you would ever think him to be with."

"They say who it was?" Carter asked, interrupting.

"They were being pretty smug about it and wouldn't say anything more. But they smirked when he returned to the office," Geoffrey said.

"Anything else happen?"

"Yes, from then on neither woman stayed long in his office. Before, he would have afternoon sessions with them but that stopped. Harriette also began to be more cheerful. I don't know why but they seemed to have some leverage over Mr. Cain."

"And you don't know why or who this individual they saw was?" Carter rushed in.

"No, I didn't then nor do I know now."

"And you can't give us any more information?"

Raleigh left the air to thicken, not uttering a sound.

"Even if we told you your two co-workers are dead. Killed probably by the same person that killed your boss?"

"Are they really dead?" Geoffrey said in genuine shock, not lost on the other people in the office.

Murdered last night at about 6pm. Where were you last night?"

"Drowning my bad luck in a bar."

"What bar?"

"I don't know but I took a book of matches. They're in my room. The matches will tell you where I was last night. I was there from about 5pm till 11pm when I went to the office."

"That reminds me, why did you try to get in at 11pm at night?"

"Because in my desk is my album of pictures that I really want to keep?"

"*I'll have it checked out and if not material to the case returned to you,*" Raleigh said gently.

"*That would be greatly appreciated.*"

"*A gesture from us barbarians,*" Raleigh tried to ease the man's sorrows. "*Are you sure there is nothing you can add to help us find Cain's murderer?*

"*If I could, I would,*" he answered, alerting both detectives to the fact there was more for him to tell.

"*Well, I don't want you to leave town until I tell you, you can leave now but stay away from the office until Mr. Alexander here gains control of the offices from us. Seeing how now you're his employee stay in touch through him should anything changes. I'll arrange for a police car to drive you home,*" Raleigh said as a way of dismissal.

"*I prefer to walk. Mr. Alexander, how do I get in touch with you?*"

"*Here's my card Geoffrey and we will be in touch with you.*"

With the last statement, Geoffrey got up and walked stiffly out of the office with its other occupants following him down the hallway and past the dividing door.

"*You're really going to give him a job until the end of the Cain podcasts?*" Carter asked dubiously.

"*In order to collect on Cain's insurance policy we need to close down the business as inoperable without him. The person coming down is our company lawyer to close out everything. With the death of those two women there's only Geoffrey to deal with. A brief separation package and disposing of the office and equipment and we're done. Easiest five million dollars I made in a long time.*"

"*Can you hold off on telling him those facts? I think he has more to impart to us?*" Raleigh asked.

"*Of course. I want these murders solved almost as much as you do. Will a $25,000 reward help you? Our citizen's group is happy to do it.*"

"*You mean you'll put up the money? Hold off on that. Rewards like that generate a lot of tips, most of which are useless, but we need to run each down, putting a strain on the department.*"

"*Your call. Let me know if there is anything else I can do.*"

"*You helped us a great deal, thanks*". Raleigh replied sincerely.

An officer rushed in as Knox began to walk out of the office.

"Raleigh, that guy just walked out of the station. Someone shot him when he exited through the garage and parking lot. He's dead with bullets in his body and face," the officer said heatedly.

"Son-of-a-bitch," Raleigh exclaimed.

"Guess he did have lifetime employment with Cain Podcast," Knox said amusingly to cover up his shock.

Forensic Secrets Saturday 12:07am

Since his last dog died, Leonard Patenaude saw no reason to go home. His father built the house to be a fortress against the world. While they lived, it kept the world out. Now the home held a gallery of memories.

Four children were raised within its walls. Two brothers died defending the country and his sister from cancer. Her family sent him Christmas and birthday cards and called only to determine if he still lived.

The terms of his mother's will said he could live there until he either left voluntarily or died. In either case, they were entitled to half the proceeds of its sale. With property values sky rocking in Skye Landing, they saw scads of money. Leonard paid the bills of the house's upkeep, long giving up hope they would share those costs. It mattered little to them but enormously to him.

On the advice of his attorney, he carefully kept all bills and wished he would be there when they found those costs deducted from their share of the proceeds. His will gave all his assets to the Police Benevolent Fund.

After training in forensic science at the University of Georgia, Leonard joined the Atlanta police department.

As his parents aged, he angled to come back to Skye Landing. Finally, the opportunity presented itself, and for 21 years, Leonard ran the Crime Research unit. It was now among the best small-town units in the country The reason was Leonard's devotion to the job. That was why he was still in the lab at midnight, staring at the bullet taken from Geoffrey Wallace's head.

Unlike the two taken from Henriette and Hilda, this was almost undamaged. The others were misshapen by the impact and travel through their brains. Because the killer was farther away from his target this time, the kinetic energy generated by firing the bullet was almost spent when it entered his forehead and brain. Still lethal enough to kill him, the shell had no energy left to exit the skull. Enmeshed in the brain's soft tissue, the bullet waited for Leonard's inspection.

Because the killing happened so close to the police station and knowing the importance of the case, he was on the scene just minutes after the event. With his compliance, Leonard's probe extracted the bullet before the medical examiner whisked the body away. The scientist had combed every database for five hours, trying to match this slug to another case. Leonard knew he had seen the bullet's twin somewhere before, thus the reason for the dogged search.

During the so-far fruitless search, Leonard kept others away. He enjoyed his work but not so much when there was such a hard nut to crack. Did he think he could crack the problem? Of course. They hadn't given him so many awards for being lazy or incompetent. He knew the solution would come.

For Leonard, the answer came as he drank his fourth cup of chicory coffee. Besides addiction to crossword, Leonard's major vice was chicory in all forms, and it was the chicory that gave him the clue. Years previously he was building the case against the woman who killed her husband and his secretary in the Red Roof Inn. While testing the gun, his chicory-infused coffee spilled on his almost completed report. This forced him to redo the report leaving out crucial data by mistake. He always remembered his vulnerability in cross-examination if the case had ever gone to trial. Thankfully for him, she pled out. Leonard mused, come to think about it; she was almost due to be freed soon.

He dug out the stained report and the ballistic photos accompanying it from his private files. Sure enough, there were the comparison photos. Bringing the image of today's killing, the match was unmistakable. The bullets came from the same gun. But that gun was supposedly locked in the evidence room along with thousands of other cartons. Knowing about the lost Couri case file, Leonard knew Amanda now had a bigger problem. His only question was who should he call and when.

Suddenly tired from his efforts, he decided to go home and call Amanda and Raleigh in the morning. He looked at the clock and realized it was morning already. Well, he'd call them later in the morning. Taking all the pertinent files with him, he went home to the house he had lived in the longest. As he expected, no one was there to greet him but ghosts.

Threats Multiply Saturday 9:05am

Faced with the new threat concerning the integrity of her department, Amanda moved swiftly. With Raleigh at her side, she tracked down the case box supposedly holding the gun Annie Crawford used to kill her husband and his secretary. Annie's father brought the 25 caliber Berretta home after being stationed in Thailand during the Vietnam War. In that conflict, all kinds of guns and other armaments were available. To meet the seller's expectations, one need only have the cash, preferably in Yankee dollars,

Before the trial, Raleigh's team tried to trace the gun's history, but it just started as far as they were concerned with Annie's father. Long dead himself, she had kept it as a memento of her father until the day she finally decided to do something about her philandering husband.

She claimed that she only intended to scare the two lovers at her elocution. She offered as proof the fact she was a dead shot. In the eyes of the law enforcement officials present, this lent more weight to the idea the real purpose of the confrontation was pre-meditated murder. To their consternation, the prosecutor believed her, as did the judge, hence the relatively light sentence imposed.

After Leonard's early morning phone call and while still in her bed, she called the prison to see if Annie was still there. Bemused by the request, prison officials nonetheless physically checked her cell. They determined she was still in the jail 76 miles away, thus eliminating her from any suspicion involving these new murders.

Understanding the effect of this new development, Amanda set about finding the gun and the murderer. She knew that if, as Leonard's research indicated, the weapon had been used in three more murders, the chances of Amanda surviving as police chief were slim, if not close to zero.

Meeting Raleigh at headquarters, they descended into the cage where cardboard cartons holding cases going to trial; those completed but awaiting appeal, and rare cases where criminals pled out but police were unsure the results would not be contested.

Consulting the master file, they made their way to the box's location high on the five-level shelving. When she saw the box looked clean against the others stored nearby, Amanda's heart sank. No dust appeared on the label section, and when they wrestled the box to the ground, it was empty save one brick designed to give it weight.

"What do we do now," Amanda said heavily.

"We solve the case. Get the gun back and act as if nothing happened. Leonard will keep his mouth shut. No one else needs to know until we find the guy.," was Raleigh's angry reply. It was not aimed at Amanda but at the person making them look like fools.

"What about the guy coming to find out about the Couri box?" was Amanda's next query.

"We tell him or her up front and ask him to keep secrets for a while."

"You think he'll agree? I think so probably will be someone I know. We'll cross that bridge when the time comes. Now, let's put this box up there and hope no one notices its clean appearance."

Not liking leaving the situation like Raleigh arranged it but having no better solution, Amanda went about her Saturday chores with little concern for them but for the sword hanging over her head. Raleigh read reports on other cases being handled by his department, something he'd neglected all week. Reading and acting on these matters did not distract him from thinking about the Podcast Murders.

When the phase popped in his head, he thought for a moment before deciding it was a good title for the case. He wasn't sure the podcasts were the reason for the murderer. Falling back on the old detectives' prerogative, Raleigh thought love or money generated or thwarted by the podcasts were the keys to these murders. The last three murders were committed strictly to protect the murderer's identity.

Threats Multiply Saturday 9:05am

When children were no longer possible for Raleigh or his wife, they resigned themselves to never hearing young people in the house. Although neither admitted to the other, it was something they both felt the loss, and it was an unspoken void in their home. Somehow, the house also seemed to fall into itself. One neighbor called it "the house of sadness."

Then out-of-the-blue Ellen's sister arrived in her big Cadillac with two suitcases, two cats, and one daughter. The cats didn't stay around long, and the vagabond lady never returned. Without further word, Ellen and Raleigh were responsible for raising an abandoned child.

Years of bedwetting, angry outbursts, and violent punching matches were followed by acceptance on the part of Caleigh. Using love and understanding, they finally succeeded in making Caleigh accept that she would never be abandoned again. Things went smoothly until her third year in high school, and a chance remark from one teacher to another about her abandonment led to two years of rebellion.

This ended when Raleigh went to Charlotte and found Caleigh naked in an upstairs bedroom of an off-campus fraternity.

No one talked about what he said or did that night, but Caleigh came home meekly and returned to her studies. After deciding she wanted to become a reporter not as an act of rebellion but out of a desire to learn skills to find her mother, she studied journalism at South Carolina University.

During summer internships and during her free time, she used every resource to find her mother. No one ever did, and Raleigh was convinced someone killed and buried her for the car and money she had. To her dying day, Ellen never spoke about her sister, just the luck of having Caleigh.

Both foster parents bit their lips when Beau came around and eventually married Caleigh. When he left her for Corinne, they both thought good riddance. By that time, they had two other little feet around the house. By mutual consent, they both decided trading Beau for their grandniece was the best bargain.

Sue Ellen learned to wrap Raleigh around her finger from an early age. She got him to promise her a Saturday outing once each month at one birthday party. As she grew older, these Saturday get-togethers morphed into luncheons with all four Butlers attending. With Ellen gone, the quartet became a trio augmented by Eleanor when her classes didn't interfere. In recent months, they were becoming increasingly more frequent.

Looking at the clock in his office, Raleigh realized it was near time to meet his two nieces. Without admitting it to anyone, he enjoyed these breaks from routine. Knowing his schedule would not permit more frequent lunches, he would not ask for more time with them.

Sadly, he reflected, Sue Ellen would be going to college, and Caleigh would be free to find another husband. There had been suitors almost from the moment Beau left. But Caleigh rejected any permanent relationship. Her fear was if her daughter got to depend on a new man, any breakup would be disastrous. She couldn't admit it to herself; she also feared not surviving abandonment herself after her mother and Beau.

Because the day was warm, they ate outside at the Parke on the Square. The food was adequate, but all three appreciated the better cuisine found in Eleanor's kitchen. The previous week, Sue Ellen had taken her first college entrance exams.

"*Uncle Raleigh they were so hard,*" Sue Ellen said.

"*Nothing important is set up to be easy,*" he replied.

"*You just say that because they only give you the hard cases,*" the youngster reposted.

"*I had to go through a lot of what you call easy cases to learn how to solve the hard ones.*"

"*But you always do.*"

"*Not all of them.*"

"What's your clearance rate?" the young girl asked him.

"Where did you get that term?" Raleigh said with surprise in his voice.

"From a book I'm reading."

"What book is that?"

"One on forensic science."

"Why are you reading that book?"

"Because this summer I want to go to a course on that in Athens, Georgia."

"What does that have to do with you?"

"Well, I can't be a policeman. Mother will kill me if I tried. Forensic scientists are really policemen without guns."

"But they do carry guns and need to pass all the same tests."

"But they don't get shot at," mother and daughter almost shouted in unison.

"In all my years on the force, I've seldom had to draw my gun."

"That's because you scare people into surrendering."

"Where did you hear that?"

"From my father, he says you scare everyone."

"I don't scare you?"

"No, because I know you're a teddy bear. But I know what you did to my father when he left mom."

Raleigh, taken aback by having the incident brought up by the one person he tried to hide it from, sought to cover his uncertainty. Caleigh rushed into the breach but only made it worse.

"Whatever are you talking about, Sue Ellen?"

"Well didn't Uncle Raleigh push Daddy down the stairs from his office and then kept whupping him for two or three blocks after he left you for Corrine Sukenik?"

"Catherine May repeated the story after hearing it from her mother. She has a crush on Uncle Raleigh."

"I'm old enough to be her grandfather."

"We both like older men," Sue Ellen teased.

Recovering his aplomb, Raleigh decided to punch his way out of this conversation.

"The man deserved it, leaving your mother with a six-month-old child. I would have done more but your Aunt Ellen stopped me."

"So you think he deserved it," Sue Ellen pressed on, wanting to know more than the two adults wanted to talk about.

"As your Aunt Ellen said at the time, it's up to your mother to decide. He's still your father and I think it's good you're seeing him."

"Oh, I'm not seeing him. He's called me and met me twice. I think he's going to run for mayor and he's worried what I would say if a reporter asked me."

"And what would you say?," her mother chimed in and asked.

"Just the facts as I know them. He left us and eventually married Corinne and has not been in my life."

"A politician's answer if I ever heard one," Raleigh said, laughing.

"Well, it's the truth." Sue Ellen said using an assertive tone.

"That it is. That it is," Raleigh said, still chuckling. *"He went into our attic the last time he was at the house. He said he wanted some pictures and things he left with you, mom."*

"The only thing he left me was you. Even took the ring he gave me as an engagement ring. Said it was his mother's. I let him but over the years, it was the only thing I ever wanted to keep that he gave me besides you," Caleigh said bitterly.

To cover the awkward silence, Sue Ellen jumped into another topic more important to her.

"Can you help get me into that course in Georgia Uncle Raleigh?"

"Yeah, I guess I'll know a few of the boys there. Write out the details and leave it on my desk. I'm going back to the office after this lunch. We have a tough case."

"Just remember Uncle Raleigh to always come back to us. We need you," Sue Ellen said, almost in tears.

"I will honey, I will."

The rest of the meal proceeded almost in total silence. All participants mulling the thoughts brought up on the warm spring day.

Why Him? Saturday, 2:45pm

Hunched over the computer screen, neither Carmichael nor Carter heard Raleigh's approach. For another uncounted time, they were reviewing Geoffrey's death. Nothing changed during each viewing. The victim exited the police lot and turned to his left. Stopped apparently by someone calling his name out of sight at the bottom of the screen, Geoffrey turned towards the caller and evidently knew him. Reversing himself, he moved towards the caller only to stop, apparently seeing that the other person held some weapon. Before he could do anything, the first shot caught him in the chest. Almost in the same breath, another bullet ripped through his face. Crumbling to the ground, Geoffrey gave one involuntary spasm and was still.

Cursing the camera's limitations, both men and now with Raleigh also sought to see any hint of the murderer.

"When they put up the cameras they thought any danger would come from the main arteries," Carmichael said to no one in particular.

"So, there are no cameras further down Howell?" Raleigh asked, *"No?"*

"No, one covers the back entrance to the police station but doesn't cover the alley all the way to the street."

"Where does Coolidge Street go?"

"Five houses down it empties into the baseball parking lot and the field itself."

"There's a link to Wilson Avenue that some people use to park their cars when shopping."

"So he walked through the lot and out to Wilson?" Raleigh asked.

"That's what we think he did. From there, he melted into the Saturday crowd.

"No cameras until the field, I suppose?"

138

"*The five home owners thought they were quite safe being next to headquarters,*" Carter replied.

"*As long as you didn't work for Cain Podcasts, you're safe,*" Carmichael chuckled.

"*So you think the murderer just walked down the street, into the parking lot, and then over to Wilson?*" Raleigh accepted their answer, relying on his men to have done an excellent job of figuring out the criminal's route.

"*We took all of the pictures from the CCTV on Wilson, but none caught anyone leaving from the parking lot that looked even mildly suspicious.*

"*But how did he know Geoffrey was going out the side entrance?*" Carmichael asked.

"*Took an educated guess and knew he could always catch up,*" Carter replied.

"*But Geoffrey knew him,*" Carmichael said.

"*Yes, that's our only clue.*"

"*That and the fact he's a good shot. That's kind of long range for someone only owning a .25 automatic. That's good shooting from 10 feet away.*"

"*Who told you the caliber?*"

"*Leonard, he said to look for a smaller gun.*"

"*He's right about the shooter,*" Carter said.

"*Let's not bandy that about for the moment,*" Raleigh said by way of warning.

Leaving the two detectives to continue their analysis, Raleigh went to his office, throwing himself into the chair with resignation. Reflecting on the sparse clues, he took out his personal case file to review their investigation. He had scarcely begun when Caleigh called him.

"*In today's conversations I forgot to tell you, that Patrolman's badge? It was Ned Barrow's idea and baby for a long time. Then old Mrs. Bancroft got on about no girls in the program and got it closed down.*"

"*Those nosy women get around. Charlie Stewart lost his job because of the druggist's wife.*"

"*He's not the only one. In less than two years, she's gotten other teachers fired and forced at least one councilman to resign.*"

"*Wonder if she's involved in this case.*"

"Well if she is, you're too late."

"Late, why?"

"She died Thursday falling down some steps in her home."

"You don't say?"

"I do say. Obituary just came in to the paper."

"Will you send it over?"

"Why?"

"No reason but I hate coincidences."

"Now Raleigh."

"Just send it over, please."

"Will do."

Not surprisingly, Raleigh's next call was to Jules, who called him back 30 minutes later.

"Funny you should call Raleigh," the medical examiner began.

"Because you think there's something wrong with Vera Stone's death?"

"Yeah, it looks accidental but I'm not sure."

"Why?"

"Two things bother me: a bruise on her neck and the body is too far off the steps."

"Then why did you okay the obit?"

"Obit doesn't mean it's an official cause of death. Just give you more time to investigate without people questioning everything."

"Smart as always, Jules. Thanks."

"Don't thank me Raleigh, you got to figure out what's going on in this town."

"I will Jules, I will."

Cameras Talk, Saturday, 4pm

Picking his way through the piles of reports generated by detectives, lab technicians, and the coroner, Raleigh chose the two lists compiled by Sawyer. Detailed to examine all the footage from cameras inside the station and surrounding the building, he sought to identify who came and went before Geoffrey.

Because the cashier for settling traffic tickets occupied the front window, there were more than 100 visitors on the previous days. Most came in, went to her window, transacted their business, and left. One of the payees was Charles Stewart, the now unemployed teacher, and theater director.

By Sawyer's count, 27 individuals went past that window and approached the duty Sergeant. All but three left without going deeper into the building. They were Knox, Geoffrey, and the reporter from the Eagle. Much to his surprise were two of the men who stopped at the front window, Beau Jenkins and Henrik Gunderson.

Raleigh picked up the phone and called Sawyer.

"Did you notice Beau Jenkins and Henrik Gunderson came by yesterday?"

"I did and meant to tell you. Gunderson asked for you and they said you were busy he wrote you a note. It's on your desk someplace. Beau asked for the chief and when they said she wasn't in he started to go back into the station till they told him you were here. He made an about face and left. If you notice all three of them were here while Geoffrey was with you."

"I didn't realize they were all around about that time. I'll try to find Gunderson's note. Look at the two sheets under your keyboard."

Raleigh found the note. It was short. "Come to my office, I have something personally for you not connected to the case," it read.

Wondering what Gunderson could have for him, he taped a stick-it note to his computer and promptly forgot about it.

Raleigh took up the second list comprised of what department personnel entered the building through the front door, just two, or the portal from the garage. According to these documents, fourteen officers or other personnel were on this paper as being in the building when Geoffrey was present, and none had left the building before he did. Raleigh breathed some relief, knowing no officer could be involved.

Raleigh went back to Sawyer and told him to take a break from tape watching to review all witness statements for anything he thought was not true or funny.

Interestingly, someone came through the back door using the code, but Sawyer could not match the code to any officer. Curious, Raleigh went out to Sawyer and asked him to pull up the video for the back door. When he identified who came in the back, Raleigh told him to track that person's movement in the building. Going back to his office to await Sawyer's efforts, he stopped by Carter's desk; he was still hunched over the screen but alone as Carmichael had gone home.

"Still looking?" Raleigh asked.

"I know there's something there that we're missing."

"Like what."

"I don't know but this guy could kill someone on the street, next to the police station, and not leave some trace."

"But he did and we need to find another way of tracing him."

"Like what?"

"Like go through Cain's papers again. With all that dirt, something might stand out."

"I'm learning more about people in this town than I ever want to know."

"Like for instance?"

"Did you know Mrs. Stone worked the bars in Atlanta as May Belle Holland until she married Mr. Druggist Stone?"

"No, I didn't know that. Adds to the puzzle, you know she died yesterday falling down some stairs."

"No, shit. Now that's a coincidence I'd look into. Do you think our murderer did it?"

"Why I stopped by. Jules thinks it wasn't an accident. So take a lab guy and go check the house and also see if there are any camera's in or around the Stone house."

"Do I think it's related to our case?

"Yes. How? I don't know, but we'll find out."

"Do you think her husband's involved?"

"What do Cain's files say about him?"

"He's doctoring his books and selling painkillers and other drugs to addicts without prescriptions," the younger detective said, seeking some sort of approval from Raleigh.

"Let Simon in Narcotics know about that and you better check on that teacher Stewart's movements yesterday."

"I don't think he had anything to do with her death."

"Neither do I but we need to cover the bases."

Usually, on Saturday afternoons, police stations are quiet, officers preparing for the nighttime rush of drunks, husbands and wives fighting, college kid pranks, and the violence of angry citizens caught up in emotions they often did not understand. These events were leavened with the drug induced tragedies that often led to death.

From his office, Raleigh observed his detectives were busy at their desk, eschewing homelife to find a dangerous killer as swiftly as possible.

Raleigh's stomach began to growl two hours later, but Carter and his technician hadn't returned. Today the building's lack of noise bothered him. Although he knew Saturday afternoons were usually quiet, the building was almost too silent. He knew if he waited some hours, things would be rather noisy.

Ask any policeman, and they report that Saturday nights generate landslide business for any precinct or headquarters. Raleigh knew the town was facing changing times and not for the better. It seemed each month the number of incidents rose so much that Daw had been forced to almost double the number of officers on the streets.

In recent months, he urged Amanda to ask the city council for five more patrolmen emphasizing the need in his final report. Raleigh was glad that was her problem but expected no detective-grade individual would replace him when he retired. That slot would go to patrol.

Promising warm leftovers as an inducement, Raleigh left Carter instructions to come to his house when he returned. He wondered what Caleigh's reaction would be to the gesture. He didn't care. She needed to start looking around for someone to replace Sue Ellen as her main focus outside of work. Her job was okay, but in an industry that was dying with little prospects for women like her, he thought she should be expanding her horizons. Maybe Carter was a good place to begin.

Questions Grow, Saturday, 8:30pm

While growing up in China, the only thing Eleanor sorely missed was line dancing. While in high school in Hong Kong, she tried to organize dances, but the sight of Asians trying to imitate their North American cousins in western clothes simply did not fit. When Eleanor returned to the states and married, her husband did not show enthusiasm for line dancing. After his death, she tried to find line dancing places around Skye Landing.

Not being successful, when one local bar was closed because of its unsavory patrons, she bought the license, found one reasonably honest partner, and turned it into The Texas Rodeo. Eleanor could be found there dancing to country hits every Friday and Saturday night. The venue was a "must play" spot for up-and-coming bands, approaching its tenth year. The bar's success contributed to Eleanor's plans for when Sue Ellen left for school.

But that was in the future. This night, she was at "The Rodeo," thus leaving it to Caleigh to put out Carter's meal while Raleigh read over his subordinate's notes concerning Mrs. Stone's death. They were sitting on stools in her kitchen, and Caleigh watched Carter wolf down his food.

Raleigh finished Carter's notes which strongly hinted at murder. The lab technician he had brought with him agreed. From where she started at the top of the stairs to where she landed, if she fell unaided was impossible. Put simply, she was too far from the bottommost rung without being flung by someone else from her home's second floor.

Another clue, she was obviously dressed for a visitor. This guest came while her husband was at work. If Jules' time-of-death estimate was accurate, the husband couldn't have killed her. No one doubted he loved her. Defying everyone's scorn, he brought the honky-tonk denizen to

Skye Landing. Almost from her first month, she set herself up as the town's arbiter of sexual misconduct. The druggist was ruled out as a suspect because witnesses saw him at his station almost every minute during the fatal day. It was left for the cleaning lady to find her when she arrived.

A macabre thought struck Raleigh when registering who found the body. One maid discovered Cain's body, and now this woman came upon Mrs. Stone. Someone might think cleaning rooms in Skye Landing wasn't easy these days and certainly didn't pay enough. If there was another victim, some other cleaning lady's poor luck, like these two women, would be to enter a room and find a body. Laughing, he ascribed the thought to the morbid humor most cops develop in the face of all the depravity they saw.

Then there was the victim herself. After reading Cain's file, they were loath to call her by her Skye Landing name, and every time either tried saying "Maybelle," both men laughed. After one or two chortles, they were forced to explain the source of their joke to Caleigh.

"You mean Mrs. Virtue used to dance in strip joints," Caleigh also starting to laugh.

"According to Cain's notes she did a lot more than that." Carter said between mouthfuls of Eleanor's cooking and with a bit of glee.

"You think that's how she met Homer?"

"Cain's team seemed to think so but couldn't prove it." Carter answered

"That wouldn't stop Cain from saying something on the air," Caleigh retorted.

"Unless he preferred to use her as a source," again Carter spoke through mouthfuls of food.

"Well, she knew where a lot of bodies were buried in this town and Atlanta," Raleigh chimed in.

"Who in this age names their baby Homer?"

"A classic professor whose only claim to fame was one book on Homer," Carter almost shouted.

"This from Cain's files?" Caleigh said.

"Yep, it is amazing what's in there. I don't know where he got it all from." Carter said.

"Ever think that's maybe how we go looking at this case?" Raleigh interjected.

"You mean track down his sources."

"I think there is just one main source who gave him access to other people Cain could shakedown for more information," Raleigh corrected.

"You think one person gave him all that's in the files?" Carter asked doubtfully.

"No, but Mrs. Stone knew where a lot of bodies were buried. And I think others gave up secrets to protect themselves. But it needed to start with someone so plugged in to this town to start the chain. What Cain didn't realize was that his original source was using Cain for his own purposes." Raleigh emphasized.

"Like my ex-husband?" Caleigh said, reacting to the conversation.

"Don't get me wrong honey when I say this but Beau wasn't up to thinking like the man we're after. Before you ask, yes I think it's a man. From the start, this case pointed to a very angry man and the more I go down the trail, the more convinced I am. But, much as I would love to get Beau out of this, I don't think it was Beau's style."

"Meaning?" she said somewhat defensively.

"Beau comes at you directly. He's an action person. This person is passive using others to do his bidding when it comes to payback." Raleigh said like a school teacher educating his class.

"Do you have anyone in mind, Raleigh," she asked quietly.

"I got a glimmer, but it's too early. Need a lot more evidence to even name him a suspect to you, Carter, or anyone else, let alone to nail this guy," he murmured almost again to himself. At this point, he laughed, realizing he had been muttering a great deal lately and not to good effect.

"You've said a lot but given us nothing, Raleigh. What do we do now?" Carter said.

"We go over the information we collected so far again and try to find additional clues," Raleigh said.

"Easier said than done," Carter replied.

"We can start with the material in Cain's file."

"I already went through those files." Carter wailed.

"Well you'll need to do it again tomorrow. There's something there we missed I know it."

"If you say so."

"I do. And now I'm going to bed, Good night."

Leaving the other two participants in the conversation somewhat taken about, Raleigh left them. They looked at each other to break the silence, and Caleigh asked him if he wanted coffee.

"Bourbon would be better," he replied.

"For that, we need to go into the parlor," Caleigh said, moving quickly out of the room.

He followed her, wondering where this conversation would take them. Moving swiftly to a cupboard, she took the Maker's Mark bottle down from its shelf and poured it into a glass marked NPA 2015.

"Where is this glass from?" Carter asked, raising it above his head to better read the seal.

"They gave Raleigh an award for his career at some police convention in Memphis. I think they used the award as a pretext to pick his brain," Caleigh said. Her glass was filled with scotch.

"Doesn't seem to be the only reason, you see awards all over this house."

"Yes, lately other departments have used Raleigh to look at some of their tougher cases. Word gets around. Cops are territorial, they don't mind if other cops help them but bristle if the media or the FBI gets involved."

"The feds are a pain-the-ass."

"They have their uses."

"Can't tell by me."

"By Raleigh, he uses them all the time. Just doesn't tell anyone."

"Now, that's interesting."

"There's a lot of interesting things you can learn from Raleigh if you open your mind," Caleigh said earnestly.

"Is this why we're having this conversation?"

"No, more like Raleigh sees something in you no one else does."

"Now that is interesting. I couldn't tell by the way he treats me,"

"How should he treat you?"

"Well, a good start with respect for my abilities."

"He's sending you out alone to Mrs. Stone and tomorrow to the files."

"Busy work."

"It's how he solves cases."

"Yeah, I heard about the candy wrapper."

"Don't let that one fool you. He always tells his fellow policemen it's the little things that trip up the criminals."

"Well, still wish he treated me different."

"Don't you know that's why you're here tonight?"

"Thought he wanted to see my notes?"

"He knew this afternoon Mrs. Stone was murdered. He just wanted to give you a chance to figure that out that as well."

"How did he know?"

"I can't tell you but on these things he's almost always right. For the moment this case has him baffled but I'll bet you he's figured out who is the murderer. He's waiting for you to figure it out as well."

"Why is he being especially nice to me?"

"If you think this is being nice you're in trouble. If you don't determine who is the killer before Raleigh needs to tell you then your days are numbered in this department."

"I didn't know I was on trial."

"You are and will be since you caught that guy from Washington."

"That was a good bust."

"Three questions the shoot team should have asked but glanced over. You going after him without any back-up? Initiating a shooting in a crowded civilian zone? You shooting while on the ground? Even I knew it was all wrong. What worries me is you still don't understand how bad it was."

"How do you know so much?"

"Because Raleigh got me to kill an editorial we were going to run about how bad the arrest was and a threat to civilians."

"Who was going to write this editorial?" Carter asked, already knowing the answer.

"Me, I've been around enough police stations to know better. Trouble is you didn't and still don't."

Gulping rather than sipping his drink, Carter reviewed what she said. Deciding he had enough to digest, Caleigh asked Carter what the Cain papers revealed about her. Feeling he had to strike back at her, he said almost nastily:

"You go out with married men."

"I thought that might be the case. I interviewed the president of a local software company. There was obvious chemistry and he asked me out. No ring or family pictures in his office so I said yes. We went on several dates and spent one weekend in Charleston. He gave me no hint he was married. He left town regularly, but he kept saying he needed to be away on business. I know I should have Googled him but I was a little blind. Three months into our relationship I came across a magazine article about him. As he was being extolled for his business acumen, the article mentioned his family was in Seattle. End of romance. His staff knew he was married and assumed I did as well. One and only time I messed up."

"Apparently Cain tried to blackmail your erstwhile friend. Seems he has an open marriage or bluffed him. Note says to check with wife."

"Hmm, I don't think she knows of his flings. But I'll call him on Monday to give him a heads up."

"Why?"

"Because any marriage is tough enough without some outsider butting in and I don't think our efforts to hide the dirt will work, somehow those files are going to get seen."

"Not if we can help it."

"You can't help it. Some people will talk."

"I'll still try."

"Good for you. For you, that's one step into learning. God knows how many secrets Raleigh carries."

"Speaking of which, will you tell me about Jenny Couri now?"

"Not yet. You still need to learn a little humility."

"Like you have a lot?"

"I've learned the hard way and hope my daughter won't need to go through what I went through."

"She seems like a good kid."

"Don't tell her but she is. I don't know how we did it but we managed to raise one heck of a child."

"When you say 'we' you mean Raleigh?"

"And Eleanor, and Ellen till she died and this whole town."

"Cain's papers say Raleigh killed his only child."

"They're lies. Everyone knows the story but won't repeat it. Whoever told Cain must really hate Raleigh."

"So what is the story? From the note in the file, Cain was going to hit Raleigh with it if he ever appeared on the show."

"Ellen had a difficult pregnancy and she was ordered to bed for the final month. Despite the bed rest, she was having pain, cramps, and other symptoms. So the doctors ordered her to come to the hospital. Raleigh took her but the trip further weakened her. For two days and two nights Raleigh stayed by her side. Something happened and they ordered Raleigh from the room. As he waited outside, things went from bad to worse and finally one of the doctors came out and asked him to choose, the baby or the mother? What choice would you make? Raleigh chose Ellen. When she awoke, she screamed at him, "You murderer!" Only argument I ever heard from them. She was in the hospital for almost a month. First few days Raleigh didn't come visit her. I don't know who convinced him to go to her. They both cried when he came into the room. Yes, he killed his child to save his wife. Everyone in town knows not to say anything about that part of his life."

"Wow. Were you there?

"I was still young but I do know that man loved that woman so much. Funny, there was a British drama on PBS about a couple and at one point she wants to have an operation so they can have children. He stops her because of the small chance of losing her. Raleigh faced the big chance of losing Ellen and he couldn't."

"What do you think would have happened if Cain hit him with that charge?"

"Raleigh would have beaten him to within an inch of his life."

"Raleigh seems a violent man."

"He can be when it comes to things he really cares about. Family! Children! Fairness! You watch him, he even treats criminals fairly. They all learn that. I've even known them to thank him after their sentencing."

"I didn't know that about him."

"There's a lot you don't know and maybe won't, but he wants you to be a good policeman."

"What do you want of me?"

"To stop looking at my crotch and wondering what color are my hairs underneath these jeans."

Brought up short by this change in the conversation, Carter realized he had been looking at the lower part of her body. It was then he remembered his vow to sleep with this woman.

"I can't help it."

"Well learn to help it. I'm at least 10 years older than you and a helluva lot more experienced."

"I doubt that."

"I know I am. Now go home. We've talked enough tonight.

"I'll dream about you."

"I won't dream about you."

"Someday you will."

"That I doubt."

"I don't."

"Good night"

Another Victim, Saturday, 11pm

The Reverend Bob was a grifter for almost his whole life. How he became a minister was being in the right place at the right time.

Fifteen years earlier, Robert Singelhoffer came to Skye Landing at the behest of Mary Hollander. At that time, she was known to her few parishioners as Sister Mary. Offering spiritual comfort in her storefront church on the last block of Skye Landing Boulevard in the downtown district, she made a bare living.

Mary supplemented her income by helping individuals hotly pursued by police to hide in her home while the manhunt was most urgent and intense. When seeking to replace herself and perhaps receive some retirement income, she turned to one of the few people she trusted. Knowing he was tired of the constant road travel his illegal activities required, she summoned Bob to offer him a chance to settle down.

"I won't sugar coat anything Bob, I have cancer. They say there's little chance for me."

"Sorry to hear that. Why call me?"

"Because I want to go home to die."

"Haven't you been able to save some money?"

"Yeah, some, but my last guest left with some of the funds I hid here."

"That's a tough break."

"Well, what else do you say about our lives?"

"True. But I don't have much money right now."

"I figured as much but I also know you're one of the few grifters I know who would honor any agreement we made."

"Nice of you to say but I don't see where there's that much you have to sell."

"I got this ministry."

"So, you think I can become a pastor?"

"I bet you'd make a great one."

"So, you'll sell me this ministry for a down payment and regular payments for how long?"

"Five years at a thousand a month."

"How much down?"

"I figure from your last scam you got $10,000 left."

"About right."

"Half to me now and the place is yours."

"And $60,000 over five years."

"Knowing you, you'll figure an angle to earn twice as much and have a home."

"This town looks dead."

"It is right now but things will change."

"Okay Mary. I want to stop traveling. Where will you go?"

"Great Notch, New Jersey."

"Where's that?"

"Somewhere in New Jersey, you don't need to know."

Bob stopped sending checks by the end of the first year. Mary was in no position to complain, being dead before that. Her brother cashed the last two checks.

Soon after taking over from Sister Mary, Bob's sermons attracted people to his storefront. As collections increased, plans took shape for a small church. When prosperity returned to Skye Landing, his church also flourished. Outgrowing the smaller venue, he bought the Baptist church building when that congregation organized its more extensive campus. All along, he made sure to maintain good relations with the other priest and ministers in town. When asked where he was ordained, he always managed to finesse the question. Finally, he found one California school willing to give him ordination papers in return for donating $1000. This satisfied them both.

Tonight, he was returning from dinner at the Gates. They were parishioners who supported his church with money, gardening, and Mrs. Gates providing the fuel for their heated sessions in his apartment behind the church.

Coming up to his apartment door, he made out the figure just out of the light. Turning towards the person, he wondered who could be waiting for him at this hour. Pastor Bob had no more time as the figure raised his arm and fired. Like the first two victims, the bullet entered his forehead and exited out the back, lodging in the door frame. Pastor Bob dropped immediately on the doorstep.

Hurrying down the street alongside the pathway, the killer left two good foot impressions. They would be there in the morning when early arriving parishioners spotted Reverend Bob's body. Unfortunately, in their haste to reach him, they obliterated the footprints. The first two policemen to arrive further covered the tracks. Only when Raleigh arrived did someone notice the remnants of the vital clue now lost forever.

Services Cancelled, Sunday, 11am

Squatting down to be closer to the body, Amanda knew she would not see anything more than Raleigh had. Reasoning television crews and reporters were watching her every move, she wanted to appear involved in the investigation. Straightening up, she looked at Raleigh and Carter.

"Any ideas?"

"Not a clue," Raleigh said honestly.

"We don't know where the Pastor fits into this puzzle. But from the fact the gunshot took him in the forehead, we can assume its connected to our other murders," Carter said, hoping he wasn't stepping on Raleigh's toes.

"He's right, their connections, we just don't know how." Raleigh came in after Carter agreed.

"What's your next move?" Amanda asked.

"Talk to whoever he saw last night," Raleigh answered.

"It was the Gates. They're over there, and they came early to do the altar and told one of our boys they saw the Pastor last night," Carter threw into the discussion.

"You go talk to them Carter. I doubt they know anything but ask them anyway," Raleigh said.

Drawing Raleigh aside, Amanda began talking in a low tone.

"Might not mean much but about a month ago, someone mentioned that the good pastor was monkeying around with some of his parishioners," she said.

"Male or female?" Raleigh asked.

"Female was suggested."

"Who told you, Amanda?"

"Now, that I can't say but it was a female member of his flock. I think she had had a fling and was supplanted." Amanda said reluctantly.

156

"You know, Cain may have been right, lot going on in this town we don't know about," Raleigh said with half-a-chuckle.

"Some of this stuff we don't want to know, Raleigh. Just thought you should know what I know."

"Thanks Amanda. I'll catch up with you this afternoon to bring you up to speed."

"I'll schedule a press conference for five; give you enough time to get something from Jules."

"Make sure he's at the press conference, he's going to need some help to stay in office."

"Will do," she said, retreating and running the gauntlet of reporters by promising a press conference at five.

Waiting until Jules arrived, Raleigh and Carter returned to headquarters after his confirmation of the time of death. Raleigh went to his office, and Carter looked at Cain's files. Daw came by his desk an hour later with the last of his office belongings. Stopping to say goodbye, he noticed the files.

"Cain's files?" he asked.

"Yes, seems everyone in town is in them," Carter answered.

"What do they say about me?" Daw asked almost too casually. Carter picked up the anxiety in his voice.

"You really want to know?"

"Not really but I'd like to hear what he thought."

"Says you have a mistress in Washington," Carter said reluctantly.

"Any details?"

"Just her first name, Miranda," Carter answered slowly.

"Well, at least he got one part right, her name."

"What do you mean?"

"She's my daughter. My wife has forbidden her to talk to me so we do it clandestinely."

"That's a relief to me. Hated knowing that mistress thing about you," Carter said.

"I still love my wife. No, now she's my ex-wife. I hope we can work it out but it becomes more and more difficult each time she does something to cut our ties."

"Like keeping your children from you?"

"Like keeping my children from me."

"Sorry, man."

"Appreciate it."

"You just proved one thing; these files aren't complete or accurate."

"Didn't think they would be."

"Wish I knew what to look for in them."

"Well, take it another way. Look for what isn't in them. Look for something or someone that should be there but isn't. That may be the lead you need."

"That's a good tip. Thanks Daw."

"No, thank Raleigh. He's the one who taught that one to me."

With that, Daw walked out, leaving Carter to ponder the advice and return to the files. He had a new direction and more respect for Raleigh. But first, curiosity got the better of him, and he searched for the file on Amanda. "Files" wasn't the right word for the index cards or sheets of paper divided by thin cardboard separators with names or titles indicating what was behind the wall.

It took him a few minutes to find Amanda's because she was lumped with another name, Hudson Combs. He was the previous township attorney, and according to the notes on two index cards, he and Amanda had one torrid affair.

But he was white, married, and about to run for state attorney general when his wife discovered the pair. Choosing his wife over Amanda, he moved across the state and was once again gearing up for the state-wide office. How Amanda felt was not recorded, and Carter tucked the information away for future use.

His lips moistened by the Amanda tidbit, he looked for Ned Barrow's file. After 15 minutes of fruitless searching, Carter realized Ned's file either never existed or was someplace else. Either way, he now had his teeth into something. What did Raleigh say by way of Daw? Look for what wasn't there.

Within minutes, Raleigh came by and told Carter to go home and get some sleep. He thought tomorrow would be an exciting day, and Carter thanked him, saying he had something to do. Both men walked out of the station together and parted at the garage.

This little tidbit made him feel more secure. Carter knew his hiring came about because Beau talked directly with Ned who greased his recruitment with Daw. The patrol chief in turned hired him without doing all the checks typically done when moving from one department to another. Daw followed the recommendation of Barrow. After gaining approval for the hire, Daw ensured Carter spoke with everyone in the department. Barrow's interview was brief, with the man seemingly intent on other matters. When he joined the detective bureau, Barrow ignored him, not giving him a welcoming handshake.

Carter didn't dislike Barrow, but like every man or woman in the detective squad, they were glad he was going over to patrol as rumored. They also pitied patrol for getting such a hands-off leader. Everyone in his department was wondering who would lead when Raleigh retired.

But the absence of a file on Ned or Barrow, whatever name you called him meant there was much to ponder. It was funny; he now used his last name. Similar to when officers use last names when hunting a suspect. Barrow wasn't one yet, but Carter's gut feeling made him queasy. He wondered if he should tell Raleigh what he found. He also asked himself whether he was going to Raleigh's house to see him or Caleigh. Either way, it was a good excuse, besides which there might be some leftovers from Eleanor's cooking. Not a bad dividend.

Press Conference Sunday, 5pm

After briefing the mayor and council leaders in their private chambers behind the city council room where the press conference was scheduled, Amanda joined Jules, so the two walked into the meeting together. Both expected the press conference to be filled with hostile questions and get worse than she thought. With each journalist jockeying for attention, the representative assembly of reporters from local TV stations was augmented by two video teams from Atlanta and one from Charlotte. There were also reporters from AP, naturally the hometown Eagle and finally, the Atlanta Constitution papers.

Seeing the mob, Jules almost backed out but decided any publicity was better than none. He weathered the questions thrown at him. Then it was Amanda's turn, and she did not fare as well.

"Is it a lunatic killing random people?" asked the local CBS man.

"No, we believe there is a pattern to these murders."

"And that pattern?"

"I'm afraid we can't divulge more about our investigation at this time."

"So, you're making some progress?" asked the NBC telecaster.

"We believe we are making some progress, yes."

"And that progress is?" asked the reporter from the Eagle sent by Caleigh to give some semblance of even handiness.

Claiming the paper's coverage was not hard enough on the police, Caleigh had been getting grief from headquarters about her coverage despite the scoops she was handing her reporters. Dark consequences were promised if the paper persisted in not being more aggressive in its columns about the incompetence of the police. This led her to assign the most virulent anti-police reporter on the paper to the press conference.

"We can't say more at this time. We believe the Reverend Bob was targeted because of his relationship with one of the other victims."

"You know this for a fact?" The AP man followed up.

"Not totally but our citizens can rest assured these killings are not random."

"Meaning they may be connected to the Jenny Couri murder," a blogger in the back of the room shouted.

"Jenny Couri was not murdered as our police investigation, two coroners, and I can testify," Amanda said with a touch of weariness.

"Henry Cain disagreed with you and died for trying to expose the truth," the Blogger persisted.

"Henry Cain was going to accuse three men all of whom have solid alibis for the time he died and were never suspected in either case," Amanda continued.

"Then why check their whereabouts when he died," the *ABC* reporter asked smugly.

"Because you the media forced us to. In this case it was asking the question: When did you stop beating your wife? The only thing linking these men to Jenny Couri was their names written on the paper wrapped around a positive pregnancy test found in her room."

"That was stored in your basement and somehow got to him." It was time for the Atlanta Constitution reporter to jump in.

"How that happened is still under investigation."

"Is this related to your current investigation?" CBS was back in the blood hunt.

"We are still looking for the individual."

"Didn't answer my question," the man persisted.

"Can't at this time."

"Can't or won't?"

With a grimace on her face, Amanda moved to adjourn the press conference.

"That will be all for today. You have your fact sheets and when we know more so will you."

Avoiding all efforts to see her, Amanda reviewed all the reports Raleigh sent her, signed the duty rosters for the next week authorizing the overtime and started for home. On her way, she thought a car was following her. Taking three or four extra turns, she became convinced. Using her phone, she called headquarters and ordered a patrol car to be waiting at her house. Three more turns and she set course for the condominium complex and the three stories home she shared with her mother.

When Amanda pulled into her driveway, the car following her slowed and parked near curb. The patrol car flashed lights and rolled behind the car. Only when its lights illuminated the second car's interior did she realize it was Raleigh.

"Just wanted to make sure you were safe," was all he said.

Amanda smiled and said thank you. The second patrolman got into Raleigh's car and he sped off. Only then did Amanda realize the patrol car would be there all night.

Amanda's Guest, Monday 10am

Amanda allowed herself to be late on the following Monday morning. Seeing the roly-poly figure of Hy Grossman, the crime reporter from the Charlotte Observer, sitting in the visitors' room made her wish she had stayed home. He was positioned to see anyone walking into the building before they could see him. Having seen her before she became aware of his presence, Amanda could not avoid the man. Deciding offense was better than defense she went up to him immediately.

"You're here early, Mr. Grossman," she started.

"Please call me Hy. I wanted to see you before going to talk with anyone else."

"About what?" Amanda played innocent.

"Can we talk in your office rather than the hallway?" he asked humbly.

Knowing this reporter was not a humble type person, Amanda assumed their conversation would not be easy. *"Let me check with my staff if there is anything that needs my attention,"* she replied.

In her office, she took up matters that could easily wait to keep the Charlotte reporter waiting until half past the next hour before having him brought to her office. Declining coffee or water, the man made himself comfortable in one of the chairs facing her.

"Outstanding press conference," the man said sardonically. *"I didn't see you there."*

"I came, stayed in the back. Wrote a great column for yesterday's Observer. Did you read it?"

"No, no one said we were in the Charlotte papers."

"Happenings in this town are too good a story to pass up."

Exasperated and defensive, Amanda took her time answering the man who now sat perched at the end of his seat. She was convinced he had more than suspicions fueling his questions. Warning bells told her to be very careful at this point. She decided on a new tack.

"Can we go off the record, Mr. Grossman?" She said in a conciliatory tone.

"Call me Hy but why should we? I'm here to get a story." He shot back.

"Because there are people involved here who could be hurt for no reason." She tried to keep her tone even.

"Seems to me only criminals will be hurt by me telling the public the true facts of this case."

"That would be true if the criminals haven't already been punished. Except one or two that apparently have crawled out from under the rocks," she said angrily.

"Whoa. Let's not get confrontational. I can go off the record but if I think your wrong about what's happened here in Skye Landing I'm going to write about it."

"So, you're one of the hyenas who think everything and everybody are fair game," Amanda felt herself losing control and her temper.

"Two failed marriages and more than one lost career gig says differently," Grossman's own bitterness began to punch through.

For some moments, the two antagonists stared at each other through their respective angers. Both began to see the other's challenge. Each had information necessary for the other. How do they create some bonds of trust? Finally, Grossman cracked.

"Suppose I told you some of what I know. Then perhaps you'll feel comfortable providing me with why I'm wrong or set me in another direction," he said to an angry Amanda.

"Well, you did investigate the three men Cain said were prime suspects," he began.

"In Cain's mind they were but never in Raleigh's or mine."
"Why?"

"Because there was no murder." Amanda said reflecting the weariness of repeating the denial.

"Someone said Raleigh told them there was."

"Who said that? Bring him or for that matter her here and let them tell me to my face."

"Now that sounds like a school yard taunt." Grossman pressed knowing he had gotten under Amanda's skin.

"Let me point out Mr. Reporter, Cain claimed one of the three men he named was the Couri girl's murderer. What's funny is he had the case file but not the interview logs. If he had them, he would have known Knox was in Atlanta, Henrik in Denmark and Charles in Ashville when she died. And remember, I said died not murdered."

In a fit of pique at this slovenly man before her, he had managed to get Amanda to reveal the hoarded evidence she was prepared to throw at Cain if he made the list known.

Rocked by her revelations, Grossman regrouped his thoughts. When he had entered the office, he was sure he would have her on the ropes by the end of the interview. Instead, he found himself doubting his sources.

Stammering, he asked her why she thought Cain was so off base. Expressing no solid opinion she laughingly said, *"Go ask your sources."* Admitting to himself that he would be doing just that when he left the building, he tried one more volley.

"Who do you think is the source of the leaks?"

"Right now I'm not sure. I will tell you this, whoever it is did not know the results of those interviews then and now."

"Someone was feeding Cain information."

"Yes, someone who wasn't here when Jenny died."

"Do you know who that might be?"

"I think I have a pretty good idea."

"Proving it is going to be the hard part."

"Not if he's as full of hubris as I think he is. He'll make a mistake."

"Who is he? I'll keep it confidential until you make an arrest. Can I have the story?"

"Why should I give it to you?"

Beau's Office, Monday, 11:05am

College and law school were not happy times for Beau Jenkins. From being one of the most eligible young men in Skye Landing to an ordinary student did nothing to feed his ego. He also found his money could have been better than many others in the school, residence halls, fraternity, and law triangle.

In Skye Landing, he was important because his father owned the local bank during the sleepy years after World War II. It was a period of prosperity followed by a slow decline as its two primary industries faced foreign competition. As the mills, clothing, and wood started to lose markets to foreign competitors, businesses that lived off their bounty withered and died.

Only agriculture survived but depended on the bank to tide them over when crops or prices were terrible. During this time, Beau's father still held mortgages from these farmers. He still sat in his second-floor office watching them bringing crops to the local cotton mills, granaries, or sidings. Folks in Skye Landing said his father could calculate how much each farmer could pay on their mortgages by judging the wagonloads. Since the bank was his, Beau's father could be a benevolent lender letting mortgages and loans slide from season to season until things improved.

Area farmers, minor timber operations, government offices, social services, and infrastructure maintainers meant the bank was slightly profitable. But the Kiwanis, Elks, and Amvets chapters closed along with the second movie theatre. Only the bank's continued presence gave some people hope the town could revive.

Town leaders knew if the area was to be saved, something radical needed to happen. Lars and Benjamin offered that hope when they proposed the community on Dane's Hill. Unfortunately for Beau, they came along too late to let his father leave Beau with the considerable fortune he thought he deserved. In subsidizing others, Beau's father hadn't built up his wealth. At one point, with the bank barely profitable year after year, Beau's father looked around for added capital. He got it from Provender, who, a decade earlier, bought a majority interest. When Lars and Benjamin brought their plans to him, both natives saw the advantages in the deal for Skye Landing. Provender was the beneficiary of the buyout with Beau's father getting enough to retire.

Most of the initial dealings were kept highly confidential. Once the son knew what was happening, Beau fought his father's decision to sell to the Danes. When he realized Provender was getting the lion's share of the monies, Beau turned his fury on him. Reserving some resentment for his father, Beau came to hate Provender and waited to deal out vengeance; striking out in all directions, Beau made dire predictions about the town and its leader that didn't pan out. He thought for sure he was doomed to leave Skye Landing forever. Understanding what the father had done for the town, Benjamin wisely gave Beau some law business and encouraged him to stay. Grudgingly, Beau stayed and decided to build his law practice.

Happily, Beau did not need to leave. Thanks to his association with Benjamin and by displaying his ability to be an excellent attorney, Beau thrived. His inability to leave women alone often got in the way of consistency. Sometimes, he dallied with his mistress of the moment rather than concentrate on his law practice. Once or twice, irate husbands brought their cases to other attorneys after finding out Beau visited their wives while they were not at home.

Because of his ability to make her happy in bed and not wanting to go through another divorce, Corinne put up with Beau's straying. While often banned to another bedroom, Beau knew he would return to the marital bed.

His relationship with Benjamin, his father-in-law, was more difficult. From the beginning, Beau's practice did well mainly because people remembered his father. Knowing new clients would come from people moving into town, he was always looking for ways of aggrandizing his appearance. Therefore, when Benjamin built his new corporate headquarters just outside of town, his corner office in the older building on Main Street became available. Beau swooped in and bought Benjamin's suite. Unstated was his feeling of not being wanted when he was not invited to join his father-in-law in his new building. Beau contented himself with the thought being in town was more likely to attract new business.

Benjamin put him on the boards of two companies associated with Skye Landing. What bothered Beau more was his rotation off these two company boards. In both cases, Beau had hoped to be named chairman, and Benjamin said it was to get new blood onto them. Beau said nothing hoping other board positions would become available. In subsequent years, he realized such appointments would not be in the offing. Fortunately for him, other opportunities opened up, and soon he was heavily involved in town businesses and some state-wide corporations.

Also, his marriage to Corinne did not quite work out as he thought. She proved her father's daughter when it came to money and investments. Although Benjamin was immensely wealthy, he had long planned for future generations. Beau knew that when he left Caleigh. Within two years, Corinne's inability to have children meant all of Benjamin's patrimony would go to his niece and nephew. Beau resigned himself to having to build his own fortune. In recent years, he invested in long-term opportunities and found himself short of capital at the beginning of the year. Right now, he was sleeping in the spare bedroom. Corrinne had been apprised of his infidelities by one of his mistresses. Beau knew this was temporary because Corinne craved his ability to make her happy in bed.

Early last year, several of his business friends thought it would help Beau if he were mayor. Letting the idea germinate for several months, he acceded to their wishes and built the campaign he now thought he was winning. Provender had been mayor longer than some constituents' lives, and Beau realized he had few enemies for one man in office that long. At the start of his efforts, Beau learned the only way he could win was by galvanizing the people on Dane Hill against Provender. He picked the only two issues they worried about: the schools and the police. Cain had taken care of one and intended to take care of the other.

All this Hy Grossman had picked up through pumping local sources, several well-spent evenings at Skye Landing bars and restaurants, and what Beau had said and implied in their meetings. As Amanda had guessed, Beau and his cohorts were the sources, and it was evident they also had feelers deep within the police, education, and, most important, town hall.

Content to use them as sources, Hy also realized they were using him and other media players in an orchestrated plan to bring down the current mayor. He also got the sense the old boy was also playing it cagey. Hy's paper circulated in Skye Landing but left local coverage to the Eagle and television stations. He wanted to know who killed Jenny Couri. As he entered Beau's offices, Hy thought it was time to sweat the lawyer a little, and Hy knew he was the newsman to do it. Entering through the glass door, he saw workers gathered around Beau's closed door. No one stopped him at the front desk, so he walked to where they were standing. Huddled around the door, they ignored him as they sought to open Beau's door.

"*There's something jamming the lock,*" the oldest woman, who was Beau's secretary, said.

'*What's jamming it?*" Beau's number two asked.

"*A key?*"

"*Even if Beau's not here, we need those Ellenville files for the depositions,*" the man said in an irritated tone.

"*What do I do?*" she wailed.

"*There's nothing for it. We need to break the door.*" He said in a tone of authority. He turned to the younger man behind him and motioned for him to act. Shrugging his shoulders and with great effort, he pushed the door open after one or two half-hearted tries.

Triumphant, the older man walked into the office only to stop in his steps. Sitting in his high-backed office chair, Beau was there, showing a look of surprise on a now-white face and a bullet hole in the middle of his forehead.

Everyone was immobilized by the sight of Beau's body except Hy. Shrugging off his feeling, Hy reached for his phone to call the office with his latest front-page scoop. He was laughing as he asked for the City Desk.

Survivor Reactions, Monday 2pm

Learning of Beau's death from Raleigh just after noon, Caleigh's first thoughts were of Sue Ellen.

She called the school's principal to keep Sue Ellen in the dark about the death until she arrived.

Organizing the newspaper's staff to get all angles of the story, she ran out of the building only to find a police cruiser waiting to take her to Sue Ellen's school.

While the car sped to its destination, she continued shouting orders over her mobile phone.

The driver cut the siren when they neared the school, and Caleigh leaped from the car almost before it stopped.

Her shoes glittering in the hallways, she and the principal found Sue Ellen in class, still unaware of the tragedy.

When Sue Ellen saw Caleigh at the store, she exclaimed: "Raleigh?" She blurted out, expressing her fear that the worst had befallen her great-uncle. Caleigh shook her head no but beckoned her daughter to come into the hallway.

"It's not Raleigh," Caleigh said.

Then who?" Sue Ellen asked.

"Your father," Caleigh replied.

"Did he have an accident?"

"No, worse, he's gone."

"How?"

"Someone shot him."

"One of the husbands whose wives he slept with?" Sue Ellen blurted out.

"No, we don't know who," Caleigh replied to the unexpected question trying to suppress a laugh.

"You always said an irate husband would kill my father."

Embarrassed by what her daughter was saying in front of the principal, Caleigh had no reply.

"Are you alright? Caleigh asked gently.

"Of course. He was my father but he was hardly around."

"You'll soon feel worse when it all sinks in."

"Oh, mother, I think you'll feel worse."

"I haven't had time to digest that he's gone. Poor Corinne."

"She's not poor and you and Eleanor always said she would chuck dad out after the kids were grown."

"Sue Ellen you been listening behind doors."

"No, my room is just over the kitchen. You'd be surprised what I've heard."

"No, I think not. But let's go home."

"No, I want to stay here. You need to go back to the paper. When I saw your face, I thought something had happened to Raleigh.

It's okay, and it's Raleigh I worry about. Not dad; he always finds a bed to sleep in, even if it isn't his own."

"Sue Ellen wherever did you here that."

"Everyone in school knows about my dad," she said. "

He's slept with several kids' mothers; I won't be surprised if Raleigh doesn't find the murderer amongst those wives and husbands."

"What kind of a daughter have I raised?"

"One who wants to get back to class?"

Unhappy with what had just transpired, Caleigh walked slowly back to the waiting police car. Sue Ellen's words echoed in her brain. Sitting in the back seat of the police cruiser, the fact that Beau was gone finally hit her. The sad part was that she was unsure whether she wanted to cry or laugh.

Added Suspects, Monday 5pm

That Beau was killed in his office surprised Raleigh who always thought it would happen in some wife's bedroom. The veteran detective, indeed his whole squad, knew how the lawyer and politician made love indiscriminately, from society matrons to college girls. The only thing keeping them from looking for an angry husband or discarded mistress was the neat hole the deceased presented in the middle of his forehead, because it was the hallmark of the killer they had been seeking since the prior week. That he was able to commit another crime before being caught stung them all.

"Beau didn't know how to keep it in his pants," Carmichael chortled to Sawyer as the men processed the scene.

"True but from the looks of this off, the killer was looking for something."

"I don't think he found it," the other detective said.

"Almost every drawer, cabinet, file box has been rifled. If he found what he wanted some of these areas would be untouched. If Beau was anything, he was neat and tidy."

"Good points. Let's not forget to put that in our reports."

"Raleigh will see that as well."

"Raleigh isn't going to be around forever, we need to make sure our next chief gets the benefit of what he taught us."

"Who do you think?"

"Don't know. Think it will be someone from out the department."

"Really?"

"Yes, you and I don't want it. That snot-nosed kid is too young and inexperienced.

Amanda will need to bring someone in from the outside."

"From Washington?"

"Why, not? The boys on patrol think Daw was great."

173

"*Not too many Daws around.*"

"*They'll find someone. As long as it's not Barrow becoming more involved.*"

"*Heaven forbid. Guy doesn't know his ass from his elbow.*"

"*He thinks he does.*"

"*So did Hitler.*"

With that, the men went back to cataloging the office. Raleigh and Carter were interviewing the office staff. They took the reporter's statement and gently but firmly ushered him off the premises. He went after covertly taking some photos of the death scene, all appearing in the next day's papers.

When the coroner and forensic team were gone, Raleigh sat in Beau's chair, ignoring the blood, and wondered what the man saw in the last moments of his life. That he knew the killer was immediately evident. On Sunday, Beau needed to let him in, past the alarm system, to gain entry to the second-floor offices. Two glasses were missing from his liquor case. So was a bottle, though no one in the office could remember which brand or type it was.

Beau's jacket was hung in the closet, and the papers on the desk pertained to Cain's company and house.

They were useless now as blood and brains were on most pages. Beau's safe was opened, and money was scattered about. The office staff said the safe held $77,000 Friday. A patrolman was dispatched to go to Raleigh's bank and get all receipts from Friday onward. The bank officials balked at giving him the information without a warrant. Raleigh got on the phone and yelled at the young bank officer, who meekly complied.

Just before closing up, Leonard Pentanaud called Raleigh to say the bullet found in Beau's office wall was from a .25 Berretta. Leonard could not, however, state conclusively that it came from the same revolver used in the previous murders, and he was conducting more tests.

With this news, Raleigh decided to end his day with some gin and tonic with his family. As an afterthought, he invited Carter, and the tyro detective accepted with alacrity. Detailing a guard for the night, the two men rode off quickly. When they arrived, one went to shower and the other to roam the house, speculating on Caleigh's Levi's. Only the latter was disappointed.

Threats Multiply Saturday 9:05am

When residents learned of the two weekend murders, fears rose even higher. Not knowing of the Reverend Bob's pasts and being all too familiar with Beau's, townspeople were total unsure if the two were connected.

After sleeping on the cases Monday night, Raleigh came to the opinion the police were dealing with two separate murderers. In her office, he told Amanda that two separate investigations should be conducted. He also bunched the Druggist's wife death with Beau's demise.

"Who do you suggest lead Beau's investigation? Amanda asked, sensing Raleigh had a plan.

"Carter," he replied laconically.

"Won't the other detectives be jealous?"

"Don't be misled. The more important case involves the other victims. They know which is more urgent to solve. They'll want to stay on the serial murders."

"Is Carter ready?"

"Of course not. He'll come to me for help and that way I can be on top of both investigations."

"As long as you square it with Sawyer and Carmichael."

"They'll be okay. These other murders are bitches. Frankly, I'm back to square one."

"What about Beau?"

"If we found him dead in bed, we all know it wouldn't be a surprise."

"What about the wife? Could she have done it?"

"In Atlanta with the kids. Solid alibi."

'Could she have hired somebody?"

"What for? She has the money. Everyone knew he catted around. I'm convinced she was going to divorce him when the kids went off to college."

"*They say she kept him around for the sex.*"

"*Many women do. Maybe Corinne did as well. But the motive for Beau's death revolves around whatever it was the killer wanted. It must be important because the killer didn't find it.*"

"*What makes you say that?*"

"*Because Sawyer and Carmichael say the killer didn't stop searching the office until every draw or cabinet had been examined. If he found what he wanted, he would have stopped, leaving some drawers unopened.*"

"*That's why you want them on your team?*"

"*Yes, we'll solve Beau's murder eventually. Right now, we have a serial killer at large and a town living in fear. I don't want to waste time on a side issue. After we get the first killer, we'll go after the second murderer. In the meantime, let Carter do the legwork. Who knows, like I've said, he's luck and just might find the killer on his own.*

"*Bring him in here and I'll tell him the news. I won't tell him any of the reasons for his good fortune.*"

"*No need, I'm sure he will think it is because he is so good.*"

"*He's your responsibility.*"

"*I'm okay with that.*"

"*You'd better be. Square it with the other detectives right away.*"

Carter's reaction was one of which they expected. He strutted into the detective's area positively gloating. Sawyer and Carmichael smirked behind his back. Called into Raleigh's office, they immediately understood why he chose Carter. Both quickly agreeing Beau's murderer was not the person they were seeking.

Working Beau's murder as he thought Raleigh would have, Carter surveyed the scene looking for something to tell him who had been in the office when the lawyer died. Finding nothing, he and his two new colleagues moved outward to the alarms, the video cameras, the sign-in sheets. Nothing gave him any hope of finding the killer.

At the funeral, Carter saw Beau's wife for the first time. The man could attract attractive women if Caleigh and Corinne were two examples. After observing her shepherding two teenagers away from the coffin, he understood why Beau gave up Caleigh. The second wife must have been something special in bed he decided. His conclusion, like most judgements in his life, was shaped by what happened in bed, his or someone else's.

Beau's murder put the town was once again in fear. Too much was happening that people could not comprehend. Jules determined he died the previous day around 6pm while apparently alone in his office. The myriad of prints and foreign DNA in his office prevented the lab scientist to even begin sorting out any visitor. Being a Sunday, the security system and video cameras were on but nothing could be gleaned from them. Supposedly able to track all visitors, Beau had disabled the back door unit in order not to record his many nefarious liaisons. Absent those sources, no one could find many clues to who killed the lawyer.

Carefully staying in the background, Amanda watched Carter as he went about the investigation. Vexing her was the manner of Beau's death. She checked and the remains of the gun in the other murders were still in Leonard's safe keeping. Adding to their perplexity was finding the bullet taken from the chair lining after exiting Beau's brains was the same caliber as those that killed Cain's employees.

This similarity, when leaked to the press, even though the striations didn't match gave the media fodder for many speculative stories. Wisely, Amanda kept her counsel and would not be drawn into any speculations about the case. Her silence didn't help her standing with the Council and only Provender's strong support kept them from ordering an investigation of the department's handling of all three cases.

Despite repeated hostile questions and having to admit they had few clues; Carter handled his first two press conferences well. He hinted police were focusing on Beau's legal cases for clues as to possible motive. After Benjamin called, Amanda told Carter to keep Beau's peccadilloes out of the news but not neglect them. Several husbands who had threatened Beau were quietly brought in but provided alibis. So were four women and his current paramour, the local real estate appraiser. Quietly, they checked Corinne's alibi confirming she was in Charlotte with the two kids which was why Beau was in his office working.

Beau's funeral on Thursday was attended by many people, some of whom were there to make sure he was dead. Corinne was inconsolable, comforted only by the fact his death was swift. News crews recorded the event and there were stories on all the nearby stations and in regional newspapers.

Corinne and Caleigh comforted each other but both were a little relieved that Beau did not die in another man's bed. Corinne's children were outwardly unmoved. Strangest of all, Sue Ellen displayed little emotion as her father's coffin was lowered into the earth. This worried Caleigh but she said nothing. At the reception afterwards, she avoided all contact with Carter, much to his anger.

Luncheon Conversation, Saturday Noon

Like three bums on a log, Sue Ellen, Caleigh, and Raleigh sat at their usual Saturday lunch table two days after Beau's funeral. Each were mired in their own thoughts. Sue Ellen was processing her first encounter with death in the family. Caleigh worried about the affect Beau's death would have on her daughter while also still unsure of her own feelings about the loss of her ex-husband. Raleigh was turning over in his mind the two cases and trying to determine how they were related.

Listlessly, Sue Ellen pecked at her salad, unsure how to ask Raleigh the nagging question she had about her father. Finally, when the silence became too oppressive she shot him a look of defiance and blurted out her question.

"Do you think some husband killed him because he was sleeping with his wife?

"No, honey, whoever killed your father had a much deeper motive."

"Like what?"

"If I know the answer to that, I'd have him in custody."

"So, you think it was a man?" Caleigh jumped in.

"Not for publication, but yes it was a man. Someone Beau trusted or thought he controlled."

Any ideas?" Caleigh pursued her questioning.

"No, but it's all related to the Cain homicide."

"In what way?" Sue Ellen joined the questioning.

"I have no idea. We have four men, three women gone and nothing that really suggests a motive for all seven."

"Three women?" Mother and daughter said in unison.

"Yes, Mrs. Stone figures into these cases somewhere."

"In what way?" Both asked together.

The Podcast Matrix Murders

"Now you're asking questions I have no answers to right now. So, let's eat and get out of here for a walk. I need to get back to the office."

With that injunction, the three finished their meals in silence. The walk afterwards was short and Raleigh hurried away. Mother and daughter were left to share a silent ride home. When the car stopped, Sue Ellen turned to Caleigh and in a grown-up voice questioned her mother.

"Are you sorry he's gone?" Sue Ellen cut to the chase. *"I honestly can't answer that question, honey. Your father lived his life his way. Not caring who he hurt or made miserable. Corinne reined him in some but the fact her father did not do more for him rankled with your father. I think he took it out on Corinne in many ways, including his infidelities."*

"But did you love him?" Sue Ellen asked.

"Till the day he died but the only good thing he ever did for me was keeping away from you."

"You asked him for that?"

"Yes. Beau corrupted everything he touched. I couldn't have him do that to you."

"Didn't I have any say in the matter?"

"No, because your father had a gift for making people think what he was doing for them was for their own good. Every time he did that to someone, they ended up hurt or betrayed. I couldn't let that happen to you. I've carried the hurt for all these years. I could not pass it on to you."

Hearing that last statement, the wall against tears broke for Sue Ellen. The howls of grief rolled out of her into the street beyond. Caleigh comforted her daughter as the youngster dealt with her loss.

Persistence Pays off, Saturday 5pm

Sawyer did not return to viewing the police department tapes until the following weekend. During the week, something in the tapes he did review bothered him. Despite gnawing on the idea throughout the week, nothing came to mind. After lunch, Sawyer sat down to begin crawling through the tapes slowly.

Before Raleigh could get into his office, Sawyer beckoned him back to his desk.

"Something has been bothering me all week. Been looking at these damn tapes for two hours. Finally, this is what I found when I reviewed the tapes. It was Chief Barrow, Raleigh. I didn't even know he had a code for that door. What's more there's something funny."

"How so?"

"Well, usually, he enters headquarters through the front door, so everyone will see him being saluted by the duty Sergeant. Yesterday, he came in through the back door, which I have never known him to use. Then it's what he does as he enters that you should see. When he enters, he props the door so it doesn't close."

"Let's see that," Raleigh said urgently.

He watched as Sawyer started the video. Ned clearly comes in the back door and bends to put something between the frame and the heavy barrier in the tape. Walking away from the most direct route to his office as the other video cameras inside the building record, Ken passes through the center hall and encounters Raleigh seemingly by accident. The video captured the two men talking, parting, and Ned going to his office. Minutes later, he is shown going down the hall and out the back door without his jacket. The two men saw that because the door was propped open, nothing registered departure.

"Strange behavior, don't you think Raleigh?"

"Yes, at least for Ned. But he didn't look or act strange when we were talking there."

"What'd he want to talk about?"

"Anything but the case it seemed."

"Wonder if he had other things on his mind."

"Ned, always has other things on his mind other than police business," Raleigh admitted almost to himself. He trusted Sawyer not to say anything to anyone else.

"What do you want me to do with this?"

"Keep it under wraps but put together a loop I can easily operate when I show it to Amanda."

"Will do," was all the detective said but he knew Raleigh had some thinking to do.

Returning to his office, Raleigh examined the roster lists and witness logs again and realized that Ned avoided having his presence recorded by his actions. As far as Raleigh could recall, he was the only one who spoke with Ned yesterday. If somehow he was gone and the department tapes disappeared, Ken's headquarters visit would be unrecorded. With the Couri file and the missing gun gone from inside the building, erasing tapes would not be difficult for the individual involved. Sawyer wondered why they weren't erased.

At dinner time, Amanda rushed into the police building, she saw Raleigh and motioned him into her office. There she closed the door to impart information on another media induced problem.

"The Charlotte papers are saying we have a suspect in custody for the murders," she started.

"News to me," Raleigh said truthfully.

"Where would they get the idea from?"

"Not from someone in this building," Raleigh replied softly.

"They wouldn't go with the story if it didn't come from someone inside this building, but who would do something like that?"

"Someone with a grudge against us."

"Against me more probably."

"Yes. That may be more of a motivating factor."

"But who?"

"What you need to do is get something out there denying it."
"No one would believe me."
"Have a news conference to discuss the case."
"When?"
"Tomorrow, at 2pm."
"Why, so specific."
"I have an idea on who we're chasing."
"Tell me now!"
"Not until I have all I need to convict. Trust me."
"Done. I hope you're on to something."
"I only need some more facts to wrap it up for you."
"I'll call our PR people."

Anger Continues, Sunday 2pm

A slew of angry reporters faced Amanda at the afternoon news conference. Looking directly at Hy who had written the Charlotte story, she started the meeting by denying any suspect was in custody. Advised by her PR people to confront the story directly, she let Hy ask the first question.

"We have it on good authority that a suspect is in custody in this very building," Hy started, worried his scoop might be getting away from him.

"If he or she is in custody, its news to me," Amanda said looking directly at the portly reporter. *"Since your story appeared I have personally questioned every officer in my department and all assure me they have not arrested or detained any suspect."*

"My source says differently."

"Bring that source to me here and now. We would love to have the suspect in custody but he or she is not. Are you prepared to name or bring your source here before all your colleagues?"

"You know we need to protect our sources," Hy said belligerently. *"And I say your source is wrong. We have leads and we are pursuing several channels but are not yet ready to name or arrest anyone."*

"My source is a high-ranking officer in your department."

"Who is he or she? Every person in my department has told me since yesterday they have not spoken to you or anyone else."

"They lied to you."

"Prove it. We are moving slowly and methodically towards solving these crimes."

"So, you know who has been committing these murders," Hy said hoping to salvage something out of the debacle of his discredited story.

"That's not what I said. We have leads. We have witnesses. We have forensic evidence. The important thing for you people of the media should report is that as of this moment we have no suspect in our custody."

While reporters shouted more questions, Amanda left the room trailed by Jules. At the back, Raleigh slipped out before the media realized he was there. Circling the Council chambers, he caught up with Amanda.

"Rough on you," he started.

"No rougher than the Washington press corps. They all hope to make it to a bigger market so the more aggressive they are the higher likelihood they'll be noticed by some news director at a bigger station or the network."

"So you're sympathizing with them?"

"To a certain degree yes, they needed to do their jobs."

"And we need to do ours. Did you really ask all of us?"

A few I ignored, like you. I couldn't reach Ned."

"No one ever reaches Ned," Raleigh mused darkly. *Then he added,*

"Come over to my house for dinner, it might cheer you up."

"I really don't feel like it."

"I figure but this is more a working dinner. I think Carter has something you ought to know about and so do I, especially after what that fat reporter said."

"In that case I will."

"Bring your armor vest and that fancy gun of yours."

"Why?"

"You'll see."

Threats Multiply, Sunday 6:30PM

When Amanda arrived late at 6:30, three more cars were in front of Raleigh's house. One belonged to Carmichael, another to Sawyer, and she was betting the last vehicle was Carter's. She left the armor in the car but holstered the Glock special given to her when she left Washington by her staff.

Carmichael and Sawyer exited as she entered the house, passing her to their cars. They greeted the chief but did not slow their progress. Amanda noted they wore armor, and both showed guns bulging from under their vests. She also saw they were not wearing suit jackets but windbreakers. When dressed like that, officers knew they were going someplace where there was police action about to happen.

She depended on Raleigh to tell her what was going on.

With the door partially opened, she entered without knocking. Proceeding into the house, she heard voices in the kitchen, and Eleanor was spooning out an entrée to Sue Ellen, Caleigh, Carter, and Raleigh. Their bantering stopped when she entered. Except for Raleigh, they all smiled at her. Eleanor indicated the seat reserved for her at the end of the table. Eleanor called it her chef's table on her podcasts, but it was the communal eating table for the family.

Drawing two small platters from the nearby dish cabinet, Eleanor put Amanda's plate in front of her, ladled the chicken dish, and picked up another pan to spoon creamed vegetables on the other side. Leaving others to talk, Eleanor started washing some dishes, seemingly unaware of the other people in the room.

Assuming Raleigh and Carter were waiting to talk to her alone, Amanda joined in the light banter from Sue Ellen and Caleigh. She noted neither Raleigh nor Carter said much. Within minutes, the food was consumed, with Amanda not tasting the chicken dish which she was sure was superb. Seemingly on some unspoken cue, Caleigh got up and signaled her daughter to follow her. Eleanor stopped washing the dishes and joined the other two women as they started to leave the room. Before reaching the door, Sue Ellen turned and rushed to hug Raleigh.

"I don't know what's going on but promise me you're coming back Uncle Raleigh."

"You know I always do, Sue Ellen."

"But tonight somehow feels different."

"Nothing's different, Hon. We're just going to talk."

"No, you're not. You're going out to do something."

"Not tonight?"

"Promise. And I'll be here tomorrow. Like always."

"Promise me that Uncle Raleigh."

"I promise."

With that, the teenager followed her mother up the stairs. Eleanor lingered to say she would do the dishes in the morning. To Amanda, it was an interesting admission, breaking Eleanor's lifetime of adherence to the rule of never going to bed before all the chores were done.

When the women had gone, Carter and Raleigh moved closer to Amanda. Raleigh was the first to speak.

"We've been looking at these murders the wrong way around, Amanda," he began.

"Meaning?"

"We've assumed from the start that Cain was the reason the murders started," he said slowly.

"Seems logical given his was the first murder."

"That's just it; I don't think Cain's death came first."

"We all know who killed Jenny Couri and they're not around anymore."

"No, this doesn't go back to the Couri girl. I think it's a more recent death."

"We haven't had a murder since that boy sliced up his girlfriend three months ago."

"Agreed but I think we haven't found the body or bodies that triggered our killer."

"*My god, you think there are other deaths we don't know about?*"

"*Afraid so.*"

"*Why do you think so?*"

"*The Reverend Bob.*"

"*According to Carter, Sawyer, and Carmichael, the Good Reverend liked to sleep with his parishioners.*"

"*I told you that in confidence.*"

"*I assure you, I never breathed a word. But all three detectives heard about Pastor Bob while talking to witnesses after the pastor's murder.*"

"*The tales I heard,*" Carter jumped in and said with some glee. "*Parishioners knew he couldn't keep it in his pants. They forgave him because they loved his preaching and outreach.*"

"*Sawyer and Carmichael also heard the same,*" Raleigh said, putting any doubts from Amanda's mind. Not that she needed much.

"*So, you think some jealous husband killed the Pastor?* Amanda asked.

"*Yes we do but not because they felt cuckolded,*" said Raleigh.

"*No, there is a lot more to this than some wife was straying and her husband being angry,*" Carter said.

"*Why do you think that?*" Amanda probed.

"*Because of the anger in the way Cain was killed. The killer had strong reasons for hating Cain at that moment. But the resentment he felt then resulted from feeling many people had conspired to hurt him,*" chimed in Raleigh.

"*What reason do you think he felt hurt?*" Amanda asked.

"*Betrayal,*" both men said almost in unison.

"*In the case of Cain, both men were gay. Cain went to Hollywood where being gay could actually help his career. The other partner remained here in Skye Landing but was forced to hide or even deny his homosexuality for some reason,*" Raleigh said ponderously.

"*Not in this day and age,*" Amanda rejoined.

"*There are still professions where being gay holds people back,*" Raleigh said.

"*So you think this somehow involves homosexuals?*" Amanda acted inquisitor, knowing the men were laying out the case for one suspect.

"*Yes. I think Cain came back to Skye Landing for one reason, to resume a relationship that ended badly for him and then to betray his lover like the other man betrayed him,*" Raleigh said.

"*How was Cain going to betray his lover?*" she asked.

"*First, let's go back. Someone had to give Cain the information he had on many town leaders, including you. That person had to be well respected and high in the government of this city,*" Carter jumped in.

"*So, this person gave Cain ammunition to blackmail people?*" Amanda asked.

"*No, he gave Cain some dirt and the podcaster used that to get more dirt. It's like the Sorcerer's apprentice, once spells he stole were invoked, the apprentice couldn't control the outcome. Once Cain had enough dirt he didn't need his lover.*" Raleigh said.

"*But the lover didn't realize what was happening until Tuesday?*" Carter argued.

"*What happened Tuesday?*"

"*Cain told his lover he was leaving town for New York thanks to Knox and his new contract.*"

"*And he was leaving alone,*" Amanda followed along.

"*Yes, Cain was doing to his lover what his lover had done to him years ago,* added Carter.

"When he was in high school," Raleigh almost yelled

"*That stupid badge gave you the clue,*" Amanda said, anticipating the realization of what was coming.

"*Yes, that stupid badge makes me wonder,*" Raleigh said.

"*Once you get a bone, Raleigh, killers need to worry.*"

"*Well there's more. I'll let Carter fill in that part.*"

"*Raleigh asked me to look at what passed for Cain's notes. I didn't see anything until Daw said to look at what wasn't there.*"

"*And what wasn't there?*" Amanda asked, suspecting the answer.

"*Almost everyone rich, or powerful, or susceptible in this town was there except one person.*"

"*Let me guess, Ned Barrow?*" Amanda grew impatient with the discourse.

"*Bullseye,*" Raleigh said.

190

Carter went on quickly. *"I also checked the logs in the records section and you can guess what I found. Four months ago, Ned signed the log and again three weeks ago. He hadn't been down there for five years prior to his first foray."* Carter reported.

"But that's not all. This afternoon, when we compared notes, neither Sawyer, nor Carmichael, nor I had spoken with Ned's wife." He went on.

"She wasn't there?"

"No, but people said she and her son always came early to talk with Pastor Bob and she always sat in the front row."

"She's supposed to be seeing her mother in Fayetteville," Amanda said.

"That was the thing that bothered me. Until I had Caleigh check the paper's obits. The mother died five years ago," Raleigh said as he put a period to their briefing.

"And you've sent Sawyer and Carmichael to sit on him until we arrive?" Amanda said.

"Yes, but we're going to wait until dawn. He'd have all the advantages if we went at night."

"Good thinking but we could call the state police to give us a SWAT team." Amanda suggested.

"We could but then they would have control of the situation and we need to get that gun he used back with as little public identification as possible," Raleigh said by way of explanation.

"And you think the wife is dead?" Amanda asked more for clarity and knowing the answer beforehand.

"And the son too," Carter said almost too eagerly.

"Why?"

"Because church gossip claimed that the boy wasn't Ned's."

"You believe that?" Amanda asked.

"I don't want to think he's dead because he's only eight years old but seems logical," Raleigh said angrily.

"So to sum up, you think Cain's betrayal triggered Ned into murdering people who betrayed him?" Amanda asked.

"If I were prosecuting this case that would be the theory I'd work on for the jury."

"*But we don't know who died first, Cain, his wife, or even someone else,*" Carter jumped in again.

"*I think the son died first, then the wife. He wanted her to know what he did,*" Raleigh said soberly.

"*Why didn't he shoot Cain?*"

"*Now, that I have no answer for you. I think he brought something they both thought was important and used it to kill Cain. Or he just wanted it to be very personal. I don't know,*" Raleigh said.

"*What about the three people in Cain's office?*" Amanda asked again for clarity.

"*Cain's employees were killed because they had seen him with Cain at some point.*" Carter jumped in again.

"*What about the druggist's wife and Beau?*"

"*Her I have no reason on Earth but Ned will have one. As for Beau, who knows? He could get under anyone's skin. Maybe it angered Ned that Beau did not support him when we chose Daw? Maybe he thought Beau knew something. I don't have all the answers, Amanda,*" Raleigh said in frustration.

"*Ned must have been around Cain's office at some point.*"

"*We would not have thought much about it.*" Amanda said.

"*We would have if Geoffrey had said something when we had him at headquarters. But remember Ned saw Geoffrey talking to me. Either he was afraid or was thinking a little blackmail. Either way he was doomed.*"

"*And I was going to make him Chief of Patrol.*" Amanda said.

"*I'm sure he thinks you should have made that decision eight years ago,*" Raleigh said gently.

"*Didn't think he was right for the job,*" she mused quietly. "*I still don't. Best thing I could do was forget what we owed him and I should've have pensioned him off.*"

"*Then we would be dealing with his suicide. Being Chief was his reason for living. Take that away and he had nothing.*"

"*Right now he has nothing and at least six people are dead.*"

"*We don't know if you weren't on his list. That's why I had you come here.*" Raleigh said.

"*Always thinking Raleigh,*" Amanda said.

"Didn't think fast enough Amanda. I believe we will have at least six dead and maybe more before this is over. Don't forget what a crack shooter Ned is? There are few people who could have killed as he did. I'm sure if we discover more bodies they will again demonstrate that ability as well."

"Then it's agreed, we wait till sun up before tackling him."

"Yes, but I'm going to call the Capitol and get a SWAT team up there. In case we can't take Ned ourselves."

"We'll need surprise on our side. If he knows we're coming, it could get dicey and others may die," Raleigh said soberly, looking at his coffee cup.

"Let's hope not. So if we're here for the next few hours how about we wash Eleanor's dishes for her?"

"You can but the last time I tried to do something like that she threw me out of her kitchen," Raleigh said laughingly. *"But Carter will dry so he gets used to it. I think he's going to be around a lot in the future, the way he ogles my niece."*

Night Hours, Monday, 5:30am

Ask any police officer, and they will name domestic violence incidents as the part of law enforcement fraught with the most danger. With emotions high, usually irrational in their focus, when police officers enter homes, apartments, or trailers, they are unsure of what to expect but continually fear the worse. When he was younger, Raleigh learned techniques to defuse most domestic situations. For him, most police incidents boiled down to reason and calmness. He hoped to persuade Ned to surrender peacefully. There were many lives at stake here, and his hope was Ned would listen to him.

Through the hours after Amanda's briefing, Raleigh was restless. Several times he had participated in actions involving armed felons.

In all of them, reason and conversation defused the situation. This time, Raleigh felt certain no matter their approach, it would end in gunfire.

Usually, he could sleep the night soundly before any police action. Giving Amanda the sofa in his living room, he had chosen the most comfortable ottoman, leaving Carter with the stiff-backed visitor's chair.

The young detective appeared to have gone off like a lighted candle blown out by the wind. Just for tomorrow's event, Raleigh wished he was Carter's age. Knowing he wasn't and suspecting Ned would be fully armed when he confronted them frightened Raleigh. The scared police officer was not afraid of his own death but of the possible killing of those around him. Despite what many think, especially Carter, shooting someone is not as easy as squeezing the trigger when it was only paper targets in front of you.

Raleigh knew that mental restraints weren't there in many cases involving insane killers or kids who go to schools or churches to make them scenes of mass murder. For most police officers, their training and sense of justice often prevented many from acting fast enough to save their lives.

Raleigh knew later in the morning his companions and himself needed to act quickly. Ned had not let his victims do anything but stare blindly at the instrument of their death. Raleigh hoped his people were able to react better.

Before Sunrise, Monday, 5:35am

Veteran soldiers warn others the night before any action often weighs more heavily on the nerves than the actual combat. Once under fire, some adrenaline will kick in, erasing all sense of self except that focused on staying alive. For Carter, the night past too slowly as he watched the clock over the mantle tick off the hours. At his belt, he carried the department-issued Glock. In the shoulder holster was the Magnum purchased when he joined the Atlanta force. In his car was the department's pump action shotgun. None gave him much comfort because he kept thinking of all the things that could go wrong in the morning.

Carter noted Raleigh still carried the revolver given to him when he joined the Skye Landing police force. He hoped Raleigh was bringing more firepower.

Throughout the night, Carter's thoughts skipped from Ned Barrow to Caleigh to Raleigh's view of him. He doubted Amanda had changed her feelings towards him but noted she listened to his contributions to her briefing.

While doing the dishes, Amanda said not one word to her detective but did wish him a good sleep. *"Well, something is better than nothing,"* he thought.

Periodically his thoughts strayed to Caleigh asleep or pretending to sleep in her room. If her daughter's room wasn't between the stairs and her door and he was sure it was unlocked, he might have tried sneaking up to her.

"The worse she could do is slap me or I might get lucky." He thought.

Almost immediately, his mind returned to what would happen later in the day.

"*Better leave that business for another day*," he finally concluded. Still thinking about those tight jeans made him squirm.

While pretending to sleep on the sofa on the other side of the room, Amanda watched Carter toss and turn. She had caught the looks he gave Caleigh, whom Amanda knew. No doubt Caleigh also saw those looks. What the woman was going to do about them was her decision.

Amanda was sure her concern right now was Raleigh. When this was over, Caleigh would make her decision. Carter did not know it, but Caleigh was in the driver's seat regarding this romance. Talk about a cougar; Amanda knew Carter had caught one by the tail. Whether he could hold on long enough to get her into bed was his problem.

Amanda was being forced to make decisions about him as well. Her problem was deciding what to do with him. Recognizing what Raleigh did, Carter was one of those detectives blessed with acumen and luck, and he would go far. Her dilemma was if she wanted him in her department? She was gradually coming around to keeping him, albeit under whatever leash Raleigh could put around him.

Let's see how he handles today's events, she finally decided. She resolved not to tell Carter how important it was that he follows the rules in today's actions. Whatever he did would affect his career in the Skye Landing police force. He would need to decide for himself what that role would be.

With that thought, Amanda suddenly silently laughed at herself. Who was she kidding? Today's action would affect everyone in town and especially her. If nothing else, recovering that stolen gun had to be high on the list of things that needed to happen this morning. Squaring her activities with the Mayor and Council also needed to be done. The worst thing was the mess Cain stirred up over the Couri girl. Somehow, that Genie needed to be put back in the jar. For Jules's sake, if no one else, this had to be done. But in the end, she realized, even if successful her job might still be in jeopardy.

But first, Amanda heard Raleigh stirring and knew Carter was awake. In search of coffee, she padded into the kitchen and found Eleanor already busy with coffee and some buttered rolls. It was then she realized it was the smell of coffee that woke her.

"*I thought you could use some fortification. Some brandy in that decanter as well as scotch under the shelf in front of you. There's coffee in those thermos except didn't know how you like yours,*" Eleanor said too brightly.

"*Black with one sugar,*" was the grateful reply.

"*The others will be up in a minute. Use the bathroom there,*" Eleanor said, pointing to a door opposite where Amanda had entered.

Gratefully, the police chief headed to the immaculate half-bath she had not known existed. Then, realizing what Eleanor did in this kitchen wondered what the woman thought about the invasion last night and this morning. Pondering Eleanor's role in the Butler household for a moment, she left that speculation for another time, grateful for the coffee and proffered alcohol. After relieving herself, adding some makeup in the mirror, and washing her face and hands, she reappeared. Sitting comfortably in stools were Raleigh and Carter. A plate loaded with rolls, jelly, and smears of butter were next to another vacant stool. So as not to wake the rest of the house, they talked in hushed tones as Eleanor puttered nearby.

"*Are we ready?,*" she asked.

"*As we'll ever be. I have the shotgun, extra rounds and a spotlight in your car,*" Raleigh said.

"*One or two cars?*" Carter asked.

"*Two, we may need the spotlights and headlights,*" Amanda said.

"*Are the state guys coming?*"

"*Yes, they're an hour behind us.*"

"*Why not wait for them?*" Carter asked.

"*Because of that gun from our records room and god knows what else we'll find. Gives us a better chance of controlling the information after this is all over,*" Raleigh said before Amanda could answer.

"*So just the five of us?*" Carter mused. Actually pleased he was included.

"*Should be enough if he doesn't know we're coming,*" Amanda said.

"*And if he does know we're coming?*" Carter asked, not wanting to know the answer.

"*Still be enough,*" Raleigh answered laconically.

At that, Amanda smiled and looked at the two men.

"Nice to know you think that's enough," she said.

"Has to be," Raleigh answered. *"Ned's set it up so we need to get to him first."*

"Okay, let's stop talking about it and get going," Amanda ordered.

Eleanor handed them a hamper of coffee and food as they left and wished them good luck. Staying in the kitchen until hearing the crunch of cars going, she waited for Caleigh to appear. Not having slept through the night, Caleigh's first stop was Raleigh's office. There, as expected, was a file for her, and it contained detailed notes on the case. Caleigh took Eleanor's coffee and read almost before sitting down. Thoughtful as she read, Caleigh rose within minutes and started for the front door.

"Will you take care of Sue Ellen," she whispered over her shoulder.

"Yes, I think Raleigh has given you the scoop of your career."

"He has, but at what cost."

"He knew what he was doing."

"Yes, but why do it now?"

"Maybe he knows something we don't."

"Well, I can't look at this gift horse in the mouth."

"Go to it honey."

"Wish me luck."

"You've got all you need."

Second Thoughts, Monday, 7:00am

Daylight was still a half-hour away as Raleigh and Amanda drove to Ned Barrow's house. Raleigh watched Carter's even spacing behind him. Grunting to himself, he threw sideward glances at Amanda. She sat there, not speaking, ruminating on God knows what. He admired her, thought she was one heck-of-a-police chief and was glad he didn't have the job. To break the silence, he asked in a neutral tone about her mother.

"Still cranky I'm not married."

"Still worrying at your age?"

"Every mother worries."

"You worry about your boy?"

"Every day I wonder where's he at? What's he doing?" Is he safe?"

"No word?"

"My ex says he's fine but gives no details. He's still mad at me for succeeding here."

"Thought he had a great job in Washington?"

"He did, till he got passed over by Daw."

"I didn't know that."

"Neither did I. Friend told me last week but we've been so busy with this case didn't make the connection. Funny, Daw never mentioned it."

"Probably, did not know what to say."

"That's probably the reason. What do we do about Carter?" She said to change the subject.

"Figure him as a good detective who'll be better over time," was Raleigh's quick answer.

"He's a hot-shot."

"Who's smart and, more importantly, lucky. Make a good head of detectives someday."

"*That day is in the distant dim future, Raleigh.*"

"*No, he's the kind that learns quickly on the job. Give him his head quickly Amanda and you'll have one Cracker Jack department,*" Carter said almost too quickly.

"*You're not going anyplace Raleigh,*" she said almost too quickly.

"*These old bones are getting tired Amanda.*"

"*What would you do retired Raleigh?*"

"*Consult. They're dangling big money in front of me to join some groups that look at cold cases and turn them into television shows and podcasts.*"

"*Seeing you on a podcast would almost be worth losing you. But I can't lose you now, Raleigh, not till all this dies down.*"

"*Till all this dies down,*" Raleigh answered.

As they turned into Ned's street, they noted Sawyer's car parked by the side of the road. Raleigh was pleased they went to the stakeout position in one car. Smart move, he thought. Amanda and Raleigh had been to Ned's house for celebrations, cookouts, and other occasions. It sat at the end of the four-block dead-end road. Ned bought the house 15 years previously when he married Victoria.

At the time, the subdivision was new, and Ned convinced the developers to sell him the two lots adjoining his home. So, in consequence, his house sat between two uncleared half-acres with abundant trees. Like everything in Ned's life, the lawn was immaculate and trimmed. Victoria loved gardening, and Raleigh knew abundant flowers and shrubs were in the back. But in the front, Ned chose to have only short bushes near the house and long stretches of lawn and driveway.

No cars were parked in the driveway. Raleigh spotted Carmichael's car parked three houses down from Ned's home. He pulled behind it, surprised the two detectives did not get out of the vehicle. Carter drove up behind them. Raleigh suddenly felt his stomach clench while waiting for the two men in front to move. He got out of the car and approached the lead vehicle. Taking the small flashlight from his pocket, he shined it into the car's interior. The passenger side window was shattered, and the engine had run out of gas. Both detectives were dead. Carmichael's head was mashed with blood and gore in the driver's seat. Sawyer's forehead exhibited the now familiar single bullet to the forehead. Carmichael's wounds indicated he had time to react, but two quick shots ended any hope of retaliation.

Raleigh deduced from the cold engine that the two men were killed early in their stakeout. Looking around, Raleigh realized the two houses flanking Ned's were vacant. Cursing himself, he realized the families were either away, or Ned had gotten them to leave. Something to check out later.

Realizing Ned had prepared for possible police action, Raleigh looked up and saw CCTV cameras on the poles beside Ned's house and further down the street. "There goes the element of surprise," he thought to himself. At that moment, the yard in front of Ned's house was floodlighted from the poles and house.

"*Knew you'd be coming Raleigh,*" a bullhorn-augmented voice boomed.

Jumping away from the car, Raleigh ran to his car to get the shotgun and his own bullhorn. Amanda piled out of the vehicle, followed closely by Carter, and both had guns drawn in each hand. Quietly ordering them to spread out, Raleigh walked towards the figure standing in the doorway. Ned was dressed in his Chief's uniform, but Raleigh suspected an armored vest was under the outer jacket.

"*Came to arrest you Ned,*" Raleigh said as neutrally as he could through his bullhorn.

"*I've been expecting you. But I can't let you take me in just yet.*"

"*Why not now?*"

"*Haven't finished what I set out to do.*"

"*Which was?*"

"*Some people need to die.*"

"*That's a cliché from some movies. Ned.*"

"*Yeah, I guess it is but applies here though.*"

"*Why did Cain need to die?*"

"*Because that little queen needed to die.*"

"*Now, who's quoting from the movies?*"

"*Ned, you know I haven't been to a movie in seven years.*"

"Not since Ellen died, I know. But then you never did treat her right. Always off gallivanting from one case to another. You always left her alone with her charities."

"You're the third person to tell me that this week but that don't change why we're here."

"You think you're going to take me, here in my house, on my grounds?"

"Yes, Ned, I think so."

"As we used to say in the playground: "you and what Army?" All I see is one nigger lady and some callow cop."

"More than enough for this assignment, Ned."

"You see this gun," Ned waved the big Magnum in his left hand, *"Punch through any vest you have. And this one?"* waving the target pistol in his right hand. *"You know what a good shot I am Raleigh. You're all as dead as those two in that car."*

"Why did you kill them?"

"Because I knew I could. That's what you never understood, you and that nigger chief. I am really good at whatever I do. Be it carpenter, police officer, or killer. You would have never caught me if I could have found that damn badge. Couldn't find Cain's key and when I went to his house never found his safe. Even got that Charlotte reporter to believe there was a suspect already in custody. Had you all running around looking for the rat who gave him that scoop. Gave you extra-work, extra-headaches. Bet he's mad and won't make what happens here today look pretty for you."

"But we're here and you're going down."

"Didn't think you would get here so fast. I thought I had more time."

"You knew the clues would eventually add up."

"You were always good at finding those little clues that led to an arrest. Cain just left one I couldn't hide."

"So you think it was the badge that brought us here."

"Yep. I killed those three that worked for Cain so you would have no connections to me.

"Once you had that clue, I knew the game was up. You finding that badge."

"That's where you're wrong Ned. It's that callow young detective that identified you. Cain and him."

"Cain?" Ned's voice wavered a bit at this news.

"Yeah, it seems he had information on everyone in town that mattered but you. This detective realized to look for what wasn't there. And lo and behold, Ned Cain had no file on you. Isn't that funny?"

"When he was in high school, he asked how to avoid being caught? I told him never to write down anything he didn't want people to know about. It turned out he didn't do that, only thing he didn't record was about us."

"You had an affair when he was in high school?"

"I'm not that stupid. We waited till he graduated. It was nice for a while but then he got too demanding. Last straw was when he called me an Old Queen. Told him to leave town or I would run him in. He said I wouldn't dare because then he would tell everyone I was gay. Took my gun and put it in his mouth and said I would kill him first. He got the message and left. Then he showed up and we got back together. Then he tells me he's going to New York and his last broadcast from town would include exposing me. I pretended to be frightened and begged him for one last chance to convince him not to. Stupid fag agreed to meeting at the motel. Even turned his back on me as he ordered me out of the room saying he had another lover coming. That's when I killed him."

"So you weren't the person spending the night? Raleigh said, surprised by this development.

"Yeah, it surprised me as well. Don't ask me who it was supposed to be. I don't know. Took his briefcase but it had nothing in it except one clean underwear and one dirty pair."

"When did you decide to kill him?"

"Knew there was something up when he agreed to the meeting. That's when I decided to kill my wife and her son. When the time came, I was careful how I arrived at the motel. Saw the woman leave and knocked on his door right away. Cain didn't waste any time, said he was going to take a nap before his next visitor came, so we could end our business quickly."

"So the killing was premeditated?"

"Just like this morning's killings are going to be."

"Not much talking then?"

"He looked at me and got a silly grin on his face. He said in a matter of fact tone that he was leaving for New York. Said I was his past, New York was his future."

"And he said he was going to out you on his program?"

"He said those words with such a malicious voice, I knew then he hated me and just used me."

"I can understand that murder but the others?"

"Well, Victoria was stepping out on me. I kept quiet when I realized that bastard child wasn't mine."

"How you know that?"

"Doctor in Atlanta told me three years ago. Said somewhere, somehow, I became infertile."

"Are you sure about that?"

"Hell yes, went to Nashville to confirm it."

"But why kill them?"

"Once I decided to kill Cain, I figured I had nothing to lose."

"Where are they?"

"They're lying on the floor in the parlor. I kept them in the freezer waiting until you arrived. They're laid out just fine for Jules. Killed the boy first so she knew I was serious. Begged for her life, but I told her it was too late. She cried that she only strayed because I stopped touching her. I told her I would spare her life if she told me who the father was."

"Did she?"

"Of course, you know people will say anything to try and save their lives."

"Who is the boy's father?"

"You're going to love this, Raleigh. It was Beau. I figured it was Beau by the way the boy walked. I just wanted to confirm it. Then I shot her."

"Then why was she flirting with the Reverend Bob?"

"That was her clever ploy in case I ever divorced her. She could wait while living with the Reverend until Beau made his big run for mayor or governor, and she could then blackmail him. Somehow she had DNA tests of Beau and the boy. They're sitting on top of her body."

"I can understand Beau and Mrs. Stone, but why the Reverend Bob?"

"Give you a clue pointing in my direction, wanted you to come after me."

"So, you want me here?"

"Yeah, so I can kill you and that black bitch of a police chief."

"What makes you think you'll succeed?"

"You're here, I'm here, and she's here."

"You're going down."

"Not by you and that bitch. After I kill you two, I'll wait for the SWAT team you ask for. I'll get a few of them before they get me."

"You really think that is how it will play out."

"Yes I do. And I got something else for you. I didn't kill Beau or that dancer bitch. Your successor's going to need to figure that out because I didn't kill either one of them."

"My successor?"

"I intend to kill you and that black bitch of a police chief."

"Why do you want to kill us, Ned?"

"Because I know you prevented me from being Chief of Patrol nine years ago. Amanda would have made me Chief if you hadn't brought in that other nigger."

"You know Ned, if you think that, I say fine. It isn't true but you were about to be made Chief of Patrol this time around."

"I know that, but only because you don't have any other candidate, and what do you say in Amanda's office: He'll screw up what Daw has accomplished."

"Where did you hear that? Raleigh was surprised.

"Like I said, I'm good at anything I set my mind to."

"Years ago, I bugged Amanda's office. It was interesting hearing her grunting under old Nate's prick. Surprised you haven't taken a dip. But then again Ellen was always enough for you."

Momentarily shocked by what he had learned, Raleigh gathered his thoughts as he noted Amanda sliding to the left of Ned and Carter moving slowly to the right. As they gained separation, he eased his gun's safety off, allowing Ned to see what he was doing. He wondered how much longer he could keep the man talking. Clearly, Ned was not going to be arrested without shots being fired.

"Ned, you don't know who Cain's lover is?"

"Not a clue. I didn't even suspect he had another.

"What I do know is this lover knew him in Atlanta and he's been feeding Cain information. Stupid bastard threw that into my face before I killed him. I couldn't figure out who it could be. If I had, he'd be dead by now."

"So you didn't tell him about Jenny."

"Why would I bring up that old case? We know the story. There was ole Raleigh doing a good deed. Made me puke but I went along hoping to be chief. But you screwed me."

"Sorry, you feel that way Ned," was all Raleigh could say, digesting this second new set of facts.

"Too bad you won't be around to figure out who it is. If she survives today, that nigger chief will have to do it. And I don't think she's up for the task."

"Think it could be Knox?" Raleigh said, playing for time.

"Knox wouldn't touch someone like Cain," Ned said reflectively.

"I wonder who it is?" Raleigh said slowly to draw out the question and time.

"Who cares at this point Raleigh, it's you and me and soon just me."

"That's big talk for a man about to be arrested and tried for six murders."

"Death penalty takes time to be done here in South Carolina."

"But still happens."

"True, but you won't be around to see me gone," Ned said viciously.

With that, the man raised his left hand to aim at Raleigh. Flopping to the ground, Carter fired first, but both rounds missed Ned. The killer looked at Carter, distracted for a second but then turned and fired at Raleigh, who was slow in dropping to the ground. But in falling, his head and neck were exposed to the bullets aimed at him. One entered his neck, the other his face. With his third bullet, Ned knocked Raleigh backward onto his back.

With Ned's attention drawn to his right, instinct rushed in as Amanda advanced towards Ned; she immediately started firing, avoiding the armor by aiming left to right to hurt Ned's arms. Her first shot hit his left arm severing his artery and causing blood to gush from the entry point. This proved at autopsy to be the wound that killed him.

Not knowing he would be dead in minutes, Ned turned towards Amanda. Realizing his left arm was not responding to his commands, he raised his right arm to aim at the police chief. Before Ned could get off another shot, Carter's fourth bullet, the only one of his to hit the suspect, entered Ned's side between the armor and pushed him into the door. Lying there and unable to get up, he bled out on his doorstep.

Ned's eyes glazed over as Amanda raced to Raleigh's side, and, at her command, Carter rushed to cover the dying man. Amanda saw it was too late for Raleigh and started to cry. Hearing her sobs, Carter kicked the man's body to assure himself Ned was dead after pulling aside the murderer's guns.

Bending down, his quick search revealed no other guns, and he wondered where Ned put the murder weapon used in the other killings. Fears the weapon was sent to different police jurisdictions swept through his mind but he turned and saw the weeping Amanda. Running to Raleigh's side, he saw it was too late. The man was dead, and Amanda was crying. He should be, too, Carter thought, but all he could think of was Caleigh, Sue Ellen, and Eleanor, and he knew they would be devastated.

"We need to find the gun before the state people get here," he almost shouted at Amanda.

"You're right, go inside and look around. If they come, I'll hold them back as long as I can."

"Will do," he said over his shoulder.

Going around the body, Carter entered the house. As he expected, it was neat and clean. He saw the two bodies in the front parlor, and both were still partially frozen. On top were the two letters, DNA tests, and the gun Carter assumed came from the box in the police evidence room. Cain's two phones and his briefcase were also sitting there. He pocketed the gun but left everything else undisturbed.

Four state SWAT members entered the house as he exited. The entire front was lit by Ned's searchlights and those set up by the state police. He saw Amanda in talks with a camouflage-dressed, grey-haired individual he assumed was the SWAT commander. Someone had already covered Raleigh's body. Looking up, he saw the Eagle press car in the street behind the hasty barricade already erected around Carmichael's car and the front lawn. He almost ran to the car and snatched the phone from the young reporter Carter thought Caleigh had sent.

"*Don't mention that anyone but the suspect is dead to the editors,*" he said harshly.

"*Why not, they're part of the story.*"

"*Because one of them is Caleigh's uncle. I don't want her to hear about it over the phone from you. Amanda will want to do it herself. Do you understand?*"

"*Do now but she's going to ask.*"

Then you say we are all safe. That will keep her until we can go tell Caleigh, and also the families of Carmichael and Sawyer. I promise we will keep it under wraps for you."

Looking up, Carter saw Jules's car approaching. There were two television vans behind him, as was his body transfer vehicle. He ran into the street and halted them well away from the scene. Jules got out of the car with his bag and walked towards Carter, displaying the gravest face Carter had ever seen on him.

"*Is it bad Carter?*"

"*Couldn't be worse. Sawyer and Carmichael in that car there, Ned at the door and Raleigh on the lawn. Victoria and her son inside the house.*"

"*Six bodies. I'd better call County to send one of their ambulances.*" He said, reaching for his phone.

"*Call Archer's for their hearse. I want Raleigh handled special.*"

"*He will be son, trust me when this gets out he will be.*"

"*He distracted Ned long enough for us to get in position.*"

"*Figured as much. Raleigh always led.*"

"*I don't know what we will do now.*"

"*We'll survive and go on. No worries about that. Just be a little bit sadder.*"

"*Amanda said I had a lot to learn.*"

"*We all do. But this may be the toughest one to learn.*"

"*I didn't realize how much people looked up to him.*"

"*You're going to find out son during the next few days. Is that Amanda there crying?*"

"*Yes, I think she killed Ned but not before he shot Raleigh.*"

"*Where were you,*" Jules demanded harshly.

"*On the ground firing away, but he had an armor vest.*"

"*Where's yours?*"

"*It's on me but I didn't trust it. Amanda simply closed in on him and kept firing.*"

"*Well, let's go to Raleigh first so we can hide his body from those Hyenas behind me.*"

"*Treat him gently Jules.*"

"*No worries on that score.*"

Hugging herself after turning over control of the crime scene to the State Captain, Amanda watched as Jules performed a perfunctory exam of Raleigh before telling his two assistants to move him behind the SWAT truck until Archer's vehicle arrived. Moving around Ned's body, Jules entered the house and went to the two bodies inside the parlor.

Removing the material from Victoria's body, he carefully bagged, sealed, and noted the contents. Squatting over the body, he saw the neat bullet hole in her forehead for what he hoped was the last time. Muttering what a great shooter Ned was, he noted the frozen state of the body and left the time of death for later examination.

Moving over to the boy, he stopped himself from cursing. At eight, he was small for his age, and his face still had the slight suggestion of surprise. There was nothing to note except the Star Wars T-shirt he wore, and it looked brand new.

Going to the door, he motioned his two assistants to cover the victims with body bags and wheel them out to their van. To distract the cameras, he told them to wheel the bodies down the driveway away from the car. Using that ruse to draw their attention, Jules knew their parade would draw attention away from his examination of the two detectives. He decided to leave Ned for last.

In comparative peace, Jules finished his look at Sawyer and Carmichael. He got the state police to erect a curtain between the car and the television crews while their bodies were extracted. Wrapping them in body bags, he ordered the coroner's van close to the car and the two bodies loaded with the screen as coverage. Jules wasn't in a particularly charitable mood to give them anything worthwhile to film.

When the van and ambulance sped away without pursuit, he decided to give the television crews, now numbered six, what they wanted: "If it bleeds, it leads." With a grin hidden by his surgeon mask, he invited the crews to draw near Ned's body.

The blood pool now covered much of the doorstep, and individuals needed to step around it to enter the house. Inviting the state police captain to join him, Jules examined Ned's body. Standing up, he said with a straight face, *"The man is dead. We will need to autopsy."*

Questions were hurled from the crowded press corps at Jules and the state official who deferred all to Amanda standing at the bottom of the lawn.

"We will have a press conference at noon," she said as they got into a state cruiser and headed towards headquarters.

On the way, Amanda issued orders for Sawyer and Carmichael's families to be brought to headquarters. They stopped by the Eagle office for Caleigh, but she had gone to her home, having learned about Raleigh's death from the reporter who disobeyed Carter's commands. They went there to find Sue Ellen hysterical and the two women consoling her. All five piled into the cruiser and went to headquarters with Sue Ellen crying the whole way.

As they expected, Provender greeted them along with two council members, Knox and Benjamin. Amanda, Provender, Knox, and the councilmen huddled in his office while Carter and other officers consoled the families as much as they could. Sue Ellen's wails could be heard around the building. With the aid of the town's PR team, brief bios of all the victims, police officers, and Ned, along with pictures, were assembled into packets. With the noon press conference drawing near, Amanda sent someone home for her spare winter uniform.

The Aftermath, Noon, Monday

Two hours before the scheduled press conference, television crews assembled in the council chambers. They knew the number dead but little else, gaining no information from the tight-lipped police officers who came and went inside the building. Surprised anger, fear, and grief made them brush aside reporters seeking comments. Unusual, as word of the morning's events filtered through Skye Landing, people began to drift towards police headquarters.

By noon, a sizable crowd milled around outside, seemingly trying to comfort each other and unsure of what had occurred. Hastily, loudspeakers were set up to carry the news conference, and then, the local stations opted to carry the conference live. CNN and Fox also decided that there may be some national interest and set up monitoring operations.

More concerned with Sue Ellen than the news, Caleigh hid her in the detective's area. She couldn't bring herself to use Raleigh's office. Just before the conference kicked off, Sue Ellen gained control of herself, burying her face in Caleigh's shoulder.

"He promised to always return," she mumbled.

"I know honey but this time he couldn't. Ned was just too dangerous."

"Then why didn't he bring more help?"

"Because more help would have meant more questions. Someday I'll tell you more."

"More than he is dead?"

"Raleigh was special and he knew what needed to be done."

"He always put his job ahead of Aunt Ellen."

"She would have it no other way."

"But she denied herself."

"When you're married you'll understand better."

"Not if losing someone hurts this much."

"Honey, this isn't some romance novel. Life is hard. Most people don't realize how many people are hurt when someone is murdered. You have your whole life. Raleigh's was almost finished. He knew that. I think he hung around until you were ready for college. He missed Ellen so much."

"But he was never home."

"They both accepted that. So stop crying and let's go out there and hear how he died."

Taking her daughter's hand, Caleigh followed a policewoman to the side of the chamber as Amanda, Provender, and Jules walked to the microphones with the state police captain already in place. After introducing everyone in the front, Amanda gave a concise report of the morning's events, omitting the fact she fired the fatal bullet into Ned. She explained Ned's motive involved his fear of exposure as a gay man.

When she finished, Jules relayed all known facts about the five other victims, not mentioning Raleigh. When he finished, the State Police captain said his department's initial investigation confirmed the facts.

The press started to clamor for more details until Provender stepped to the mike and, by his scowl, quieted them for the moment.

"What Chief Harris left out was the extraordinary effort by Detective Captain Raleigh Butler to convince the culprit to surrender. When that effort was not producing the desired outcome, Raleigh then engaged him so that the Chief and Detective Williams could achieve positions through which they were able to effectuate the demise. Unfortunately it was too late for the culprit's wife and son. For that we are all greatly saddened. For their efforts today, Detectives Henderson and Winston are being posthumously promoted to Lieutenant and Raleigh Butler to Chief. Flags in the city will be at half-mast until the end of the month. Now if you have questions, we will hear them, but remember this investigation is still ongoing."

Like raw meat to lions, the press corps seized on the invitation and shouted questions at Amanda. Deciding to take the most offensive first, she replied to the CBS-affiliate reporter's query on why they didn't wait for the state police SWAT team.

"When we arrived on the scene, we found our colleagues dead. At that moment Chief Ned Barrow switched on spotlights illuminating us to him. We were forced into the confrontation not initiating activity," she replied evenly.

"But you suspected Chief Barrow before sending the two detectives," NBC asked.

"Yes, we had developed evidence from different sources pointing to Chief Barrow. We wanted to convince him to come down here where we could question him."

"But he was expecting you?" The Fox-affiliate anchor asked.

"Yes, seems he was following our investigation by means we have not yet established and knew he was now a person-of-interest," she replied.

"Can you tell us what got you focused on the chief?" yelled the AP bureau staffer.

"Among Mr. Cain's papers was his badge from a police-sponsored program headed by then Lieutenant Barrow when the victim was in high school. It got Chief Butler thinking and as we all learned over the years, when Raleigh got to thinking, criminals were doomed," she said with a touch of melancholy.

"That one clue?" the AP man said with a touch of doubt.

"Yes, as police departments around the state and country will tell you, Raleigh had a knack for piecing out the one clue to break a case."

Stepping in as Amanda temporarily loss her focus, the State Police captain reminded the audience that many of Raleigh's cases were studied in courses at the state-run crime school.

"Doesn't seem to me enough in one badge to warrant bringing in the Chief of Patrol," the AP man persisted, egged on by his fellow news people.

"Parallel to that we developed information indicating a closer relationship between Mr. Cain and Chief Barrow. That and the continued absence of the chief from his duties began to form a pattern."

"Why did he kill his wife and son?" asked the national television crime show producer.

"Of that we have no firm motive as yet," Amanda responded.

"Why Mrs. Stone?" Back to CBS.

"As yet we have not established his motive." Amanda answered quickly.

"The three Cain employees?" NBC quickly followed.

"Because they had seen him with Mr. Cain, and he was afraid of blackmail or exposure."

"The Reverend Bob?" a blogger from Charlotte asked.

"We think it was jealousy, but no firm motive as yet," replied Amanda.

"You seem to be implying that all these murders stemmed from the Chief's jealousy, but if he was gay, why was he jealous of the Reverend Bob?" a thoughtful journalist from the Charlotte papers asked, seemingly innocently.

Recognizing the trap being set, Amanda answered him carefully.

"As we said earlier, the investigation is still ongoing. As to the man's motives we are still trying to determine them. Jealousy is the only one that fits right now but we may need to revise it in the future. Ned left three notes which we have not fully reviewed."

"Why kill Beau Jenkins?" Caleigh's reporter asked waspishly.

Amanda stepped in to answer the question. *"At this time we have no motive for that murder, but are working on the assumption that Mr. Jenkins knew something the murderer did not want revealed."*

"What information was that?" the reporter persisted.

"At this time, we do not know, only that his office was thoroughly searched after Mr. Jenkin's murder. This leads us to the information theory but the investigation is ongoing."

"If the motive turns out to be jealousy, why didn't he target you or former Chief Daw?" the Charlotte reporter asked again innocently.

"Good question and one Raleigh posed to me last night when he had me come to his house, rather than go home. I think that saved my life," Amanda said.

"So, you think you might have been a target?" His questions were incisive.

"I don't want to flatter myself or take on anything. We have some idea of what went on in Ned's head thanks to Raleigh but not everything. What we do know is he killed up to eight people in cold blood and terrorized this city. Beyond that until we have more facts, we can't say," she rejoined.

Other reporters wanted answers to their questions, and he relinquished the floor. Looking at Amanda, his face indicated they would be asked at a different time. Other reporters threw questions at her for another 15 minutes, but they quickly saw when her answers became repetitive that there was nothing more to be gleaned beyond what had already been saying. As the conference petered out, the CBS reporter threw out one final query.

"Who killed Jenny Couri?" he shouted over the noise of equipment being dismantled.

"Again, I can state with absolute certainty, Jenny Couri was not murdered," Amanda said wearily.

"Try telling that to our viewers," he shot back.

"I hope you will tonight on the 6-o'clock news," Amanda said in an attempt at humor.

"Fat chance," playing the game, he replied.

With that exchange, the conference ended but not the vigil outside police headquarters. It continued until Caleigh, Sue Ellen, and Eleanor walked out and the crowd gave them a cheer. Sue Ellen broke down again and they were hustled away in Provender's limousine.

Somber Parting, Friday, 9am

Working with the state technicians and driving her troops hard, Amanda assembled the thick case file for the assigned prosecuting attorney to sort out the final details of the Podcast Murders. With no other detectives left in the bureau, she was forced to name Carter head of the department. Liking the SWAT captain and his approach to the case, she asked him to temporarily take over as Chief of Patrol. They slipped into an easy relationship with the first days, and she mused about offering him the job permanently.

When Jules finished his autopsies and confirmed her bullet killed Ned, she got grim satisfaction. Carmichael and Sawyer were buried Thursday, with many townspeople joining the funeral processions. The posthumous pensions would be higher thanks to Provender's unilateral decision, for which some council members were unhappy. But given public sentiment, they were not going to publicly complain. Today was Raleigh's turn, and she knew it would be an ordeal. His viewing caused massive traffic jams around the funeral home, and Caleigh's decision to walk from that venue to the cemetery would add to the chaos.

Amanda had arranged for neighboring towns to send officers to patrol Skye Landing while her entire force marched behind the hearse. She had not realized the town would have hordes of officers from other instate and out-of-state departments who were arriving. Apparently, Raleigh worked with many more departments than she was aware of, noting the high number of chiefs among the mourners. Amanda began to realize Raleigh spent his time helping other departments without shortchanging his force. Despite his prominence within the police community, the graveside ceremonies were going to be mercifully short, as per Raleigh's request found with his signed will.

Buttoning her tunic, Amanda looked up to see Provender in the doorway of her office. The Mayor was dressed in the dark suit he reserved for solemn occasions.

"Quite a turnout there, Amanda," he said in greeting.

"Wonder how we're going to feed them afterward?" She asked, almost to herself.

"Township set up facilities at the knoll behind the cemetery. I've never seen so much police brass in my life. Did Raleigh really help all those departments?"

"You should see the messages on the police net. Never knew we had such an impressive man in our midst," she said.

"Come on you knew all the work he did."

"I did but wonder now when the man slept."

"Probably didn't. Don't think he was the same after Ellen died."

"No, guess not. Anyway, why are you here?"

"I'll try but know from experience he's really into the gun angle."

"Every little bit helps. But telling people that murdered boy was his son won't help anyone."

"I think you're wrong but I'll abide by your wishes. But don't blame me if he finds out from somewhere else."

"Just Carter and you know."

"I think Jules figured it out."

"Hmm, hadn't thought about him. Guess I'll need to wander to his office and set him straight."

"I don't think he'll say anything."

"He might if it could ease the pressures on him. People are admitting he's grown into the coroner's job and maybe they should keep him. Which reminds me, how's young Williams doing leading the detectives?"

"Only had to ream his ass once this week. But other than prodding him to stop thinking about Caleigh's crotch he's doing fine. Raleigh thought he should succeed him."

"Do tell? Raleigh knew how to pick talent. So will you?"

"Between you and me the answer is yes. I'll let him sweat for a time, but really have no choice. The two patrolmen up next for the detective department are so green, they make Carter look like a 10-year veteran. They'll all three will need to learn on the job and fast."

"They have a good leader in you."

"If I'm allowed to stay."

"If I have any say you will. But we have another problem." *"What?"* Amanda asked but thinking she knew the answer.

"About the gun that killed most of the victims," Provender said.

"The gun?" Amanda blurted.

"That pesky Charlotte reporter got wind that there might be something fishy about the gun we ran the ballistic tests on."

"It blew up while we were test firing it. End of story."

"Yeah, seems he's not satisfied with Leonard's explanation of its loss," Provender went on.

"It was a good cover story. The barrel exploded during testing."

"Saying it happens all the time doesn't quite make him believe us. He says it's too convenient."

"He's right but how else explain we can't match the bullets. We know it was the gun stolen out of the evidence room, but we don't need to admit it."

"True, but be careful of him. He's smart and determine to find something bad in this town."

"You could find bad in any town."

"We just did."

With that, the mayor left to allow Amanda to dress fully for Raleigh's funeral. When the entourage started, she suspected he would take up position next to her in support, and she just wished it was Raleigh there.

New Facts, Friday, 9:30am

The door swung open to reveal a bustling detective bureau. The coroner hurried into Amanda's office while she was still getting ready for Raleigh's funeral. He blurted out his news, leaving her scrambling to keep up.

"I just got back the results from taking all the DNAs of our victims," Jules began.

"What did they prove?" Amanda asked, bracing herself for bad news. Jules shook his head. "You've got a tough case here, Chief."

"In what way?"

Jules took a deep breath. "Nobody involved is the father of that boy—not Beau, Reverend Bob, or anyone else on our records."

"The chief thought it was Beau."

"That's what the paper on their bodies said."

The DNA wasn't his. Besides, he had a vasectomy at least ten years ago.

"Are you sure?"

Jules nodded. "I checked twice. He had a procedure that doctors stopped using years ago because it was so painful."

"He was shooting blanks all these years?"

"That's why there aren't a bunch of little Beaus running around town."

"One more thing, I talked to the judge who handled Corinne and Beau's custody fight over Sue Ellen. He said both sides agreed the child was Caleigh's and Beau's."

What's its importance?"

"Usually the lawyers are clamoring for this from day one, in hopes something may

220

pop. The judge thought it strange and told them so, but both parties just shrugged."

"Thank god for little things. You don't know who the boy's father, then?"

"He wasn't Brother Bob's. Nor anyone else in this case."

"But the chief was covering all possibilities when he shot the good reverend."

"What about the druggist's wife?"

"What about her? We don't know why he killed her."

"Or if it was really him. What if there was a deeper reason, perhaps something hidden in her past? Maybe she knew something she shouldn't have."

"You think there is another killer?"

"I'm coming around to that more and more each day I live with this case."

"It's time for us to give Raleigh a proper send off."

"He sure left us some big questions."

"We'll need to get some big answers."

Surprising Day, Friday, 10am

Weather is much discussed when people gather together for funerals. Not wanting to face the specter presented by the coffin or ashes, most mourners deal with the awkwardness of their own future mortality by using this banal topic to avoid its reality. By providing good weather at Raleigh Butler's funeral, mourners' small talk revolved around the women or the coming summer. A slight breeze cooling the immense crowd on Friday morning chosen for his burial came with the mild weather.

The coolness enabled police officers and other officials to lower their car windows to enjoy the weather. Between patrol cars and motorcycles, more than 100 vehicles were strung out on the streets leading to Archer's funeral home. Disdaining the proffered hearse, Caleigh accepted the AMVETS's offer of their gun carriage for his coffin. It stood outside the funeral home, a white horse hitched to its tongue. Archer's two sons and regular pallbearers carried the casket to the waiting transport. Five pipers from different cities started playing Amazing Grace upon seeing the coming burden. Their wail drowned out the huffing and puffing needed to place their burden on the carriage's rear. When the coffin was loaded and secured, horse and carriage lumbered forward slowly.

Following immediately behind the flag-draped coffin were Caleigh, Sue Ellen, Eleanor, and Amanda. As the carriage began to move as if by universal consent, townspeople threaded their way through the police vehicles to form up behind the city council. Not missing a chance to steal some publicity, the Governor suddenly appeared accompanied by Knox and 10 other political leaders and elected officials. Wisely, he took up station next to Provender.

Each piper took up the song in turn, so there was only the lonely sound of the single instrument. Never a religious man, Raleigh would have laughed seeing the Protestant, Catholic, Jewish, and Black clergy form a single line among the mourners. Behind the civilian throng, the Skye Landing police force marched in formation. Bringing up the rear were the police units.

Less than one mile separated Archer's establishment from the Good Hope Cemetery, where Ellen waited. Once or twice, Caleigh looked back at the mourner line, realizing for perhaps the first time how many people Raleigh had impacted. She looked for Carter but realized the townspeople were between him and the police marchers.

When the cemetery was laid out, the founders chose to locate it on the hill overlooking the town. Any road leading to its gates was, by necessity, upward inclines. The street they were on was not steep but still slightly uphill. This was the reason many other townspeople were already at the gravesite when the procession passed the main gate and wound itself to the open grave.

Caleigh saw many wheelchairs and walkers lined up, but noted spaces next to the gravesite for her and others left open. In the front row was Henrik Gundersen standing behind his wife. Knowing her condition, she was amazed the woman would come. But then, looking around, she saw people Caleigh knew seldom ventured far from their homes. To the side, an honor guard of uniformed Marines stood at attention. Caleigh had forgotten. How could she have? That Raleigh had been a Marine.

Raleigh's non-attendance at any church made deciding who from the local clergy would lead the ceremonies difficult. It was taken out of everyone's hands by Benjamin Goodman. Using his generous contributions as a subtle wedge, he got agreement from all faiths that the retired Episcopal Bishop who lived in town would make an excellent gravesite religious leader. If there was any reluctance from any clergy, Benjamin merely reminded the cleric that Raleigh deserved the high churchmen at his send-off. Before the funeral day, he also sent checks to all of them. Most said they were attending because they knew what Raleigh had done for their flocks.

Not expecting his presence, Caleigh could still make room for the Governor alongside the family. Wordlessly, he thanked her and indicated he wanted to speak briefly. She turned to the Bishop and pointed to the Governor, and he understood immediately and nodded back. For 15 minutes, people assembled around the graves as the workers put Raleigh's coffin on the railings preparatory to lowering it into the prepared site. Motioning for silence, the Bishop intoned a prayer. He then told the crowd the Governor would speak first.

Anticipating a long narrative, Caleigh was surprised when the usually bombastic politician took a plaque from an assistant who somehow managed to wriggle his way next to him.

"On this sad occasion, I want to add the state's condolences for the loss of Raleigh Butler. Many officials and state police officers know of his contributions to bringing justice to South Carolina. Perhaps you citizens may not be as aware. We all knew Raleigh as a man who served his community. Many policemen enforce the law; Raleigh enhanced it by making the law work for people. It is with heartfelt sorrow but also joy that I proclaim today Raleigh Butler Remembrance Day and announce the dedication of the new State Police barracks one mile from here as the Raleigh Butler Barracks. May he go with God and be forever remembered. Thank you."

Presenting the plaque to Caleigh, the Governor whispered words of encouragement and sat down to applause. With the shortness of the opening moment, the ceremonies lasted an hour but seemed to fly by for everyone. In the end, Provender invited all present to the luncheon at the local knoll behind the cemetery.

Holding up better than Caleigh expected, Sue Ellen broke down as Raleigh's coffin was lowered into the earth. Since learning of his death, she had cried almost constantly. Throughout the week, Eleanor helped Caleigh comfort the teenager. But she was inconsolable. The only good thing was her grief helped the two other women avoid thinking of their own loss.

Knowing they needed to go to the cookout, they piled into Amanda's police cruiser and proceeded slowly to the grounds. Five huge lines around the knoll indicated where the food stations were. Taking seats at one of the long tables, sympathizers swarmed around them. Food was brought to them, but no one ate. When the surrounding crowd thinned, Henrik took the opportunity to pull Caleigh away from the table.

"Forgive me, but I must get my wife home. She is extremely tired," he said, thrusting an envelope into Caleigh's hands.

"What's this?" she asked.

"I tried to give this to Raleigh Friday. Ellen entrusted this to me four weeks before she died."

"For Raleigh?"

"Yes, she came to my office several years ago. We were good friends because of her charities. I thought she wanted another contribution. But, no, she said people were commenting that Raleigh was neglecting her. She said they chose their life and she did not feel neglected but rather blessed. Despite her reassurances, Raleigh was beginning to doubt what he was doing. She said having told these things in person, she wanted to tell him again if anything happened to her. I think she knew she was ill so she told Raleigh the things in this letter again so he would not dismiss them. People will talk about marriages and how they work. But no one knows about any marriage but the two people involved. I know how yours works, she said to me, so I know I can depend on you to choose the right moment to give it to Raleigh. She said it was a sacred trust. On that basis, I agreed to keep the letter. She died not a month later. I debated telling Raleigh about the letter then, but his grief was too much. I kept it while watching for any signs he needed to know how she felt. Then last Thursday both Provender and Knox told me they regretted saying something to Raleigh about neglecting Ellen. I talked to my wife and thought about it overnight before trying to give him the letter Friday but he was too busy. Now it is too late but I think you should have it."

"Thank you Henrik, I'm sorry you didn't get a chance to give it to him. What's ever in it would've helped him because he was grieving about neglecting Ellen."

"I got that impression when we last spoke, He was a great man."

"Yes, he was. Now go back to your wife and thank her for us for coming today."

"It was the least we could do."

With many thoughts, Caleigh returned to the table, putting the letter in her handbag. She decided to talk with Eleanor about what they would do with it when they were alone.

Passing up the opportunity to meet with constituents, the Governor did not go to the knoll. But almost everyone else did. Booze and beer were supplied, and the day passed with telling and retelling Raleigh stories. Soon, these stories soon morphed into police tales in general and, from there, into other topics. Many an officer said that if Raleigh had been there, he would have enjoyed himself. People left as the day wore on, and visiting lawmen drifted home.

Hearing so many things about Raleigh, Sue Ellen's tears started to dry, and pride in being part of his family began to take their place. At one point, the Captain in charge of the state student CSI program came by to tell her a place in the summer program awaited her, and she almost jumped for joy.

From the corner of her eye, Caleigh saw Carter hovering, waiting for an opportunity to talk to her. She kept him waiting by maneuvering to the other side of the table. Putting the table between him and her made it more difficult for him to act nonchalant in approaching Caleigh. Being aware of the dynamic, she increased his anxiety by doing just that.

For most of the day, Caleigh was able to avoid talking to Carter. The loss of Raleigh and rumors of her impending job loss put romance at the bottom of her list. Sue Ellen was requiring her attention, as were the myriad of details associated with Raleigh's death.

The township attorney informed her she was a beneficiary of Raleigh's city and state insurance policies which kicked in with his death on duty. Ironically, even though adopted by Ellen and Raleigh, she could not receive his pension. But all the monies he paid into the program would be refunded. She did not expect that Raleigh would give her and Eleanor the house on a 50-50 basis. That they could live together was not doubted, but she would need to talk to the woman who was so much a part of their lives.

When the sun began to set, the knoll emptied of people. Silently, township employees and volunteers started cleaning the waste littering the ground. Carter thought this would be the moment to swoop in, but

Caleigh forestalled him by entering the waiting police car with Amanda and Sue Ellen. Eleanor said she would stay behind and collect all of the cards and notes dropped off by people all day. She also wanted to invite the caterer to her show. The police car roared off, leaving Carter angry, frustrated, and alone at the field's entrance.

Doubt Follows, Monday, 9:55am

Once again, Amanda allowed herself to be late on the following Monday morning. Seeing the roly-poly figure of Hy Grossman sitting in the visitors' room made her wish, once again, she had stayed home.

"Okay, I'll listen to what you have to say," she agreed reluctantly.
"Well to start, how sure are you that the chief acted alone? Some people in town think he had an accomplice."

"That's one I can answer immediately. He acted alone in the killing of Mr. Cain, his three employees, Mrs. Moore, the Reverend Bob, wife and son."

"But is the boy really his son?" Grossman asked disingenuously.

"Do you have information to say differently?"

"Seems most parishioners thought the boy was the Reverend Bob's and that's the reason he's dead."

"Right now we have no reason to think differently. We have not done DNA tests on the boy or the Reverend Bob."

"Ah, that brings us to another sore point."

"Who's sore?"

"Some people who think Beau Jenkins should have been Mayor. They say your people are sloppy letting things like his murder pass without nailing down exactly why he was a victim."

"Wasn't any reason to dig deeper. Ned was jealous and thought his wife cheated. Let's face it, Beau, Mr. Jenkins did dally outside his marriage."

"Marriages," Grossman immediately interrupted.

"Marriages, if you will."

"What did Ned say during the confrontation?"

"Afraid you'll need to wait for the official report," Amanda said in a weary tone.

"Did he deny killing Mr. Jenkins?"

"What gives you that idea?" Amanda asked warily.

"His death doesn't fit the pattern nor any indication the Chief had a motive to kill him," Grossman shot back again

"The Chief was not all together rational," Amanda retorted. *"But he had a reason for the other deaths but not for the town sin finder or the would-be mayor."*

"In time we will find the motive in both cases," Amanda said neutrally. *"That's another thing, you're sure everything he said was recorded in your official statements?"*

"Yes, as best we could remember," Amanda said.

"Your detective seemed a bit hazy when I talked him."

"Probably being cagey and worried what I would do to him if he said too much. Someone apparently told you wrong information in the past."

"Care to know who that was?"

"You need to protect your sources," Amanda couldn't resist the jab.

"It was Chief Barrow," Hy said as if to explain his false report

"Why should I believe you now? You're pinning the false report on a dead man."

"I have no proof. The tip came from a burner phone. Do you have a list of phones in the chief's possession?"

"As a matter-of-fact, we do. Give me your phone and we'll check all numbers."

"Fat chance, the other numbers will lead whoever care to my regular sources."

"Well then, there's nothing we can do to prove your claim."

"Why are your people so careful?"

"Because they have a job to do and don't need reporters jumping on their investigation. There are loose ends to tie up."

"So there is more?"

"No, I just like to keep tight control on news so what people hear in the media are the facts as best we know them. People and what I really mean is the media will seize on anything to bolster their own theories."

"But still, I wonder if the Chief said anything more. I can't find anything but the statements from Detective Carter and yourself."

"Wasn't anyone left but Detective Carter and myself."

"*And you made sure you killed him.*"

"*I tried to save Raleigh's life. Didn't do a good enough job.*"

"*The police chief in Charlotte says he's amazed you got him at all. His vest was the best on the market and covered almost his whole body.*"

"*I aimed to disable him, pure luck his artery was severed.*"

"*Noticed your bullets hit home and Carter's didn't.*"

"*One of his did and stopped the firing.*"

"*But people are also saying Cain was on to something with the Couri girl and you somehow got Ned to kill him for you,*" Grossman threw out.

"*And let him kill all those other people including my three detectives,*" Amanda said angrily with a sarcastic overtone.

Shared Confidences, Monday 10:30am

Neither participant was happy with the just finished conversation. As she watched Hy retreating form exit the station, Amanda motioned Carter to join her. Eager for anytime with the chief, Carter rushed to her office. Amanda sat pensively looking at Ned's phone logs.

There was something in them that Amanda had not yet teased out but felt there was a message if she could only find out the code. Seeing which documents she was studying, Carter thought it was time to venture some opinions in the hopes Amanda might respond with information about his future.

"Do you think the Chief was the source of the leaks?" Carter asked. *"Until I had that talk with that reporter, yes I did. But now I'm not so sure. I will tell you this, he did not know about the results of those interviews before I just told him. And neither did Cain."*

"What interviews?"

"The ones we conducted back then that conclusively proved the three men he was about to accuse were innocent."

"You mean they had alibis?"

"More than that, the Couri girl wasn't even pregnant.""And you had proof?"

"Of course, we had the autopsy report. We had the DNA of the pregnancy test strip. And none of those men were in town in the days before or after her death."

"How Cain could have gotten it so wrong?" asked Carter.

"Someone was feeding Cain only what was in the evidence box."

"But the evidence box is supposed to have all that information."

"If this were a murder case, yes but it wasn't a murder case, remember."

"Raleigh said she was murdered."

"She was and the murderer was punished."

"How? Who? When."

"Nobody's business now so its best laid to rest. Cain's dead, let's let the noise die down."

"Some people think it still is."

"The story died with Ned. Whoever is selling out this department doesn't know the truth."

"How will you find out," Carter asked in a seemingly neutral tone.

"Look for someone who wasn't here when that girl died."

Time Heals, Friday, 10:30am

For Amanda, the only good note during these weeks was convincing the SWAT captain to retire from his wider state duties and accept the Chief of Patrol position full-time. In their time together, she learned the need to keep up with his crew of young tigers as SWAT commander at his age was becoming a chore. What he didn't tell Amanda but she suspected, the real reason was his wife's continued fear for his safety. Raleigh's death was her final straw and she demanded he leave his position.

With Carter as acting chief detective, Amanda advanced two patrolmen to the bureau. Some of the work from all three appalled her but she recognized they were all in a learning curve. Almost reluctantly, Provender said he would run for another term as mayor. This time, under a new editor, with Caleigh named columnist-at-large, the Eagle decided he was out-of-touch with today's emerging issues. With Beau gone, the paper hinted at its preference for anyone but Provender was their choice for mayor.

Her high school term about to end Sue Ellen put aside most of her grief for Raleigh and started to look forward to working in the state crime lab that summer. Caleigh arrange for her to stay at the home of its director. This eliminated one of Caleigh's concerns her daughter might have too much freedom away from home. Sue Ellen began to receive material in preparation for the summer class. What awed her was the amount of material at the lab associated with Raleigh. Without admitting its advantages, she reveled in the fact she was his niece which made her special in their eyes.

Unhappy at losing her editorship, Caleigh took Provender's advice and accepted the columnist role until something came up that she wanted to do. Deliberately, she avoided Carter to concentrate on Sue Ellen and her new job. Plus, she had other things to consider.

When all the figures came in concerning Raleigh's insurance and pension, Caleigh realized she was almost a millionaire. She turned to Henrik for advice. He got his people on building a conservative portfolio for her daughter and her. It truly saddened her to learn they were leaving but it was obvious his wife was not going to long survive.

Only one other sour note to all of this was Eleanor's reaction to learning she was half owner of their home. She didn't like it because of the tax consequences and the fact she planned to leave once Sue Ellen was in college.

"I planned to find a house in Charlotte," she admitted to Caleigh.

"You mean you were ready to leave?"

"Yes, Raleigh knew that I wasn't happy here."

"Because he was ignoring you?"

"Gracious no, did you think I had eyes for that man. No, he was a one-woman man, make no mistake. I never saw him as a future husband."

"Then why did you stay all these years?"

"Because it was comfortable and having the three of you around gave me companionship and love. Almost as good as a marriage," Eleanor said looking away into her kitchen.

"But what did you plan to do in Charlotte?"

"What I was doing here but only bigger."

"I can see that in you."

"Yeah, I suddenly have the urge to be an what they call an entrepreneur," she laughed.

"Wish I had that urge as well."

"I know you'll find something."

"Maybe I should get married. I can still have kids."

"As long as it's not to that Williams fellow."

"You mean you don't like him."

"Yes. Call it what you will but I think there is more to that man than meets the eye."

"Really?"

"Yes, I do and I think if you ask Amanda, she'd agree."

"I was thinking to let him up a little from the iron I've used to keep him away." Caleigh mused.

"Don't do anything until you have a heart-to-heart with Amanda. She may give you more to think about than me."

"In the meantime, if you really want to move to Charlotte, I'll buy your share of the house once everything with Raleigh is settled."

"Hold off on that while I catch my breath. You're not the only one who misses that man."

Caleigh was still going over in her mind what Eleanor said during their meeting when she dropped into the police station to give Amanda Raleigh's police issued revolver. Technically, she could have kept it but wanted no reminders like that in the home when Sue Ellen returned. Amanda was in her office talking with Carter when she arrived.

He quickly got up and sidled close enough to her to make an exaggerated inhale of her perfume. She chalked it off to his immaturity and let him pass without comment. The two older women looked at each other their faces betraying mutual amusement.

"What brings you to my office?" Amanda threw an open question at Caleigh.

"Returning Raleigh's official revolver."

"You can keep it."

"I don't want it around.

"Then I'll keep it."

"Expected that would be your response."

"Something else on your mind?"

"Yes, it's something Eleanor put in my head."

"Sensible woman, so go ahead."

"It's about Carter."

"You mean your would-be lover who is still wet behind the ears."

"Is it youth or something else, Amanda?"

Seeing the seriousness in Caleigh's manner, Amanda got up and closed the door of her office. It had taken a specialist four hours to find the bug Ned put in her space. Since then, they were back three times checking the office before she was satisfied it was safe to talk freely in her space.

"You want an honest answer or one that will send you into the arms of that man? It's nice for women our age to have young men panting after us, especially one like Carter who could get just about any younger woman?"

"The truth as you see it, Amanda."

"Then I'll tell you. I don't know why but I don't trust the man. It's only been two weeks since everything happened with Ned so I have time. But the more I work with him and in his company, the less comfortable I feel about him. Maybe because Ned fooled me but I think not, it's something else and I can't put my finger on what it is. But I'm still not sure. My new Chief of Patrol hasn't said anything but I get funny vibes from him about Carter."

"Men aren't built to hold back," Caleigh said.

"True, but he's new and really doing two jobs: his old one until they get someone to replace him and the work here in Skye Landing. He also doesn't know how I feel about Carter."

"You do keep feelings about people to yourself."

"Need to in this job. But I've been doing background checking on Carter."

"Why?"

"Because I don't want another psycho Ned in my department."

"Ned preceded you here," Caleigh protested.

"Still, one of things your ex-husband kept saying that is still resonating with many people is the fact we do no psych evaluations in this department before hiring. Turns out we did no background checks on the last eight patrolman hires. We can thank Ned for that but the buck stops with me. I looked at Carter's file and noticed there is no recommendation letter from the Atlanta police department. In Washington and most other places, when another department doesn't send a letter of recommendation, that's a real red flag to tread carefully. At the least the absence of such a letter requires calling up the previous department."

"So what are you doing?"

"*Well, a friend from Washington retired into working for one of the security firms. I asked her to do some sleuthing on all eight of our most recent hires.*"

"*Dangerous,*" Caleigh commented.

"*Interesting is more like it. Based on what she's uncovered I need to let three of them go.*"

"*Do they know what you're planning?*"

"*Now, don't get going as a reporter. You can have the low down on Carter or be a reporter, but you can't have both.*"

"*For Sue Ellen's sake, I'll remain a bereaved woman making sure she's not being conned.*"

"*We're both being conned, my friend reports.*"

"*Oh no?*"

"*Carter was encouraged to leave the Atlanta police force.*"

"*Why?*"

"*Now that's interesting. My friend couldn't get an answer but thought it had something to do with leaking information. Sound familiar?*"

"*Oh no? You have anything else?*"

"*Not yet, but I had one of the new detectives going through Cain's receipts and other material. Not his blackmail or porn collection but his office materials.*"

"*Is he finding anything?*"

"*Nothing definitive but receipts for trips to Atlanta covering the time Carter was on the police force there. Cain broke some interesting cases in Atlanta. Or rather I should say said a lot in public about cases the police knew the suspect but couldn't prove them guilty. Cain comes along and names them, taints the jury pool, and gives the department nothing new to prosecute*"

"*You think Carter gave him the material?*"

"*Someone did and the same thing happened here. Two and two can sometimes make four.*"

"*But why Skye Landing? Why not a bigger city for their next scam?*"

"*Because it would have been difficult for Carter to get on another police force.*"

"Oh, I see, he could here because background checks weren't being made?"

"Precisely and I think Carter could get on the force because of one reason."

"Because Ned wasn't doing his job."

"Because Ned wasn't doing his job and someone knew he wasn't."

"Who do you think in this town?"

"Your ex-husband," Amanda dead-panned her last bombshell.

"Beau?" Caleigh replied in amazement.

"Surprised me too but seems good ole Beau has been busy the last few years."

"I thought Corinne kept him on a tight leash?"

"Provender gave me some insight into that marriage. Seems things weren't going smoothly and Benjamin gave him a big check to beat Beau."

"Good for Benjamin. But what has Beau been doing?"

"I'm not sure yet but last week I told everyone I needed to go to the Capitol for some female tests," Amanda said laughingly.

"Once you say that no one asks any more questions, am I right?" She joined in the laugh.

"Too true, so I hopped a plane to Atlanta and found out a bit more. What is important are the names on some surveillance logs they were kind enough to share with me."

"Let me guess. Carter, Beau, and Henry Cain."

"One more, Ned Barrow."

"Where?"

"The Golden Slipper off of West Peachtree."

"A gay joint?"

"For transgender and the like."

"I may not have liked my ex-husband but I know he was definitely not playing for the other team," Caleigh said seriously.

"The meeting was logged three years ago and I think it just happened to be a convenient place to meet. Beau's a lot of things but not gay."

"We both agree on that."

"Three years ago Cain broadcast some pretty serious things wrong with the Atlanta police department. He was leaked private material by someone

they never could identify publicly. But I did confirm Carter was asked to leave the department about that time. They couldn't prove he gave Cain any confidential records but they didn't want him around. He caused them great embarrassment with Cain's revelations."

"Why did he come here?"

"Now, were speculating Caleigh but I think Beau was thinking ahead and wanted to hurt Provender."

"Seems logical but where does Ned fit in?"

"This is the problem I have. Where does Ned fit in?"

"Whatever Ned did for them was because of Cain. When Cain betrayed him, it was the last straw in a lifetime of perceived betrayals."

"So you don't think he killed Beau or the Stone woman?"

"Neither did Raleigh."

"Ned did kill Cain and those others but I think it had nothing to do with what Cain was cooking up with Beau and Carter."

"I think Beau was the ringleader. He wanted to be mayor. Provender stood in the way. Beau needed dirt on Provender and needed someone inside the police department."

"And you think that someone is Carter?"

"It all goes back to Atlanta. Mrs. Stone. Carter. Cain."

"So you think Carter's interest in me has more to do with something bigger."

"Yes, and somewhere behind all of this was Beau or what he did or wanted."

"Wouldn't put it passed him. Even in death he's vexing me."

"But why is Carter still sniffing around with Beau dead"

"I don't know. Maybe he just likes older women. But maybe there's something more he needs."

"Like what?"

"Neither Provender or I can figure out."

"You've been talking to him about this and me?"

"Had to, needed someone smart I could trust. He fit on both counts."

"Why are you so sure about Carter?"

"Don't try to run away from this, Caleigh. I'll give you one hard fact. Ned obviously didn't tell them about Jenny Couri. If he had, they wouldn't

have been barking up that tree. Now I figure you've teased out what happened with Jenny so that makes it eight people who know the whole story. Raleigh, the murderer, Jules, Provender, Sawyer, Carmichael, Ned and you. If Ned was in cahoots stands to reason he would have said something. Notice, he made himself unavailable throughout the manhunt. I think to avoid talking to Carter."

"You know, come to think about it, Carter kept insisting on knowing the whole story. Especially after Raleigh told him she was murdered."

"Have you seen him since Raleigh died?"

"Not for his wanting to try. I keep putting him off."

"Take my advice; don't ever be alone with that man. I don't know what I'm going to do with him but I know he won't be part of this department much longer."

"What about Beau's murder?"

"Well, that is an interesting problem that I have no answers for now."

"Do you think his murder can be solved?"

"Yes, I will need to do it for him."

Avoiding Explanations, Friday, 11:30am

After agreeing to talk again the next day, the two women parted. Carter tried to intercept Caleigh at the front entrance but the woman scooted out the rear entrance. Frustrated, Carter vowed to see her that next day. In the meantime, he kept digging in Raleigh's files trying to find mention of the Couri case. He need not have bothered. Long before his death, Raleigh had siphoned the file from all four places it was duplicated at headquarters.

Since her visit to her doctors in the capitol, Amanda had kept her distance from Carter. He sensed the wariness in her approach to their meetings. More significantly, there had been no further mention of giving him the chief of detectives' job permanently. Keeping his head down was a new experience for him but felt it was the prudent course until things resolved themselves.

Besides, the good citizens were giving him all the attention he craved. Around town, when he walked into any store or office, there were murmurs of recognition which he enjoyed. Still, Amanda's reticence worried him but also woke up his ego. While her games bothered him, they also gave him a challenge. Carter wanted to make sure his ego won.

Despite Caleigh's attempts to keep away from him, Carter was feeling pretty cocky. Here he was running the detective bureau, pursuing an awesome chick, and confident his past would not catch up with him. Beau's death eliminated any chance Amanda would learn he was the leak in her department.

The first thing Carter did when he opened Cain's case files was to look for any mention of Ned's relationship with Cain and Beau. Thankfully, there was none. When he had discovered Cain was the victim, he decided not to disclose his relationship with the deceased. A quit call to Beau had silenced any disclosure from his office. Ned's absence from the office alleviated any fears he would say anything to Raleigh. After all, it was Ken and Daw who had failed to follow procedures in his hiring. Any blowback would hurt them, not him. After all, wasn't the newest detective a proud capturer of culprits?

He had stumbled on the Couri case while looking through some old records involving child abuse cases. Although scanty, they were enough for Henry Cain to start his campaign against Amanda and Provender Cain was angry at the town for turning itself into a thriving metropolis. Three years previously, when they met in Atlanta, Cain quickly saw what Beau's ambitions were and was happy to team with him to find dirt to drive out the current administration.

After Cain's death, Beau hinted he would tell Amanda the source of her leaks if Carter did not help him. After one or two threats, Carter agreed. Twice in sealed envelopes he gave Beau material that was in turn slipped to the dumb new editor at the Eagle. With each negative story, the mayoral candidate was getting good ammunition to overthrow Provender. That codger was a Neanderthal in Carter's opinion.

Despite losing Cain, Carter was figuring ways of making money in the town he had decided to adopt. Anticipating pickings would be easy because up until now Skye Landing had relatively escaped the ravages of drugs, transient population, and corruption. In short, it was as clean a town to be found in the second decade of the 21st Century. Finding ways to make money when Beau was mayor Carter knew was going to be easy.

Judging by the reports he'd reviewed, the townspeople were generally law abiding. Adding some protected gambling, drugs, and prostitution could be kept sub-rosa. With him running the department, protection money was just one of the ways he hoped to build his retirement stake. He just had to remember to be patient and not greedy.

Walking back to the detective bureau, Carter saw Amanda looking at him. Suddenly, his confidence deserted him. The thoughtful look on Amanda's face worried him. She was not the type he could fool for long if he wanted to run things in Skye Landing.

Already, he was significantly past the first 48-hours after a murder and he had no suspects. He needed to identify one soon or Amanda might turn the case over to the state investigators. Carter could not let that happen.

But first there was the matter of Caleigh. He would deal with her tomorrow, Saturday at her house.

Desperate Suitor, Saturday, 1pm

Combining Confederate Remembrance Day with its Fourth of July celebration enabled Skye Landing to enjoy the best of both traditions. Privately, Provender knew the days of the combined celebration were numbered but since his ancestors had fought with Robert E. Lee, he was determined to enjoy the day for as long as he could. Each year, the celebration was more-and-more about other causes.

Today was not the time to dwell on the future. Knowing there was still time before the celebrations started Provender was sitting in Eleanor's kitchen enjoying the heated sandwich placed before him. He didn't know what was in it but the taste was delicious. He would make Delilah get the recipe. Smiling and thanking Eleanor, he turned to Caleigh and spoke gravely.

"That ex-husband of yours was one pain-in-the-ass."

"He's gone. How can he be bothering you now?"

"Well, to start, he made me run again."

"Don't kid me, you love being mayor. And so do the citizens."

"Maybe you're right but Beau's petition for putting the high school on Dane Hill just got enough signatures we need to address it."

"So you will squash it."

"No, afraid this time I'm going to lose. The board and council are going to site it up there despite everything I say."

"How did that happen?"

"Your ex-husband got them to doubt my integrity."

"How?"

"Before he died, he ginned up some papers to convince the council to look at the funding for the high school labs we put in last year."

"Thought Benjamin, Knox, and you paid for them?"

"We did but kept it quiet. Just got it done because parents on the hill wanted the labs in their new school. But Beau hinted we somehow made money on the deal and wrote all of it off on our taxes."

"Didn't you clear everything with the board and council?"

"We did. Had an auditor keep tabs on the money. But shucks, I know I took the costs off my taxes," Provender said.

"I imagine Knox and Benjamin did the same."

"Yes, but there's a little-known law in South Carolina says our returns can be audited if we declare contributions over a certain amount."

"Does that bother you."

"Course not. I push the tax man like everyone else but I can stand any audit. It's just that we three never tell people when we make donations. Now we'll have every charity after us. Damn nuisance saying no."

"Didn't Beau know they'll find nothing?"

"He knew it but just by asking for it raises doubts in people's minds."

"The when did you stop beating your wife routine."

"Just about it."

"Why come to me?"

"Thought you might have some sway at the paper to stop them from running the story."

"'Fraid I can't, this new guy thinks you're a dinosaur that should be put out to pasture. If it were up to him, he'd do the same to me."

"That's what I thought. Just hoped. Need to figure some way of keeping it all private. He sure played dirty your ex-husband."

"I thought I knew him but realize now I never really comprehended how low-down he could get. Wish I had something to help you, but I don't."

"Do we ever really know the other person?"

"I hope to know someone to spend the rest of my life with."

"You will Caleigh, I just think he hasn't arrived yet."

"If you mean stay away from Carter, Amanda has given me reason enough."

"Take that warning seriously. There is something there I don't like."

"I agree with the mayor," jumped in Eleanor. *"I think he's the last person on my list."*

"Good for you," Provender said as he took his hat and left.

Departing soon after that, Provender walked slowly down the path from the house where his car waited. Eleanor left soon afterward in her car for Atlanta. Caleigh was alone in the house.

Anticipation Grows, Saturday, 2:30pm

Finding a way to being alone with Caleigh required him to sit in his car waiting for others to leave. As he sat with coffee growing cold in his lap just up her street, Carter thought of all the love he could give that woman. Confident in the power of his masculinity, he was sure one afternoon with him would eliminate all doubts she might have had about their relationship.

She wouldn't be the first older woman to succumb to his love making. More times than he remembered, in his past, his sexual magnetism earned him rewards from both women and men. He saw no reason Caleigh would also not fall under his thumb.

Since he was 13, women always gave him what he wanted, particularly older women. Whether it was his mother for movie money; an aunt who stole his virginity; the school nurse who taught him more about sex than his health education teacher, they all succumbed to his rakish charm. Except for his mother, they all gladly laid themselves open for him.

Sometimes the love making led to frenzied actions of sexual aggression on his part. Twice as a teen he was arrested on rape charges but each time the woman involved recanted. Thinking him older, both gave him teasingly invitations only to discover a firm "No" did not stop him. Afterword, when told his age, they dropped their charges. Carter was convinced it was their other sexual experiences when compared to his performance as the reason for their withdrawals of charges.

What he couldn't resolve was the feelings he had for men. Particularly men like Henry Cain. Males with power or fame were the men he gravitated towards. Cain was the first but in Hollywood he learned other men were vulnerable to his looks and bedroom skills.

When Cain was forced to leave Hollywood, Carter gave thought of staying behind and finding another benefactor. But his over aggressive pursuing of one producer's neglected wife and her reaction to his aggressive love making persuaded him to leave town also, before the heat really got intense.

Meeting the stewardess was fortunate for him. Still, when things weren't going well in Atlanta, Carter had no shame in reaching out to Cain. After coming to Skye Landing, Carter felt he'd found the town to settle down in and eventually own some part of its wealth.

When Raleigh took an interest in him, Carter looked for signs the interest was sexual. Finding none, he was unable to accept the older man's interest was in utilizing his talents to help them both succeed. But the fool went and got himself killed, rendering him useless to Carter.

That was another thing about Carter, when a person was no longer useful to him, he discarded them. Witness what he did to Cain. And Carter had no reason, when at a later date he needed them, not to ask for help from the people he discarded. Feeding his ego they often did not say no to his requests.

The anticipation any sexual encounter woke in him resulted in two conflicting feelings fear of rejection and a desire for power over another human being. These two sides translated into frenzied love making bordering on violence. More than once he found himself throttling his companion on the bed. His repeated actions scared the stewardess in Atlanta. When he left, she counted herself lucky.

Two other women thought he raped them. Often, he fixated on one woman until he managed to get her into bed. Once consummated, he often lost interest.

He thought Caleigh might be different. Since the first time he met her, he had trouble controlling his feelings and his prick. Maybe she was the one to enable him to end his bisexual yearnings. What he knew right now was impatience.

Sitting there like some ordinary would-be lover, there existed within him some anger. Aware the anger had gotten him in trouble before; he wanted to control his actions. As time passed in the car control became more and more difficult.

It was all Caleigh's fault. Carter was peeved at her for keeping him at a distance since Raleigh died. He understood her reluctance but he was growing impatient. Just thinking of what lay under those tight jeans made his prick spring to attention in the car and he almost ejaculated.

When she avoided him at headquarters, he decided to wait no longer. Today was the day whether she wanted to be with him or not he was going to strip away those jeans. It was his turn to call the shots in this relationship.

Skye Landing was a new beginning for Carter and opened many opportunities for someone like him. Cain's death derailed some of Carter's hopes. Raleigh's demise ended most of the rest. Raleigh promised an avenue to advancement in something legitimate. The day Raleigh died was the day he decided to build an illegitimate empire.

Reviewing his options in Skye Landing he summed them up as better without Cain than with the podcaster. At first, when he learned Cain was dead, it shocked him. Not only were they co-conspirators but also long-time lovers. Which side of the dominant passive equation he belonged on was still something not fully resolved by Carter. He loved to screw women but he craved power which was best obtained through men. Women were playthings, he thought of them as objects. To Carter, Caleigh was such an object, but also, new to him, a love interest.

Carter saw in Cain someone to learn from and follow. No one doubted Cain was strong. His only failing was thinking he was smarter than everyone else. Ned proved him wrong and Cain paid with his life. Carter thought he was smart but knew others were smarter. He just thought of himself as stronger and willing to take chances others avoided.

For as long as he could remember, Carter detested weak men. These feelings started with his father. Carter expected more from the man who managed two hardware stores so easily. He kept his family well provided for but never wanted to be more than what he was. His mother gave up teaching when he was born. Raising him and his siblings was the most important thing in her life. Unlike his siblings, Carter was not satisfied with the life provided by their parents. He always wanted more for himself and knew he would not get it from them.

Both were born, raised, and lived their whole lives in Winnetka. Carter's constant truancy meant by 16 he was regularly visiting Chicago using money cajoled or stolen from his mother. During one such jaunt, he met Henry Cain in that city during a day when school didn't appeal to him. Hardly a virgin when it came to girls and women, Cain introduced him to the gay life. The result of that encounter and the days spent with Cain was continued indecision regarding his sexual preference.

In Chicago gathering background for the script he was working on, Cain admitted to himself, writing wasn't his game. Turning one man's movie concept into the first draft screenplay wasn't working too well. He was in the city to soak up atmosphere and implant it into the script. The assignment was given to Cain by one gay friend in Hollywood along with some cash. If successful, Cain would have a screen credit and another step up the production latter.

Weeks into the project, Cain was having little success putting words to paper. Walking the city to avoid working, Cain spotted Carter on the street, struck up a conversation and invited him to his apartment. It was the scene of Carter's first homosexual encounter. One Carter found extremely enjoyable. Regularly through the end of his senior high school year and first semester at Columbia College, Carter romped with Cain.

Early in their relationship, Cain showed him his photo collection of women stripped to their panties. Later, when Cain saw how much Carter enjoyed the pictures, he showed the boy his more private video collection of nude women. In these videos, the women were posed in obscene ways and clearly showed in their faces how much they detested what they were doing. Because the camera lingered more on the faces than the bodies, Carter soon understood Cain enjoyed the expressions far more than the nudity. From that moment, Carter found ecstasy in the collection and more importantly, found ways of expanding it. In his videos, the camera lingered on their bodies. Also, Carter was often shown inflicting the humiliation on the victims.

As success came to Cain, his need for these sessions abated. Carter soon became the collection's custodian. He added to it with two hookers he arrested but did not charge in Atlanta and one working girl there in Skye Landing.

When Carter found his landlady snooping in his rented room stashing them there was out of the question. Seemingly in a generous mood, Cain offered to keep them stashed in his private vault. Carter realized his mistake when the search of Cain's house found none.

Planning ahead, Carter was prepared to volunteer to screen them when they turned up. He was perplexed when they eluded the search team when police finally opened the safe. Carter had dreaded them being found and wondered where Cain kept them. He thought Cain's employees might have had them but in his brief encounters with them they showed no signs of recognition.

In the first days of the investigation, Carter conducted several clandestine visits to Cain's house and office. These visits failed to turn up the tapes. When on the weekend, Beau contrived to visit the police station, the lawyer went up to Carter and with a smirk asked if the police had found all of Cain's tapes.

The encounter convinced Carter that Beau had the tapes he needed to suppress. Carter was shocked, but he could understand why Cain gave them to Beau. It was Cain's way of paying Carter back for his betrayal.

They say there is no one more vicious than an old queen. Carter thought an old queen who had been betrayed was someone worse. The ironic part Cain had been only 10 years older than Carter. But Cain had those years in Hollywood to learn how to betray anyone.

As his assignment in Chicago petered out in failure, Cain decided to return to Hollywood. Carter went with him abandoning his college career and his family. His parents in turn were almost relieved to see him depart. His mother saw in him the seeds of evil she feared he would pass on to his two younger siblings. His father had long since written him off.

Hollywood was a revelation for Carter. He quickly learned to trust no one, not even Cain who pimped him out to one movie producer in the hopes of more work. What the episode did for him was make him realize no one would look out for him but himself. The event also showed that Cain was selfish enough to do something like that to someone he supposedly loved. Carter filed that away for future payback.

When things petered out in the entertainment centers, Cain turned to podcasting. Fortunately for him, he had a talent for it. When the political podcast fizzled, he took the one listener's tip and went to Peoria to see about the crooked sheriff.

Taking Carter with him, he saw a way of using the now 21-year-old to help bring down the Sheriff. But Carter had other ideas. On the plane out from Las Angeles, one older stewardess fell so hard for Carter she invited him to come to Atlanta and live with her.

Seeing opportunity and not convinced Cain would ever amount to anything that would benefit him, he followed her to Atlanta. Moving in with the stewardess, within three months he cleaned out her bank accounts, slept with her best friend and took the exam for the police force. During the last months of their relationship, Carter had become more brutal in his love making. So much so, the woman was glad he left.

Because the force was rapidly expanding at that time, his wait between taking and passing the exam and being called for interviews was short. He passed all but the psych test. Reading the psych review board as him desiring to achieve greater humility, Carter played the role to the hilt and was admitted to the next class. The board did require him to serve an 18-month probationary period rather than the one year normal rotation. Carter settled in on the other side of town away from the stewardess and discovered he liked police work.

While Carter labored in Atlanta, Cain was heartbroken by Carter's defection but went about achieving the fall of Sheriff Arturo Gonzalez.

When fame started to roll in, Cain gained nationwide attention. What saddened and angered Cain was Carter's defection. Quietly, he thought about revenge. When Carter called him, he secretly smiled.

Knowing he was on thin ice within the department, Carter called Cain about the problems he had found in the Atlanta police. Cain saw his opportunity. More in hopes of furthering a reconciliation with Carter than interest in uncovering fraud, he went to Atlanta. To both their apparent delights, Carter and Cain renewed their romance. The Atlanta revelations added to his fame but at the price of Carter's job.

Before, he could return to Chicago with Carter, Beau Jenkins appeared. Someone mentioned Cain's program to Beau. The attorney had a unique capacity for remembering people and things associated with each person. He saw opportunity for both himself and Cain.

Planning to run for mayor, he needed to find something bad about Provender. He also knew if he found it or publicized the facts, people would say it was mudslinging. But if the well-known podcaster made the charges, Beau was in the clear. Beau initiated the call to Cain who remembered him. They agreed to meet in Atlanta.

Uncomfortable meeting at the Golden Slipper, he brought Ned with him. Neither did Carter or Beau know of Cain's previous relationship with Ned. Both men pretended their only contact had been the boy's police group. It was the sole time all four men met together. Just their luck the Atlanta police were suspicious of Carter and logged the meeting. Also, that a fan dancer saying goodbyes also was in the club that day. She was leaving her sex club employment to marry a pharmacist from South Carolina.

Carter thought ruefully of the pharmacist's wife, who saw his picture when he caught that Washington suspect. Carter found out quickly that the woman wanted more sex than her husband could provide. Since his notoriety, she had demanded Carter provide the extra dollop in her life. When her demands started to include money, Carter used Ned's murder spree to eliminate her. Before his death, Raleigh hinted although she was murdered, he didn't think the serial killer ended her life.

Unaware they had been photographed; Beau, Cain, and Carter hatched the plan to bring down Provender and Amanda. When it was put to Ned, he only agreed to hire Carter but told the three conspirators they would get no help from him.

Sometime afterwards, Cain and Ned resumed their relationship. Sitting in his car waiting to brace Caleigh, Carter now surmised Cain always intended to strike back at Ned in some way along with himself. What Cain did not admit was the possibility Ned would react so murderously. The deaths of Pastor Bob, Ned's wife and the boy were only incidental damage.

No one yet suspected Carter was the one who gave Cain the evidence box for the Couri girl. At the time, they thought the revelations were serious. With little to go on, they were meant only to provide additional scandal fodder.

Carter was surprised when Raleigh said she had been murdered and her killer given some sort of justice. To Carter, that meant whoever did kill the girl had gotten away with the crime through bribes. Bribes meant money, and he wanted some of it.

Before his murder, during their last meeting, the night before he died, Cain protested his love for Carter. But he was leaving without Carter and, the detective now knew, giving the tapes to Beau was his revenge for the hurt inflicted when the young man deserted him and went to Atlanta.

Cain did not realize he was signing Beau's death warrant by putting him in Carter's path. In Cain's thinking, Beau's possession of the videos, stuck Carter in this hick town under the thumb of a man almost as devious as himself. In devising this plan, Cain had inflicted the perfect revenge. Only Ned's rampage trumped Cain's enjoyment of this revenge. Carter was caught, or so Cain thought. That first weekend after Cain's murder, Carter had the solution to this trap.

With those videos sitting somewhere as a time bomb under his future, Carter went to see Beau to demand the tapes back. In his office on that Sunday, the lawyer laughed in his face. Angry, Carter shot him almost reflectively with a 25 caliber Beretta, similar to the one that killed the other victims. When a thorough search of Beau's office failed to turn up the tapes, Carter Immediately knew the murder was a mistake.

But it was done. He knew the videos were someplace in Beau's orbit. Right now he was stumped. What he wanted most from Caleigh besides seeing what color the hair under her jeans were, was any hint as to where Beau might have hidden those tapes. As long as he didn't have them, his life here hung in the balance. If someone found the tapes; examined them; and saw his face, they might start asking questions about who murdered the lawyer. He had been lucky that the Hollywood porn tape found in Cain's safe had not been examined too closely for any of the participants to be recognized as a young Carter. That secret, at least, seemed safe.

He had made other older women give him their secrets, she would as well. He would start afternoon in her bedroom, whether she let him in or not. It was time to show her who was boss in their relationship.

Voices Above, Saturday 3pm

Seeing no one enter or leave Caleigh's house for an hour, Carter locked his car and walked casually down the street and up the porch steps. From his past visits, he knew the door was unlocked. Wanting to surprise Caleigh, he turned the knob slowly, and Carter was taken aback when he found the door locked.

Momentarily stopped, he pulled out a credit card and tried sliding it between the door and the post. That ploy didn't work. He moved over to the window next to the door. Testing it, he found it unlocked. Quietly, he pushed it up enough to squeeze into the house.

Despite it being mid-afternoon, the house was dark. No lights showed on the first floor as he padded through the rooms. After he inspected all the first-floor rooms, he surmised Caleigh was upstairs, and since Carter was not hearing her walking about, he was pleased to think she might be taking a nap. The thought of her in bed made his prick go to attention. Feeling a little pressure as it strained against his pants, Carter unzipped his fly to display it as he walked softly up the stairs.

Almost reaching the top step, he suddenly heard voices talking low with an occasional giggle.

The sounds made him stop, trying to decide what to do. In halting, he made some noise which stopped the conversation. Caleigh's bedroom door opened, and she stepped into the hallway.

She was naked, her body white against the dark hall.

"What are you doing here?" she asked almost hysterically.

"I came to give you the best love you ever had," Carter said without thinking.

Caleigh looked at his erect penis, which was rapidly diminishing.

"With that?" she said, not knowing what else to remark.

"Other women have craved it and always asked for more," Carter said, stung by her taunt.

"Well this woman doesn't, so get out of my house."

"Not till I know who's in that bed with you."

"What business is it of yours?" Caleigh said as she became aware of her nakedness.

"Because you're mine."

"Since when?" she said in a voice betraying her growing fear.

"Since the first moment I saw you."

"Get out of my house now,"

"Not until I know who's in there with you."

"Leave now, or I'll call the police."

"I am the police."

"You're an egotistical maniac."

"Don't ever call me that."

"I just did," Caleigh said while realizing her mistake.

Carter drew out his gun and pointed it at the woman.

"Are we going to find out who's in that room or do I shoot you right here?"

"You're not going to do anything but leave this house," Caleigh said he a voice that did not betray her fear.

"Then I guess I'll need to shoot you and whoever's in that room."

Carter raised the gun to shoot Caleigh in the shoulder when Amanda came out the door, her gun held in two hands. Unlike in Ned's case, she aimed for Carter's body, putting one bullet in his lower right and her second almost square in his chest.

Carter tumbled back down the stairs to end as a crumbled heap on the first-floor landing. As naked as Caleigh, Amanda took a deep breath and put the gun down on the floor. Looking at the small pistol she picked up where Carter had dropped it, she turned to Caleigh and shrugged.

"Looks like we know now who killed Beau."

"But why?" was all Caleigh could say.

"I don't know if we will ever find out but I'm willing to bet this gun will prove to be the murder weapon for Beau."

"Why did he think I would succumb to his blandishments?"

"*Because apparently a lot of older women did.*"
"*He was crazy.*"
"*As a fox. He had a lot of people fooled, including Raleigh.*"
"*Yes, he did. Let's get dressed before we call everybody.*"
"*You know of course we're through in this town?*"
"*Why do you say that?*"
"*Because I just shot my second officer and had three others killed. Even Provender can't stop the City Council from asking for my head.*"
"*I'll get the paper to support you.*"
"*They're just waiting for something like this to fire you. Just wait.*"
"*What will you do if they oust you?*"
"*No, it's what you will do and what we will do together. There's still the matter of the Couri girl's death.*"
"*I thought talk about that had stopped.*"
"*It hasn't and I think that fat reporter from Charlotte won't let it rest.*"
"*Let's get dressed and maybe we can brazen all this out.*"
"*No way, when they ask for our clothes and they have no powder stains on them, someone will put two and two together.*"
"*Well, at least we had Charlestown and today.*"
"*And many more days if you're game?*"
"*I am, but what will Sue Ellen think.*"
"*That her mother is really hip.*"
"*Perhaps.*"
"*Well, at least Carter got to see what color hair was under your jeans.*"

THE END OF BOOK 1

LOOK FOR CALEIGH JENKINS AND AMANDA HARRIS IN OUR NEXT PODCAST MURDER MYSTERY. HERE IS THE FIRST CHAPTER.

Who Killed Teenager Jenny Couri?

Walking beside the excavated ditch prepared for the sewer line, Hy Grossman, for the umpteenth time, anticipated the thrill of meeting a new news source. The paper sheet offering to reveal who killed Jenny Couri was in his pocket, and it asked him to encounter the informant in this construction area.

In the past, the veteran journalist earned some of his biggest stories by meeting in outlandish locations. Once meeting a source behind a mortuary as services was being conducted inside the crematory. In the months after the so-called Podcast Murders were solved, Hy became editor of the local newspaper to further his quest to determine who killed the 19-year-old beauty 13 years ago.

Arriving in the morning mail, the note was very specific about where and when the meeting was to occur. With the meeting request was a copy of the coroner's report on the girl's autopsy to prove the writer had knowledge of the case. Hy noticed the top and bottom parts of the page were cut off. Evidently, the writer knew of the hidden, encoded information contained in documents spewed from a computer. This cut off one way Hy could check on who he was meeting.

Faxing the document to a friendly coroner in North Carolina, the expert reported it looked genuine and was from a novice medical examiner indicating the girl died of some natural but unknown cause. The report also suggested that additional tests needed to be made.

These findings indicated to Hy he might be meeting someone who might give him some material to finally bring this case to the public's attention.

When the Podcast Murders were solved, many people, Hy included, continued to doubt Jenny Couri's death resulted from some natural cause.

Despite continued police denials, Hy and others believed Henry Cain's claims the teenager was murdered. So much did Hy think the girl was killed he became editor of the Skye Landing Eagle just so he could pursue the case on the killer's home ground.

In the months since coming to town, Hy wrote periodically about Jenny's death, each time receiving official denials. Judging by the approving letters he received, many other residents agreed with him. Thanks to the internet, interest in the case was becoming a worldwide topic.

Despite the publicity, except for some crackpots offering man-from-mars theories, there were no legitimate leads until today's letter. Amanda Harris, the disgraced ex-police chief, had openly derided his attempts to reopen the case. The mayor backed her up, as did the current chief. The opposition made Hy even more convinced there was more fire where the smoke that Henry Cain raised centered.

Still smarting from Amanda's rejection of romance, Hy also wanted to prove her a liar. Now that she and Caleigh Butler had this private investigation firm, he was hoping to ruin their reputation by piercing this wall of denial. That hick mayor, 30-odd years as a community leader, also deserved some payback.

All this went through Hy's mind as he picked his way through the group of new homes being built in one of the last sections of Dane Hill opened to development. In front of him loomed someone hiding in the dark outside the cone of light thrown by the single bulb at the construction site. Seeing the figure, Hy quickened his step, glad he was not on a wild-goose chase.

"Glad to see you," Hy said loudly.

The specter said nothing, carefully staying out of the light. Coming to the top of the dirt mound between the two figures, Hy tried to see the informant better. The informant raised his left hand as if in greeting. Perplexed by the gesture, Hy looked at the figure's hand. To his horror, he saw a gun. The brief flash illuminated the scene. It was followed by two more blasts. All three caught Hy in the chest, the last as he toppled into the ditch, which was specially prepared for him.

Without bothering to determine if Hy was dead, the figure put the gun back in the coat pocket. Removing it, he put it in the hole, picked up the shovel used to dig the original pit, and methodically began covering the body. When finished, there was no apparent difference between that area and the surrounding construction site.

Carefully, to avoid leaving any tracks, the figure moved to the opposite paved street and walked out of the development. From a superficial inspection, no one had visited the construction site that night.

* * *

About the Author

D.J. Laing is the pen name for the Wilmington, DE couple who have produced numerous nonfiction titles in the past. This book is their first collaboration in the mystery genre. They have been producing and hosting a variety of podcasts since 2005.

JoAnn M. Laing, after stints at Chase and Citibank, has been a senior executive for Sara Lee, Olivetti, and First Advantage. Honored as an alumnae leader by the Harvard Business School, she is also a graduate of Syracuse University. She blogs All About Small Business, tweets daily on advanced technologies, plus created and funded a non-profit, The-NREF.org, to encourage robotics learning.

Donald Mazzella is an internationally experienced journalist who, for the last two decades, has been heard by more than two million unique listeners each month, hosting Small Business Digest. He has also appeared on numerous news and popular media outlets, commenting on a variety of topics. He holds BA, MA, and MBA degrees from New York University.

Thank you for reading.
Please review this book. Reviews help others find
Absolutely Amazing eBooks and inspire us to keep
providing these marvelous tales.
If you would like to be put on our email list to receive
updates on new releases, contests, and promotions, please
go to AbsolutelyAmazingEbooks.com and sign up.

For sales, editorial information, subsidiary rights information
or a catalog, please write or phone or e-mail
AbsolutelyAmazingEbooks
Manhanset House
Shelter Island Hts., New York 11965-0342, US
Tel: 212-427-7139
www.AbsolutelyAmazingEbooks.com
bricktower@aol.com
www.IngramContent.com